The Tree

By Russell Gregory

Cover Design: Kirstin Leong

"When I use a word," Humpty Dumpty said in rather a scornful tone, "it means just what I choose it to mean - neither more nor less."

The question is," said Alice, "whether you *can* make words mean so many different things."

"The question is," said Humpty Dumpty, "which is to be master-that's all."

Through the Looking Glass, and What Alice Found There.

Lewis Carroll

Alice laughed ... "one ***can't*** believe impossible things."

"I daresay you haven't had much practice," said the Queen. "When I was your age, I always did it for half-an-hour a day. Why, sometimes I've believed as many as six impossible things before breakfast."

Through the Looking Glass, and What Alice Found There

Lewis Carroll

Contents

Chapter 1 2019 5
Chapter 2 2019 11
Chapter 3 1979 21
Chapter 4 2019 37
Chapter 5 1979 49
Chapter 6 2019 54
Chapter 7 1979 63
Chapter 8 2019 67
Chapter 9 1979 75
Chapter 10 2019 80
Chapter 11 1979 88
Chapter 12 2019 98
Chapter 13 1979 109
Chapter 14 2019 117
Chapter 15 123
Chapter 16 131
Chapter 17 141
Chapter 18 152
Chapter 19 163
Chapter 20 173
Chapter 21 185
Chapter 22 190
Chapter 23 199
Chapter 24 206

Chapter 25 214
Chapter 26 223
Chapter 27 240
Chapter 28 250
Chapter 29 262
Chapter 30 264
Chapter 31 266
Chapter 32 269
Chapter 33 The next day..275
Chapter 34 8 hours later..279
Chapter 35 10 hours later......................................283
Chapter 36 20 hours later......................................286
Chapter 37 4 hours later..289

Chapter 1 2019

The tree lay across the gardens of the two houses. At first, Adam thought his eyes were deceiving him. He had only come down to the kitchen to run a glass of water from the sink; an attempt to soothe his parched throat and ease his banging headache. He had intended to go back upstairs afterwards and get some more sleep. Glancing out of the window, while he was waiting for the water to run cold, that was when he had seen it. Now, he stared, open mouthed, motionless, as if frozen in time, then blinked and looked again.

"What the …?"

It had crashed through the fence between the two gardens, smashing it completely. Huge and motionless, like a gigantic bridge between the two snow speckled lawns, it lay perfectly parallel to the two houses, tiny snowflakes swirling gently around it and through its branches.

Adam struggled to think back. It had been late, maybe 2 or 3, when the taxi had dropped him off this morning. Taxi, oh God! How much had that cost? He didn't dare to check his wallet. He wondered … had he looked out of the window then? Hmmm, probably. There was an empty water glass on his bedside table when he woke up this morning. Actually, was it still morning? He turned and checked the kitchen clock. 1.30. It was the afternoon. He groaned and turned back to the window. So, he probably had stood at the sink to fill a glass with water sometime last night. He hadn't noticed anything then, but it would have been too dark anyway. He certainly didn't remember hearing anything. Then again, he didn't remember a great deal from yesterday. He'd had a few drinks before he'd even arrived at the party. Must have been pretty pissed by the end. He could vaguely remember the countdown to the New Year at midnight and … had he kissed that girl, the tall blonde one? He looked around for his phone and spotted it on the fridge. Walking across to pick it up, he could see that he hadn't turned it off last night; the battery would be low. Damn! Sitting down at the kitchen table, he pushed some dirty plates and cups into the middle, set his glass of water down and entered the password onto his phone. A series of texts popped up on the screen.

Good morning handsome x

Hope you're feeling okay xx

Last night was fun xxx

Phone me xx

They were all from Lucinda.

Lucinda. Oh God, that was her name, the tall blonde girl. And he **had** snogged her. Now he remembered. Oh God! He took a long drink from the glass of water, swirling the last mouthful all around his teeth and gums to try and take away the stale taste of last night's excesses. Had he done anything more than that? Oh, he really hoped not. He was already seeing two girls. Twice now he had nearly been caught out. He really couldn't handle any more. He wondered why he did it, really. An ex-girlfriend, Alexis, had told him that he was insecure and needed affirmation. He thought it was probably a lot simpler than that really. It was just that, when a pretty girl smiled, it made him feel good and want to ask her out and then, before he knew it, they were dating. He winced slightly. He should probably stop doing it.

Plugging the phone into a charger dangling from the socket over the fridge, he returned to the window, rubbing at the misting on the glass with the sleeve of his blue towelling dressing gown before peering out through the thickening ferment of snow. It was beginning to stick on the ground now and on the branches and the trunk of the fallen giant. He drank the rest of the water in the glass then refilled it. He had never really taken much notice of it before, probably because it wasn't in his garden, but he seemed to remember that when he had first moved in, half way through September, it had conkers on it, or something very like conkers. Nature had never been one of his strong points.

He leaned over the sink and moved his head closer to the glass, so that he could get a better view of the garden next door and the back of the house. There was no movement. No surprises there then. He was only aware that someone had moved in last month because of the gleaming new Renault Clio on the driveway and the occasional sounds of banging and crashing through the shared wall. Apart from that, he had neither seen nor heard anything of his reclusive new neighbour.

He looked back at the branches of the tree covering his own garden. He was pretty sure that there was a shed of some kind under there somewhere. Although he'd been in the house more than three months, he'd never paid much attention to the garden. In fact, come to think about it, he'd never actually been out there. He'd seen some chap mowing the grass a couple of times. Presumably that was something Jerry had arranged. Maybe he'd mentioned it. Adam thought back to when he had first offered him the house as a short-term house-sit while he sorted out something more permanent.

"Go on Adam. You'd be doing me a big favour. I need someone to house sit while I'm in LA. It's not good for a house to sit empty."

Jerry had said, "While I'm in L.A…" like he wanted to sound casual about it, like it was no big thing. Adam knew it **was** a big thing really. He also knew that Jerry was going to be earning a lot of money. Maybe he was embarrassed about that. And so he should be really; Adam wished he could get a break like that. His own career had come to a bit of a lull, just as it seemed like he might be making some progress and attracting some attention. Well, that was how he liked to think about it, anyway. And when he was talking about it, he would say he was in between jobs, or else taking a rest from the daily grind while he planned a big project. In his darker moments, when he was being entirely honest with himself, he had to acknowledge that, so far, he had merely assisted in the making of a couple of minor documentaries. But those moments were few and far between. Honesty was overrated.

"Well, I don't know Jerry." Adam had never lived outside of a city before. And Kent, well, it was a long way from where he wanted to be. And he didn't drive. Well, he'd never needed to. And relying on trains and buses was all very well in the city but a real pain if you were going any distance out of it. You could get a cab, of course, but fares to get out into the countryside would cost a bomb. However, if Jerry was offering it for free…

"Go on. I won't charge you any rent. You can just pay the utility bills."

That had clinched it. Since he didn't actually have an income at the moment, that solved more than a few problems. Besides, if he needed to stay in town there were plenty of sofas he could call upon if necessary, not to mention the odd bed, just as long as he could keep their owners from finding out about each other.

Adam sat down at the table again, massaged the stubble on his chin, and pondered what he should do. One of his reservations about looking after a friend's house was that he might have to take some kind of responsibility for it. He shook his head slowly. Responsibility wasn't one of his strong points either. Another ex-girlfriend, Trudy, had told him that. But really! Was it any surprise? He was the only child of parents so busy with their careers that he had spent most of his childhood at boarding school or being looked after by a nanny during the holidays. When was he supposed to develop a sense of responsibility? Yet now he had a tree to deal with. Except, wait a minute, it wasn't

Jerry's tree. It was next door's tree. Adam nodded slowly. All he needed to do was to make it clear to his new neighbour that this was their problem, not his. He smiled to himself, leaned back and laced his hands behind his head. Perfect. It would even give him an excuse to go round and get a look at his mysterious neighbour.

Chapter 2 2019

Adam took a last look at himself in the bathroom mirror. Not great, but it would have to do. He had spent some time trying to undo yesterday's damage. Cold water had successfully tightened up the bags under his eyes. He had shaved carefully and used his fingers to apply the moulding wax to his hair, ensuring the right combination of stylish and casual. Mouth wash and cologne ensured that he would smell sweet if it was appropriate to get up close. He realised that the neighbour could be an old crone, or a man for that matter, but he never took risks with his appearance. You never knew when opportunity might present itself and you needed to be ready when it did. Besides, he had a hunch about that new Renault Clio.

He stepped into the bedroom and checked the overall look in a full-length mirror. The combination of designer jeans and a pastel blue shirt was, he decided, suitably casual but with just a hint of how good he could look when he made an effort. The banging headache had subsided to a distant throb. He was ready.

Adam had to walk down the snowy path, through the gate and along the pavement in order to approach his neighbour's front door. It gave him an opportunity to make a more considered appraisal. The house was severely neglected. Melting snow was dripping from a gutter leading up to the gable end and there was paint peeling from all of the window frames and sills. The front garden was seriously overgrown. It looked as if it was gradually returning to the wilderness it must once have been, long ago. Winding creepers were slowly strangling the life out of the snow-tipped rosebushes lining the path and the lawn was a knee-high conglomeration of shaggy grass and weeds, fighting each other for light. As he passed the Clio, he looked through the window of the driver's door. Two hair bands were looped over the gear stick and a small pair of leather gloves lay on the dashboard. He nodded involuntarily and smiled. His hunch had been right then. He had been right to spend that time in front of the mirror.

The most striking thing about the house was that the curtains were drawn, all of them. They looked faded, ragged even, in places. Adam tried to remember how the windows had looked before the new occupant arrived. He was pretty sure that at least some of the curtains had been open. So, his neighbour liked privacy. Interesting.

Reaching the door, he looked for a bell or knocker. Finding neither, he gave five smart raps on the door with his knuckles and stepped back a pace to wait. Nothing. Not a sound from inside. After a minute of waiting, he stepped forward again and used the side of his fist to pound more forcefully. This time, after a few moments, he heard some movement from inside. There was the click of a key being turned and then the scraping of bolts. The door swung open to reveal a young woman blinking out through thick, black rimmed spectacles from the dimly lit hallway. She was dressed in a dusty looking, dark blue boiler suit. Looking past her, Adam could see piles of books and papers and a rolled-up carpet lining the hallway. Her hair, shoulder-length and mousy, was secured into an untidy pony tail by a hairband like the ones Adam had seen in her car. She wore no make-up and there was no jewellery on show. Adam glanced at the fingers of her left hand, but she was wearing a pair of yellow rubber gloves, the like of which he had only ever seen on elderly relatives doing the washing up. She was most definitely not, Adam decided, his type. And yet, he was intrigued. Her eyes were startling beneath the dark frames of her glasses, vivid blue and piercing, appraising him as he stood on her doorstep. Statuesque in the doorway, one hand still holding the doorknob, she waited in silence.

Adam took a step forward, smiled and extended his hand.

"Hi, I'm Adam. I'm your next-door neighbour."

His greeting was delivered with a confidence synthesised from an upbringing of privilege and entitlement; his public-school accent, his boyish good looks, these were tried and tested assets which had opened many doors for him in the past.

The young woman remained motionless and silent. Only her incisive eyes signalled that she had heard him and was evaluating his intentions. Adam, deflated by her lack of response, wondered if, perhaps, she did not speak English. Still, the offer of a handshake was clear. This was not the kind of reception he was accustomed to. He stifled his irritation and tried another approach.

"The tree, it's fallen down into my garden. I thought we might talk about what we're going to do about it."

As he spoke, he realised that she had completely wrong-footed him. He had intended to say that it was her problem and that he wanted it removed. Instead, he was offering to discuss a solution. What was it about her? Her expression was aloof, impenetrable. It gave her an air of mystique. In an odd way, he was beginning to rather fancy her.

"Can I come in?" he offered. "It's a bit cold out here. We could discuss …"

"No," she broke in, holding her hand up to reinforce the statement.

She continued to study his face, registered the puzzlement in his expression, then added, "I'll come over to your house. Fifteen minutes."

With that, she shut the door and slid the bolts across, the sound of her footsteps fading as she retreated back down the hallway.

Back home, Adam executed a strategic clear up of the key areas of the house with the practised skill of a man who was accustomed to unexpected visits. He threw the shoes and slippers littering the hall floor into the cupboard under the stairs. He would keep her away from the lounge. In the kitchen, he piled dirty plates, bowls and cups into the dishwasher and disposed of packets and tins into the kitchen bin. He was just giving the table and work-surfaces a quick wipe when his doorbell rang.

It was decidedly not the transformation Adam was hoping for. She had clearly showered and changed but her hair was still scraped back into that unflattering pony tail and she still wore no make-up. She was wearing a long, black, woollen coat, with black wellington boots poking out of the bottom. A triumph of functional over stylish, Adam decided. He stepped back with his right foot and gestured with his right hand towards the kitchen at the end of the hallway.

"Thanks for coming round. Please, come on in."

She stepped inside, looked along the hallway, then looked down at her snowy boots. Shrugging, she bent down to pull them off, stood them together on the mat, then strode purposefully towards the kitchen in her bare feet. Adam trotted behind, meaning to invite her to sit down, but she was several steps ahead of him, pulling out a chair and seating herself before he had a chance to speak. Unbuttoning her coat, she pulled it open without taking it off, revealing a powder blue jogging suit. As Adam sat down in the seat opposite her, she leaned forward, clasped her hands together and placed them on the table. No wedding ring or engagement ring, Adam noted. In fact, no jewellery of any kind.

"Can I get you something to drink?" Adam offered. "Tea? Coffee? Juice?"

She gave him a curt smile. "Just some water please."

Adam nodded and moved to the sink to run the tap until it was cold. As he waited, his hand under the stream of cooling water, he looked out at the tree.

"Did you hear it come down? The tree. Do you know when it fell?"

He looked back over his shoulder.

"No." She shook her head. "I'm a heavy sleeper. Nothing wakes me."

As Adam filled the glass with cold water, he pondered on her accent. Northern maybe? He had never been further north than Birmingham. He wondered if they were all as direct as her up there. Turning, he placed it on the table in front of her and sat down.

"Well, I suppose we need to do something about it. Get rid of it, I mean."

She cocked her head slightly to one side and observed him quizzically. Smiling that same, curt smile she answered, "I've managed to find a firm that will come out tomorrow. Couldn't get anyone for today. They're going to cut it up and remove it."

Adam sat back in his seat and laughed. "Wow. You don't hang about do you!"

Her eyes narrowed slightly. "I'm sorry?" Her tone had a slight edge to it.

Adam was perplexed by her response. He tried again.

"What I meant was," he clarified, "it would take me days to get round to sorting out a problem like this. You seem very organised and efficient."

She seemed to relax a little, the hint of a smile on her lips.

"I'm not working today. It seemed sensible to find a solution today rather than waiting until tomorrow."

It was the most she had said so far. Adam was encouraged.

"Oh right, yeah. Good thinking. So ... what do you do then? For a job I mean."

She tensed again. That same narrowing of the eyes. Adam found her completely unnerving. He took evasive action.

"Sorry," he laughed. "Didn't mean to interrogate you. It's just that, being neighbours, I thought ..." He tailed off, unsure how to continue. The truth was he didn't actually need to know what she did. He was merely trying to make conversation, to get her to open up a bit. Trouble was, she just didn't react like women normally did to his advances. He tried another tack.

"Look, I'm Adam. I'm a film editor. Freelance."

Adam looked across at her but she made no acknowledgement. Girls were usually impressed by this, but Clio Girl showed no flicker of interest. In truth, he hadn't really achieved much in the film industry, so, if he was going to get this girl's attention, some embroidering of the truth would be needed. This **was** a strong point of his.

"You may have seen some of my work. I've made a few documentaries for the BBC and I've worked on a couple of films that made it to some of the independent cinemas. I'm looking for my big break now, an opportunity to do something more commercial."

He rubbed his thumb and first finger together to signal that he was looking to make some money from this. She remained impassive for a painfully long moment then, unexpectedly, her face changed. Understanding spread across her face and she giggled, almost girlishly. Standing abruptly, she held her hand out across the table.

"I'm Alice," she exclaimed. "Pleased to meet you."

Startled by this sudden change, Adam stood and exchanged a handshake with her. Her hand was softer than he had expected. As they sat down, she continued with this new effusiveness.

"I'm just in the middle of changing jobs actually. I've been doing cyber security since I left university, you know, protecting businesses from snoopers and hackers. But I wanted to work from home for a while, so I'm taking a break from all that."

Adam nodded, grinned and willed her to go on.

"Yeah, so I'm setting myself up as an independent genealogist."

Adam mimed his comedy puzzled face, head on one side, eyes wide, fingers stroking his chin. Women usually loved it, his little boy lost look, but Alice just look confused.

"Err… I'm not totally sure what that is," he quickly intervened.

She smiled again. Adam was beginning to love that smile.

"Oh, it's just a professional title for someone who researches family history and draws up family trees. It's always been an interest of mine. I just thought it would be something I could do for a while until I decide what I want to do next."

She paused and looked down for a moment. "And ... it will give me a chance to ... do some work on the house."

"Ah yes," Adam responded enthusiastically. "I've heard some of your handiwork through the walls. Looks like you've got your work cut out there."

Once again that look of surprise on her face. More like panic this time. Adam intervened quickly.

"Well, I take my hat off to you. I've never been one for DIY myself. I take it you've bought the house if you're working on it."

She shook her head and looked away.

"Inherited it. From my mother. She died recently."

Adam gasped. The bald statement hit him like an electric shock. He hated to be in contact with anything raw like terminal illness or bereavement. He just had no idea how to respond. Shows of emotion were frowned upon in his family. Any kind of emotion, really. He couldn't remember his mother and father ever showing any real affection to him or, indeed, to each other. It just wasn't the "done thing" in the Parkinson household. And at school it would be regarded as a sign of weakness, exposing you to merciless mockery.

"You're totally lacking in compassion." That's what Melanie had said to him. It was just before they broke up. She, of course, was at the other end of the spectrum; cried at the drop of a hat. And it **was** only her cat that had died. Was that really a cause for tears? Oh, well. On this occasion, however, he was surprised to find that he could feel genuinely sorry for the girl. She looked very young to be losing her mother. There was no mention of a father either. She looked a little forlorn.

"Oh my God, I'm so sorry," he responded quickly. "I really didn't mean to pry. I'm terribly sorry about your mother."

Alice nodded and rewarded him with a wistful smile.

"Thank you."

She stood, buttoning her coat and looked across at Adam.

"I need to be going. Lots to do before tomorrow."

Putting on her Wellington Boots at the door, she turned and held her hand out once again.

"Lovely to meet you. And thank you for the water."

Adam took her hand, holding onto it a little longer this time.

"Lovely to meet you too. I hope we shall see more of each other. Maybe tomorrow when the tree surgeon comes."

She nodded, almost shyly, turned and retraced her snowy footprints in the garden path.

Chapter 3 1979

Sir Blake Montague MP surveyed the crowd, his eyes glittering with satisfaction; the ballroom was nearly full now. He adjusted the sleeves of his dinner jacket over his shirt cuffs then smoothed back his dark, black hair with a hand heavy with gold rings, swivelling slowly to check off the revellers. His usual Westminster cronies were there, Lord Farquar, the Earl of Burford; always good to have a bit of influence in "The Other Place." He was pleased to see Bernie had made it. Blake had been instrumental in his selection as Speaker in the Commons. He hadn't seen the girl who was clinging onto his arm before but he knew it wasn't his wife. She looked young enough to be his daughter. That was good too. Blake made a mental note to have a word before Bernie had drunk too much, just to clarify that he was expecting a few favours in return. He spotted DI Karen Turner standing alone, watching the revellers. He wondered what she was thinking. She looked very out of place, a glass of fruit juice in her hand, holding herself very upright and tilting her head back as if to avoid a bad smell. The stink of privilege probably. Blake smiled; to be fair, the room probably reeked of it to a woman with a background like hers. She hadn't been born into money, Blake knew that. In fact, he knew a lot about her; always good to do thorough research before entering into a business relationship. She had needed to work hard to get where she was. Still, she had made it this far and now she wanted what they had. Excellent. Always good to have an extra member of the police force on board. With a few words in some well-chosen ears, he could accelerate her promotion to DCI and position her where he needed her to be. In the meantime, he had a proposition he wanted to put to her later.

The party was in full swing now, the DJ kept having to increase the volume of his music to stay on top of the increasingly voluble guests. There was a hum of barely subdued excitement; they sensed that the games were about to begin.

Blake felt a touch on his right elbow and knew immediately that it would be his Personal Assistant, Tabitha, just checking in as he had requested. Without even turning to acknowledge her, he nodded, almost imperceptibly, to indicate that he was ready to receive her report.

"All of the guests are here now Sir." She spoke very close to his ear, just loud enough for Blake to hear her, no more than that, her voice confident and reassuring. The vowel sounds of her South East London upbringing had almost vanished, Blake noted, particularly in this august company. Pity really; he rather liked it when she betrayed her poverty hardened core. It gave her a bit of an edge. Authentic. Like a gangster, he thought. Rather sexy really.

"The Chinese Ambassador is in the Derby Room with a call girl, the MD of Good Bet is in the library with your lawyers, ironing out the last few glitches in the contract." The tone of her voice changed slightly and Blake could imagine the smile of satisfaction on her pretty face.

"I popped in earlier to have a word," she confided. "I think the MD is beginning to see it from our point of view now."

Blake smiled. She was a force to be reckoned with. He knew it would be a mistake to change the basis of their relationship but he was finding it increasingly difficult to resist her attractions; her smooth contours, her artfully plaited black hair, the light reflecting from the glossy, dark skin over her sharp cheekbones. He suspected she might be as devastating in bed as she was in the boardroom.

"Thank you, Tabitha. How about my family?"

"Dora is in bed ..."

"And my wife and son?"

Blake sensed that her pause indicated problems.

"I did introduce Freddie to the call girl you chose for him. I believe she has tried very hard to seduce him, but he hasn't responded. She said that she thought he was under the influence of alcohol or drugs. Apparently, he's rather volatile this evening. Perhaps we could try another time."

Blake growled with anger. He did not like it when people defied him. He was running out of patience with that boy.

"And my wife?"

Again, there was a pause.

"I'm sorry, Sir, I'm afraid she has invited Mr Shaw."

Blake spun round, his face contorted with rage.

"What?"

Tabitha bit her lip. "She is more than a little bit drunk and appears to want everyone to know that she is having an affair with him. I'm sorry."

Blake clenched his fists involuntarily. A vein pulsed angrily in his right temple. At times like this, Tabitha was very circumspect in how she dealt with her employer. She had seen what he could do. She had seen what others like him could do. She hoped that Audrey would be okay.

"Okay. Thank you, Tabitha."

Blake had reassumed his smooth, calm exterior almost as quickly as he had lost it. Inside, Tabitha knew from experience, he was seething. She couldn't say that she really blamed Lady Montague. Everyone knew about her husband's numerous affairs. He made no attempt to hide them from Audrey. Tabitha had heard him taunting her, just to provoke a reaction. Only last week, he had waited until she was within earshot so that he could use her as an audience to the humiliation of his wife.

"I must have been mad to marry you Audrey. I should have looked at your mother and foreseen what you would turn into."

His voice had sounded casual, as if it was a throwaway remark. Tabitha knew better. It had been calculated to wound her, to probe for weakness and exploit it. Poor Audrey had not been able to resist a response to his cruelty.

"You married me for my money, Blake. And now, I am what you have made me. I am your monster."

He seemed, to Tabitha, to enjoy the demonstration of power, humiliating anyone who crossed him. It was his self-affirmation. Audrey was no pushover; Tabitha respected her resilience, her bravery. But Blake had worn her down over the years and now she was making some bad choices. Parading Winston Shaw around the room as her new lover would give her only a temporary victory. Blake's revenge was likely to be swift and cruel.

Tabitha enjoyed her job; she was very well paid, and working for Blake gave her access to powerful, influential men and women and their businesses. He was, unquestionably, an impressive operator. After a brief spell in his father's law firm, he had risen, in only eight years, from one of the youngest MPs in parliament to one of the most powerful back-benchers of his time. Still only 34 years of age, his inherited wealth and ruthless ambition had enabled him to assemble around himself a phalanx of politicians, judges and police officers who were happy to turn a blind eye to his illegal deals as long as they were well rewarded for doing so.

When Tabitha had taken the job, she had known none of this. It had seemed like a wonderful opportunity, too good to miss. It had been her intention, at that time, to use the experience she would gain as a stepping stone, knowing that, when the time came for her to move elsewhere, she would be better connected than anyone she knew. And in just two years, she had, indeed, gained the kind of experience that a more mundane post would never have afforded. But now, two years on, she had grave misgivings. Would he allow her to move on? Would he let her work for someone else? Over the two years of her employment, he had gradually grown to trust and then to depend upon her. Her knowledge of his business affairs, and more particularly, his abuse of his position as MP, rendered her too powerful to be anywhere other than in his camp.

Two years previously, Tabitha could not have conceived of the hypocrisy and corruption that thrived in some of the highest levels of society. Surely, she had thought, as she had begun to witness Blake's illegal deals and manipulation of judges and police officers, someone would blow the whistle sooner or later and bring his own empire crashing down upon him. Later in her life, she would reflect upon her naivety. But it would not be until the Jimmy Saville scandal broke that she would finally understand how corruption, backed up by power, could thrive and endure in plain sight until the source of the abuse was no longer alive to bear the consequences of his or her actions.

Meanwhile, she had come to recognise that Blake would rather ruin her than let her leave him for someone else, she was sure of that. And she sensed a more pressing concern; he had been looking at her recently as if he had more in mind than a business relationship.

Tabitha swept the room with her eyes, assessing the guests' readiness for the next stage of the evening's entertainment. She still didn't feel entirely comfortable in the company of such distinguished and wealthy people. She was a gate-crasher and they knew it. Moreover, she was well aware of the irony of her status here, a dark-skinned girl in a room full of white people where, centuries ago, the Montague's slaves had served at parties such as this one. She could see only one other black girl in the room, probably a hooker she surmised. Technically, she would be an escort, paid handsomely to accompany her date for the evening. However, if her date wanted sex at the end of the evening, then that was almost certainly part of the contract. Tabitha recognised that she too was at the beck and call of her employer. Living in the house, as she did, she was required to be available at all hours of the day and do whatever was required of her. Moreover, like the slaves that the Montague family had owned in the distant past, she was effectively invisible unless her service was required, which meant that all of the depravity and degeneracy of the family was played out before her eyes as if she wasn't there or as if her opinion was of no account. Like the escort, she was very well paid for her services, but there was no escaping from the politics of the relationship.

Tabitha spotted Blake's wife, Audrey. She thought that her new lover was looking distinctly nervous at the way he was being paraded in front of the guests. They, in turn, circled like sharks, sensing that there would be blood once Blake realised that Audrey was trying to humiliate him. Not so different from the power struggles of her childhood, Tabitha decided. The pimps, the dealers, the punishment beatings, it was all here really, just dressed up in tuxedos and ball gowns and legitimised with titles and positions on the board.

Growing up in a tough council estate in Peckham, the only wealthy people she had come into contact with were the drug dealers and the pimps. She had been recruited by the former as soon as she entered high school, delivering wraps of crack and heroin to users. They had seemed so impressive and successful to her at that young age, with their trainers and their gold chains and their cars. It was everything that she had wanted.

Her early education in the world of supply and demand had excited her. Her schooling in the commerce of the streets had taught her that, while ordinary people toiled in factories and shops or worked as cleaners for low wages, there was big money to be made by those people who showed enterprise. She had loved it that the money she earned was enough to keep her mother out of the hands of the pimps and put food on the table. She had graduated by pulling a concealed kitchen knife on a boy from a rival gang who was dealing on her territory, slashing him across the face. Her bubble had only burst when the police had mounted a concentrated campaign to clean up the area and the dealers had been arrested in a synchronised swoop upon the streets. In the power vacuum that ensued, many of the younger dealers had fought to seize power. Punishment beatings had been used to demand respect and to demonstrate supremacy. Recognising her ambition and keen intelligence, the emerging junta had been expecting that Tabitha would pledge her loyalty, taking a position within the power structure, but by now she had developed the maturity and vision to realise that the power of street crime was illusory and would act only as a temporary respite from the poverty of her upbringing. Recognising that escape lay in gaining a more conventional education, she had persuaded her mother to pester the council until they had moved them to an estate on the other side of the borough, where the school was much better and the distractions were less intrusive. Here, she could focus on moving up into the tier where the real power dwelt.

She sensed Blake sliding right up close to her from behind. She froze. Was this the moment where he overstepped the boundary of employer and employee?

"I think it's time to get the screens out," Blake whispered, his voice slow and dangerous. "It's time for some fun." The final word was loaded with irony.

Tabitha had already instructed the catering staff on how to arrange the screens stacked against the wall behind the bar. She needed only to catch the eye of the young man overseeing his catering staff and they snapped into action like scene shifters on a London stage. Tabitha wasn't quite sure what Blake had in mind, but she feared the worst, particularly for Audrey. The screens were quickly arranged into a continuous barrier across one corner of the ballroom. The guests gradually organised themselves in front of the screens, pointing at the little pink curtain in the middle of each one, numbered from one to ten, making suggestions to each other about what they thought they were for. As Blake approached the music decks, the DJ handed him the microphone. With his usual sense of the theatrical, Blake waited until the audience chatter subsided to a quiet hum before addressing them.

"Good evening my Lords, Ladies and Gentlemen. Thank you all for gracing us with your company here tonight at our … humble gathering."

Speaking with the gravitas developed through an upbringing of privilege and affluence then eight years of addressing his fellow MPs, Blake waved his hand to underline the lavish reality of their surroundings, the elaborate chandeliers, the family portraits on the wall, the expanse of blue velvet curtaining. His voice was thickly sardonic.

"Good to see that so many of you distinguished gentlemen have brought your ... wives with you tonight."

Blake paused to allow his audience to snigger, looking around the room and nodding with mock seriousness to indicate that he recognised that most of the men had actually brought their mistresses or, in some cases, a hooker with them. The wives were few and far between. They were recognisable by being, on the whole, more appropriately aged for their escorts than the array of pretty young women who looked as though they might still be in their teens.

"And our first game tonight," he continued, "will test just how well you know those ... wives."

More polite tittering from the crowd as they tried to imagine what Blake was planning.

"It's all quite simple really," Blake went on. "It's a matter of whether it's lights on or lights off in the bedroom. If it's lights on, then you gentlemen really should know what your lady's fanny looks like by now. And you really should be able to identify her just by that fanny alone. So, behind the screens please ladies, get those fannies out and, once the curtains are drawn back, let's see them through the cut-outs in the screens."

There was a sharp intake of breath from the guests followed by some heated exchanges between couples. Blake noted with pleasure that there were some very flushed female cheeks all of a sudden. There were a number of young women he did not recognise. They would, doubtless, have been expecting more refined entertainment then this. It was a strict rule, though, that nobody should talk about the games that took place at his parties. Clearly, they were unprepared for such crudity in such a select gathering of the rich and famous.

A young woman in a bright red ball gown, slit up to her thigh, bounded from the crowd and slid behind the screen to a bawdy cheer and round of applause. A hooker, Blake surmised, with the promise of a bonus whispered into her ear. She was quickly followed by four more women, each one celebrated with a cheer.

"Come now, ladies," Blake's voice was close to a sneer now. "So bashful? Surely not! Remember, what happens here stays here. It's just a little bit of harmless fun after all."

He surveyed the men. Some of them were feeling the pressure now. They too were flushed, struggling between the conflicting demands of not offending their escorts while trying to impress Blake and the other men in the room. Blake pondered with amusement what promises were being whispered right now into the ears of ladies in order to entice them to take the plunge.

When the ninth young women had moved behind the screens, Blake held up his hand to take back control of proceedings and indicate that he needed no more volunteers. He was very aware that it was mostly hookers with a few easily bribed mistresses that had responded. There were no actual wives there. However, he was reserving the final spot for one particular wife.

"Audrey dearest," Blake's voice dripped insincerity, "come and stand by me darling." His voice ended with an edge that Audrey recognised all too well. It would be dangerous to disobey him when he was in this mood.

As she approached him, he lowered the microphone, put his other hand to the side of her head and pulled it gently towards him, as if to reward her with an affectionate kiss on her cheek. As his mouth approached her ear, he whispered with angry venom, "If you don't get behind that screen right now, I'm going to have two of my men take your new paramour outside and cut his balls off," then kissed her gently.

Pulling back from the embrace, he lifted the microphone and smiled. "And my dear wife, just to show what a great sport she is, has volunteered to be fanny number ten. Let's give her a round of applause."

As the clapping and the cheers filled the hall, Audrey stared in fury at her husband, feeling the blood throb at her temples. He nodded back arrogantly, smiling for the sake of the audience, enjoying the moment. She knew that his threats were never empty. She had seen what he could do when crossed. She did not fear for herself, but to disobey Blake now would be to put Winston in grave danger. Tossing her head, she stalked furiously across the floor and around the back of the screen.

Once all of the women were in place behind the cut-outs, Blake signalled to Tabitha to draw back the ten sets of curtains, then reverted to the jovial host running a harmless party game.

"Come now gentlemen, let's not dally here, we don't want those cute little pussies to catch a chill, do we? Who's going to start us off?"

There was much hilarity as the escorts of the women tried to identify them, with mixed success, much to the entertainment of the crowd. Tabitha, at Blake's request, had stationed herself at the edge of the screen and was signalling to the men whether their guesses were correct or not. The onlookers responded with cheers and groans like fans at a football match. It was, Tabitha realised, equally tribal. It was at moments like this that she was at her most uncomfortable, helping Blake to manipulate and humiliate his guests in the guise of a harmless party game. She shrugged and continued to smile as if it were just a bit of fun. These were his version of the punishment beatings she had witnessed on the streets of Peckham, reinforcing his power and his ability to hurt anyone who crossed him.

Blake held up his hand to signal that he wanted to speak again. He waited for the rowdy guests to be absolutely quiet so that he could speak without raising his voice.

"So, I think it's my turn now. And if I can't identify my own wife's twat after all these years then shame on me."

He walked up and down the screens, stopping to consider each set of genitals through each cut-out then returned to number five. He stroked his chin thoughtfully then turned to face his excited audience.

"Could be this one. Its looks to me like the only fanny that has had two children popping out through it. And from what I hear, one of those children has been popping back up there from time to time."

It was spoken with a neutral tone, as if it was just a throwaway comment, but Tabitha knew the derision that lay beneath the surface. The guests, silent at first, were beginning to murmur now. Many looked puzzled by the comment but others had been at a previous party where Audrey had made her unfortunate comments and were quietly explaining it now to the others.

It had been at a party five weeks previously that Blake had lost patience with his teenage son. Frustrated by Freddie's failure to find a girlfriend of his own, Blake had hired a prostitute to pretend to be a guest at the party and try to seduce him. When the girl had come downstairs in tears, frightened to tell Blake that Freddie had taken her to his room only to show her his collection of homosexual pornography, Blake had exploded with fury, re-directing his attack at a very drunken Audrey.

"Good God woman, this is all your doing. No wonder he's a Nancy boy. You've spoilt him rotten. At his age, I couldn't keep it in my pants. If he fails to provide an heir, it will be all your fault."

"You still can't keep it in your pants," she had retorted scornfully. "He's a sensitive boy, that's all."

And then she had made that unfortunate comment which had pushed Blake into a fury.

"One night in bed with me and I'd soon straighten him out."

It was just a joke, a drunken quip from a defensive mother. But for Blake it was the final straw. Tabitha had needed to whisk Audrey out of the room for her own protection. She had taken her to a hotel and told her to stay there for a few days until Blake calmed down. When she had returned, he had continued to seethe and smoulder with rage. Tabitha had sensed, when the screens had been erected, that Blake had been planning his revenge on

Audrey, but she hadn't thought that even he was capable of such a total public humiliation of his own wife.

Once word had spread, through all the guests, of the events of the previous party, the mood became sombre. The women were shocked, either that a member of their sex could be so badly maligned or else that it might possibly be true. Some of the women tugged at their escorts, clearly disturbed by the outcome of the game and wanting to leave, but very few of them actually departed. Few of the men were confident enough to risk a show of disapproval. Meanwhile, Blake snapped back into his benign host mode.

"Good game everybody. Good game. For all of you good sports who played, there is a bedroom upstairs for you with champagne on ice. And for those of you with a more adventurous outlook on life, I have procured some recreational drugs for your entertainment and delight."

He tapped the side of his nose and winked widely around the room.

"Just remember everybody, what happens here stays here. Okay? We don't want any Nosy Parkers, do we? Tabitha, can you sort out anyone who wants coke or acid? Thank you darling."

Tabitha smiled, nodded and went to the safe, reflecting ruefully that she hadn't progressed so very far from the high school girl on the streets of South East London selling cocaine and heroin wraps.

As the music restarted and the guests tried to rekindle the party atmosphere that had been so viciously spoiled, Blake approached the attractive woman in her late thirties who had been standing alone throughout the game.

"Evening Karen. Glad you could make it."

Blake was solicitous and respectful, all signs of the wisecracking host gone. Time to do some business.

"Step inside my office. I have a proposition for you."

Chapter 4 2019

It was an angry rasp from outside which broke into Adam's sleep and startled him awake. He stumbled, wide-eyed, to the window and opened the curtains. The whining clamour was coming from the base of the tree and its perpetrator was a man dressed in black overalls and a matching baseball cap with some bright yellow ear protectors looped over the top of it. In his hands he was firmly gripping a bucking chainsaw, working his way up from the base of the tree, cutting it into long, thick logs. No point in going back to bed then.

Selecting the warmest looking pair of trousers in his wardrobe and a tee shirt, Adam dressed quickly and then set about gelling his hair and trimming his stubble down to a more fashionable length. He paused in the kitchen to drink a glass of water and check his phone for texts. Predictably, most of them were from Belinda and Nadia. Mercifully, Lucinda seemed to have been discouraged by the lack of a reply to her texts and had stopped communicating. That was something anyway. He scrolled through them quickly.

Where are you?

Why haven't you replied?

Are you okay?

There were a few stronger ones.

What the hell is going on?

Phone me …now!

Adam sighed. This was a mess. He needed to do something about it before it blew up in his face.

Realising that the chainsaw had gone quiet, he glanced up through the window. It was Alice; she was talking to chainsaw guy and looking over to where he was pointing with the yellow ear protectors which he had removed from his head. Intrigued, Adam snatched a ski jacket from the hook by the door, laced on a pair of boots and went out into the garden to investigate. The snow was still lying fairly thick on the ground but starting to melt in the early morning sunshine. He screwed his eyes up against the glare of the sun as it bounced off the snow. He could barely see Alice and the guy in the flood of light from her garden, but by shielding his eyes with his hand he spotted a place where he could step over the smashed fence and approach the base of the tree. He crunched his way across the garden, smiling into the glare so that Alice would know that he had seen her and was on his way over.

Alice was not smiling. In fact, once Adam was close enough to see her expression, she seemed positively displeased by his presence.

"Good morning." Adam ignored her look of disquiet and attempted to conjure some warmth. "Lovely day for a bit of wood chopping. How's it going?"

"What do you want?" Alice was positively icy in her response. Her expression, though, spoke more of anxiety than vexation.

After the previous day's encounter, Adam felt better equipped to deal with her disarming directness. She was, after all, he reflected, an expert in cyber security. The IT student in his Halls at Uni. had been a little bit spectrumy. Maybe that was it. Maybe, like him, she just didn't have any filters when she was talking to people. He smiled generously.

"I was intrigued to see if there was any indication as to why the tree came down. It looked pretty healthy to me." He turned towards the tree surgeon and raised his eyebrows to introduce the question. "Any ideas?"

The man nodded thoughtfully and pointed to where the roots squirmed out of the base of the tree like a nest of petrified snakes.

"Lightning strike. You can see the scorch marks there."

Sure enough, Adam could make out a blackened area of charred wood which started at the base of the trunk but went right down into the roots.

"Funny thing though," the man said, massaging the back of his neck with a gloved hand, "normally a lightning strike will sever the trunk but leave the roots in the ground. This one seems to have knocked the tree right over, ripped the roots from the earth. Never seen one like it." He nodded to underline the irregularity of the case. "It's like it's been hit by a massive bowling ball."

As Adam paused to process the image that the tree surgeon had just presented, Alice took his arm and started to pull him gently towards her house.

"It's getting cold out here," she declared firmly. "Let's go inside."

Adam was about to allow her to lead him indoors, but the tree surgeon was enjoying his new, more responsive, audience and wasn't ready to relinquish him yet.

"Anyway," he stated loudly, provoking Adam to turn back towards him, "as I was just telling your neighbour, it's uncovered an interesting looking object buried under the tree."

He pointed into the hole in the ground at a large, glass jar, caked in mud, with a black screw top lid exposed from the earth.

"I was just cleaning the mud off it when your neighbour came out," he confided to Adam. "Looks like an old-fashioned sweetie jar from one of them old-style shops where they measured out the sweets with scales and put them in paper bags." He dropped the volume of his voice as if he thought they might be overheard. "I thought maybe someone had hidden something in it and forgotten about it."

He took a pace back and folded his arms as if to say, 'What do you think about that then?'

Adam turned, smiling, to Alice, only to see that her face had crumbled. She was clearly disturbed by the discovery of the jar. She was shaking her head from side to side slowly, muttering something too quietly for Adam to hear it.

"Sorry?" Adam asked her. "I didn't catch that."

She shook her head more vigorously now and turned her piercing eyes directly upon his.

"You need to come inside Adam," she urged him, more insistent now. "We need to talk."

She renewed her hold on his arm and eased him firmly back towards her house.

"I'll need to pop over to another job," the tree surgeon shouted at their retreating backs. "I got a call just before you came out to say there's a tree blocking a road. I'll need to go and clear the road first and then I'll be back to finish this."

Alice raised a hand to acknowledge that she had heard but she did not turn around.

Once inside the warmth of Alice's kitchen, Adam unzipped his jacket and slipped it over the back of a chair. Slumping into the seat, he looked up at her with his most winning smile.

"Any chance of some coffee? The chainsaw woke me up and I came out straight away to see what was happening."

Alice shut her eyes and exhaled heavily. Clearly it wasn't what she had in mind. She paused, then straightened to her full height, breathed in, then returned the smile.

"Of course," she responded brightly. "Only instant I'm afraid."

She held up the jar, made eye contact and raised her eyebrows, waiting for a signal to continue.

He nodded and grinned. "Perfect. Hot, wet and strong is all that matters."

As she waited for the kettle to boil, she flicked a couple of glances at Adam, unsure of how to continue. He seemed even more bouncy than normal. It worried her.

"So," he declared suddenly, his voice low and theatrical, "a mystery. Buried treasure, summoning the powers of the heavens to strike the tree down with a thundery bolt and liberate it from its ancient lair."

"What?" She turned to face him, bewildered by this sudden outburst.

He shook his head and smiled. "Sorry. Got carried away. It's just that … well, I've been looking for some ideas for an original screenplay. I told you, didn't I, about wanting to make something more commercial? Well, this could be it. It's a brilliant opening scene."

Too excited to remain in his seat, he stood up and started to circle his hands, swirling them in front of his body.

"We start with mist, swirling around the tree. The music is mysterious, ominous, rising in volume. Then, CRACK," he raised his voice and threw his hands towards the ceiling, "a huge bolt of lightning shoots across the screen and sweeps the tree out of the ground, leaving it to crash down onto the fence between the two gardens." He calmed his voice, lowering the volume until it was barely above a whisper. "We see smoke rising from the base of the tree. The camera zooms slowly towards it and then, through the smoke, we catch sight of it, the mysterious jar of treasure. The music becomes …"

He trailed off and put his hand behind his head as he thought.

"Well, it depends upon what's in the jar doesn't it? If it's something amazing we need, sort of … magical music. You know, like it's the lost ark of the covenant or something. But if it's something evil we need brooding, dark music. It just depends."

He took a step closer to Alice and held out one hand. "We need to open it. We need to see what's inside."

Alice took a step backwards instinctively and raised one hand, palm facing Adam. Her expression was one of distress. She was clearly not comfortable with this outburst of energy and excitement. In order to gather herself, she turned to finish making the coffee then turned back and placed it on the table.

"Sit down Adam."

Her voice was glacial. Her anguish was unmistakeable. Adam sat down, his elation extinguished like the flame of a candle as it is pinched out.

She took a step back, removing her glasses and placing them on the kitchen counter. Adam had never seen her without her glasses before. Those eyes. Their brilliance was unnerving. Adam felt himself being drawn in by them. Folding her arms, she looked down on him and gently bit her lip before beginning.

"The thing is, Adam, I think I know what's in the jar."

There was a weariness in her voice, as if the knowledge was draining away her energy.

"You do? So, what is it? Don't keep me in suspense."

Adam tried to rekindle the energy he had created with his account of his opening scene, but she shook her head sadly, dousing his enthusiasm.

"It's just a time capsule, that's all."

Seeing his puzzled expression, she continued.

"We did them at school once. It's like ..." she paused as she searched for the words, "it's like a record of who you are and what you have done and what you want your life to be like. It's a kind of snapshot of your life. And you can include photos if you wish. And you can put in objects which are important to you ... and ideas about what is going on in your life and what you would like to happen. It's private, like a diary. In fact, you could include bits from your diary if you wanted."

She paused to allow Adam to assimilate all this and understand its purpose.

"And then you bury it," she continued. "You bury it and set yourself a time when you're going to dig it up again." She looked towards the window and smiled thoughtfully. "The idea is that you look at that snapshot of your life in the past and compare it with your present life. And you decide whether your life has turned out how you thought it would."

Turning back to Adam, she regarded him indulgently and shook her head.

"It's not likely to be very exciting. It's certainly not treasure. And it wasn't buried for us to dig up. It's for its owner. For us to open it would be like reading someone's diary. It's personal. It would be wrong for us to intrude."

Adam was not to be dissuaded so easily. This all felt like he was being fobbed off. He wasn't sure why she was doing this, but he definitely wasn't prepared to be put off by such lame arguments.

"Diaries are good. Lots of good films have diaries in them, Bridget Jones, Adrian Mole…"

"And Anne Frank," Alice interjected darkly. "The thing is, once you have seen it, you can't unsee it. What if there's something really awful in there? What if something dreadful happened to whoever put it there? What if," and she paused for several seconds, "what if whatever you find in there is really distressing and it upsets the rest of your life?"

Adam was struck by the poignancy of her words. The more time he spent with this woman, the more she surprised him, and the more he was captivated by her. But, at the same time, what she was saying was nonsense. And it certainly wasn't going to prevent him from following a story. Why be frightened of something a child had buried in their garden as a school project? He sprang to his feet, took his coat off the back of the chair, and started to put it on.

"Come on Alice. It's an adventure."

He opened the back door and bounded back down to the foot of the tree. By the time that Alice had caught him up, he had already stooped down into the mud and retrieved the grimy jar. He held it up in two hands, grinning like a little boy, and gave it a gentle shake as if it were a Christmas present and he was trying to guess the contents. Without warning, the glass shattered in his hands, scattering the contents of the jar over the melting snow.

"What? Oh, sod it. Quick, before it all gets wet," exclaimed Adam.

Between them, they snatched up all of the objects and papers from the ground, Adam giggling all the while. He placed the objects in his pocket and between them they carried the documents back to the house. Once inside the kitchen they laid everything out on the table then sat back on opposite sides. As Adam reached across to inspect one of the documents, Alice leaned across to take hold of his wrist. Impatient to get started, he tried to twist out of her grip, but she held him firmly.

"Last chance, Adam," she cautioned.

He shrugged, confused by her lack of excitement. What was wrong with the woman? "Last chance to what?"

She frowned, releasing her hold on his wrist and pointing a finger at him as if she were a school teacher, about to give him a scolding.

"Thanks to your clumsiness, everything is out of the capsule. And it can never go back in," she added. She inclined her head towards him to underline the significance of this. "The contents are back in the world from which they came. And they will need to be dealt with." She paused as she thought how to express what she needed to say in a way that Adam would understand it.

"The thing is, it doesn't need to be you that deals with it." She had moved on from scolding him now; there was genuine concern in her voice. "Like I said before, once you have seen it you cannot unsee it. Once you look at it, you are involved. There is no going back."

Adam was completely mystified by now.

"What is it that you're so worried about?" he asked. "You said it wasn't likely to be very exciting. There's something you're not telling me."

Alice blushed. "I'm sorry," she confessed. "I was just trying to steer you away from it. The fact is, I have a bad feeling about this. Why hasn't the person who buried it returned to retrieve it? I just have a sense that something bad may have happened." She shrugged and gave him a wan smile. "I was trying to protect you from being involved."

Adam was perplexed, unsure whether to feel flattered or patronised by her protectiveness. He hadn't pegged her as a woman who would be susceptible to feelings and intuition. It began to dawn on him that she was, in her odd way, demonstrating a level of care for his well-being, albeit completely misguided, and that he had just ignored all this and gone charging in to try to get some material for a film. It was his turn to feel embarrassed.

"I appreciate your concern for me, Alice, I really do. And I'm sorry if I've seemed a bit giddy. Fair enough, I got a bit carried away with the film thing. But I don't want you to think I'm being flippant. If you've got bad feelings about this then I respect that. It's not that I don't value your intuition; I do think you may be right; it might be that something bad has happened. But if there's something wrong here then I don't want you to face it alone. In fact,

I'd be honoured if you'd let me share the responsibility for this. After all, I broke the jar."

As he was speaking, Adam increasingly realised that he did really care for this woman and he wanted her to care about him too. He hoped his speech could repair some of the damage he had done by ignoring her warnings and appearing to disregard her concerns. Not that he thought for a moment that there was anything to worry about really, but she clearly did and he wanted her to know that he saw that now. As he spoke, he reached across with both hands and lightly held hers, giving the slightest of squeezes for what he hoped she would interpret as reassurance and sincerity.

After a few moments of tense silence, she broke the tension with a lop-sided smile.

"Okay then."

Adam smiled back, still holding her hand. "All for one and one for all."

When Alice looked puzzled, he said, "The Musketeers?"

When she shook her head, still confused, he added, "Never mind. There should be three of us anyway. Let's see what secrets the tree has been hiding all of these years."

Chapter 5 1979

It had been a difficult year for Martine. Since graduating from drama school, she had struggled to find work. Oh, she had been to plenty of auditions, but she never got past the first stage. The room was always packed to the rafters with experienced actresses, and it seemed to Martine that they were all hugging and kissing each other and talking about their role in this play and their tour with that company and oh, the director was such a sweetie. It was, she decided, like a gigantic club with exclusive membership. She had done a couple of roles for alternative theatre groups, performing in tiny upstairs rooms in pubs to audiences which were often barely more in number than the members of the cast. It was experience of a sort, but it didn't count for much. It wasn't at all what she had imagined.

Martine had dreamt of being an actress for as long as she could remember. At school, her vivacity and confidence had always earned her a key role in the annual productions. Looking younger than she actually was worked well for her in local amateur dramatics too. She could play little girls while she was well into her teens, bringing her maturity to the role while still looking the part. As a teenager, performing in a local theatre, she would imagine herself in a top London theatre, taking curtain calls in front of an applauding audience which would rise to its feet when she took her bow. She would fantasise about late night parties with famous actors and actresses, reading her reviews in the papers the next day.

For the past three months she had been paying her rent by serving burgers and fries at the local McDonalds. Before that, she had been a nanny to a spiteful brat in Kensington whose parents left her to bring up their neglected offspring while they worked long hours then went on to parties and corporate entertainments. All the while, she was having to lie to her mother in her weekly phone call from the pay phone at the bottom of the road. She could sense her mother's anxiety, knew she was dying to come up to London to sweep her back to the comfort of the suburbs and a job in the bank or the library. Her dreams of stardom retreated further and further with each rejection, but she wasn't ready to give up yet.

"It's good Mum. I'm getting parts. Not big ones yet, but that will come with time. I'm getting the experience I'll need for when the big part comes along."

Deep down, she had gradually come to recognise that the all-important first break wasn't going to come and find her; she needed to make it happen.

As she walked down the stairs of Blake Montague's country manor house, Martine felt a deep sense of foreboding. She was deeply disturbed by everything that she had seen and heard that day. Blake Montague scared her, his wife appeared to be completely unhinged, his son, Freddie was a deeply disturbed young man and she, Martine, had failed dismally with the mission that Blake had given her.

She should never have taken Sharon's advice. They had been in the local pub together, celebrating Sharon's success in landing a part in a new movie.

"You lucky thing. I've been to dozens of auditions and I never even get a call-back. How did you do it?"

"You need a powerful friend, Martine."

Martine sighed. "And where do I find one of those?"

Sharon leaned in so that they could not be overheard.

"Blake Montague."

"Who?"

"He's an MP. And a business man. Got fingers in lots of pies, if you know what I mean."

Martine didn't really know what her excited friend meant, but if this guy was a possible route to success, then she was interested.

"Okay, so how do I make him my friend?"

Sharon smiled enigmatically. "He's a terrible old letch darling. A girl has to use whatever assets she's got to get ahead in this world."

Martine spluttered on her drink. "What? You slept with him?"

Martine rolled her eyes. "Oh, come on, it's no big deal. Actually, it was rather a lovely evening. He took me to The Ritz for supper and then to his apartment in Kensington. There was champagne on ice and caviar." She made a face. "Actually, I could have done without the caviar. Too fishy. Champagne was lovely though. And silk sheets on the bed." Sharon ran her hands through her hair and closed her eyes momentarily. "I could get used to living like that."

"So, you had sex with him?" Martine's eyes were wide with amazement. "And then what?"

Sharon shrugged. "I told him I was looking for a part in a movie and he told me he'd see what he could do for me." She smiled, leaning back in her seat. "The casting director actually called me and told me to come for an audition. How about that then? After my audition, he told me on the spot that he could definitely find something for me. Called me the next day with the offer of a part."

"And what about this Blake man?"

Sharon shrugged. "I think it's all about the pursuit and the conquest for him. Since he had me, he's been a perfect sweetie. I've been to a couple of his parties since then. He behaved like nothing had happened." She grinned. "Even introduced me to his wife."

Martine had been too shocked to respond to Sharon's offer of an introduction. In fact, it had rather spoiled the evening and she had made an excuse so that she could go home early. However, after another five failed auditions and a phone call with her mother, she had recognised that she was getting close to giving up on her childhood dreams. After a sleepless night, turning her options over and over in her mind, she had telephoned her friend and asked for an introduction.

And now she was regretting it more than she had ever regretted anything in her life. She had come to the house just three hours previously, expecting to find Blake alone, ready to seduce her. She had prepared herself mentally for that. To her surprise, however, he had taken her through to a large sitting room, introduced her to his wife and told her his whole family were at home. And then he had explained, with his crazy wife chipping in from time to time, what he wanted her to do.

"I want you to seduce my son, Freddie," he had said.

Chapter 6 2019

Adam started by pulling towards himself the two objects that lay before them, while Alice picked up and glanced at each of the documents, putting them back on the table in some kind of order. He paused to watch her. Her hands moved deftly, her fingers pale with nails cut very short, arranging the papers methodically and purposefully. The speed with which she worked intrigued him. He wondered what she was thinking. Why had she tried so hard to keep him away from the contents of the time capsule? It was almost as if she had half guessed what might be there. Sensing that she was being watched, Alice looked up and frowned. Adam looked down at the table and picked up one of the objects in front of him.

"This is just a dog collar," he commented, holding a light brown leather collar up for Alice to see. "No name or identifying marks on it. All it tells us is that the person who buried the time capsule also had a dog."

"Try the locket," she responded. Was there a hint of impatience in her voice? She nodded towards a blackened silver locket on a long chain upon the table. "See if it opens. There might be a photograph inside."

Adam picked up the heart-shaped locket and revolved it in his fingers to investigate a way of opening it. It was engraved with what looked like the leaves of a plant or a shrub with a hinge on one side and a tiny clasp on the other. When Adam pressed it, the locket sprang open to reveal a tiny faded picture of a woman's head and shoulders on one side and a lock of hair on the other. He held it up for Alice to see.

"What do you think? Could this be who buried the capsule?"

Alice looked over the top of her glasses without moving her head. She smiled indulgently. "Try to think like a detective. If you were putting together a time capsule, would you include a heart-shaped locket with your own picture in it?"

Adam felt put out, like a little boy who had just been told by a strict teacher to concentrate. Had she meant to put him down or was she just unaware of the effect she had? He hoped it was the latter. He decided not to take offence.

"So who then?" He scratched the stubble on his chin. "Mother perhaps? Sweetheart?"

Alice nodded. "Could be. Or else a close friend or family member maybe. There are some photos in the envelope there." She inclined her head towards the table. "See if you can find the same woman in any of those."

Adam pulled out the photos and lined them up in front of himself on the edge of the table. He was immediately drawn to a picture of what appeared to be a family grouping. There was a man and a woman standing together with a girl and a boy in front of them. They were all laughing, as if the photographer had just cracked a joke to get the expressions he wanted for a happy family scene. Adam held the picture in the locket in front of it. A match, he was certain of it. Yes, the woman in the family scene was definitely the same as the one in the locket. He was about to demonstrate his success to Alice but, looking up, he could see that she was engrossed in a page of a letter that she was holding in one hand with the rest of the pages held in the other. He resisted the temptation to receive some praise for his discovery. Okay then, he would play the detective and impress her.

He looked back at the family scene. It's a colour photo, he noted, so not really ancient. The family seemed to be in some huge room like a manor or a castle with leaded windows and large, dark paintings on the wall. Maybe a day out to a stately home, he mused. The clothes and the hairstyles looked dated. Adam realised he was a little out of his depth on this aspect but he recalled family photos of his own parents and grandparents back in the seventies and eighties. Yes, that would be his guess.

He put the photograph down and picked up a picture of a girl who was squatting down on a red carpet so that she could cuddle a large, white, fluffy dog. It looked like a poodle to Adam, though it had not been clipped into some prissy shape like he expected poodles to be and it was a good deal bigger than any poodle he had seen before. He pulled it closer to his face to examine the dog's collar. It was light brown with what looked like a brass buckle. Adam looked back at the collar on the table. Yes, that was it. The collar in the jar belonged to this dog and was probably put there by the girl in the picture. He glanced back at the family scene. Bingo. It was the girl at the front of the picture. She looked a little older than in the family scene, maybe early teens he guessed, but definitely the same girl. He replaced the photograph on the table and picked up the last one. There she was again, only this time she was in a garden with a much older lady. He examined the background of the picture, the fence, the lawn, the flowerbeds. Could it be this garden? Glancing across at Alice to check that she was still absorbed in the letter, he stood and made his way across to the window. Holding the picture up, he compared them. The garden in the picture looked very different in terms of the bushes and shrubs, but the fence could easily be the same and the flowerbeds were a very similar shape. There was just one major difference. There was no tree.

He had not heard Alice moving but he sensed her presence just behind him. He looked over his shoulder to see that she too was comparing the picture and the garden.

"What do you think?" he ventured. "Could it be the same garden?"

She nodded. "Definitely. The photo was taken before the tree had grown."

Adam pulled a face. "I wish we'd asked the tree surgeon to estimate the age of the tree. That would have helped us to date the photo. We'll need to ask him when he comes back."

"Forty years old." She gave him a winning smile. "I'm guessing that Dora planted the tree as a conker on top of her time capsule so that would date it at 1979."

Adam frowned. "That's a guess, right? You can't be that certain about the age of the tree."

Alice raised her eyebrows. "You really are a townie aren't you? You just need to count the rings."

Adam blinked in incomprehension.

"I asked the tree surgeon to cut me a cross section of the trunk so I could count the rings," she explained. "It's like a code. Each tree has its age encoded within the wood. Every year it grows one more ring. This tree has forty rings."

Adam grinned sheepishly. "Okay then, Alan Turing, I bow to your superior knowledge of tree code." He paused. "Wait a minute, you said Dora. Have you learnt something from that letter?"

Alice winced. "I've learned a great deal. Some of it's not good I'm afraid. Sit back down and I'll show you."

When they were both seated, Alice held up the first page of a letter so that Adam could see that it was addressed to Dora. She held the final page next to it. There were just two sentences on the page. 'I'm innocent, Dora. Please believe me. Freddie'

Adam nodded to show that he had read them. "Dora and Freddie. Are they the children in the picture?" He slid it across the table for Alice to examine.

"Yes, I think so, though Freddie wasn't a child by the time that he wrote this letter. He was in jail, serving a life sentence for the murder of his mother."

Adam blinked hard as he took this in. He shook his head to signal bewilderment. "Why would he do that? They look an average happy family in the picture."

Alice shook her head. "Clearly there was something wrong, really. As for Freddie, he wrote this letter to his sister to protest his innocence. The evidence was against him but he claims in the letter that he was framed by his father, Blake. He begs Dora at the end to believe in him. He sounds pretty desperate."

Adam leaned back in his chair. "Wow. What a story. Do you believe him?"

Alice shrugged once more. "He sounds like a very messed up young man. He tells Dora that he's off the drugs now and determined to prove his innocence. He accepts that he's messed his life up but he's pretty bitter about his dad. He also wants Dora to know that there was no truth in the rumours about him and his mum Audrey."

"Rumours?" Adam queried.

Alice shook her head dolefully. "That's all he says. Something bad, I think. He sounds desperate for Dora to believe in him."

Adam was beginning to get very excited about this story. It had the potential to be a real mystery thriller. He could see, however, that Alice was looking quite upset about it all. Was this what she had meant when she had talked about having a feeling that something bad may have happened? Adam was increasingly convinced that Alice knew more than she was sharing with him but he decided to keep that to himself for now. In the meantime, he needed to demonstrate empathy and contain his enthusiasm for the unfolding story as best he could.

"So, anything useful in the other documents?"

Alice put the letter down and picked up a single sheet and looked at it with a compassionate smile. "This is a poem from Dora to her dog, Jakey."

She looked across at Adam, who did his best to look equally wistful. "She tells the dog he's her only friend. She's very lonely without her mother and her brother. It's pretty sad stuff." She held it out for him to take.

Having read the poem, Adam stayed silent and stared at his hands for a few moments in an attempt to signal to Alice that he too was moved. Secretly, he was pleased. Sad kid with a dog; that could add a nice extra dimension to the film script.

He pointed at a pencil-drawn picture of a tree. "Dora's work?" he queried.

Alice emerged from her melancholy and smiled more brightly. "Yes. I think it was her idea of what the tree would look like when it was grown. On the other side there's a family tree. Kind of a metaphorical connection I think."

She flipped the sheet over and turned it towards Adam.

"So, at the top you can see grandparents for both parents. Blake and Audrey are the parents below them. Audrey took Blake's name when she married him, Montague."

Adam held up a hand to halt her. "Wait a minute. Blake Montague?"

She nodded. "That's right. The Tory MP. Shouldn't be too hard to find out more about what happened."

Adam grinned broadly. It just got better and better. Too late, he caught Alice's disapproving stare and wiped the smile from his face.

She pointed to the last remaining sheet on the table. "This one is the mystery document," she said. "It's in code." She held the paper up to demonstrate. It was covered with rows of numbers, organised in groups of three.

Adam felt a thrill pulse through him. Yes! This was the clincher. This would be at the heart of the intrigue within the story.

"What, you mean like spies use?" he laughed. "This little girl is a spy?"

Alice shook her head sadly. "I told you, didn't I Adam? The time capsule wasn't meant to be found by someone like us. She's coded it because it's secret … because she doesn't want anyone else to know what's in it."

Adam cocked his head to one side and screwed his eyes up. "So, why put it in there then?"

Alice sighed deeply. "I can't be sure, but I think that something really awful happened and this was Dora's way of coping with it. I think she put all of the trauma into the jar and buried it; an attempt to purge herself of whatever happened, to remove it from her life. She put the conker on top so that nobody would find it for a very long time. Maybe she thought she would be dead by the time it came to light. I think the coding was her insurance policy, just in case somebody found it before she died."

Adam turned his eyes away to consider this for a moment. Yes, she definitely did know more than she was sharing with him. Looking back, he found her searching his face for a response to what she had said. He met her gaze coolly.

"Do you think that you can crack it?"

She returned his gaze steadily. "I've spent much of my life working with code. I've got a few ideas about what she has done here so, yes, I think I can probably crack it. The question is whether I should."

Adam was puzzled. "Why not? It's the key to the mystery."

She shook her head slowly. "It's the awful bit. That's why she coded it. It's not for our eyes. It's meant to be buried and forgotten. I keep telling you Adam, once we've seen it, the awful truth is back out in the world again. Whatever it is, we'll know about it. And we may have to do something about it. This is our last chance to put it all back in the ground where it belongs."

Adam's eyes widened in disbelief. "No way Alice. This story needs to be out in the open. There's a strong suggestion here that an injustice has been done. Freddie might still be in prison for a crime he didn't commit. We can't back out now Alice. You have to crack that code."

Alice held his gaze for a moment, breathed deeply, then looked down and shuffled all of the documents together.

Chapter 7 1979

As Martine walked towards Blake Montague's study, she could hear the muffled sounds of an angry exchange taking place behind the closed door. Clearly, he was on the phone, as she could only hear one half of the altercation, but she could hear enough to confirm that he was as nasty as she had suspected when she had met him earlier that day. He had been all smiles and charm when explaining to her why he had hired her to seduce his son, but she had sensed an undercurrent of malice and ruthlessness. Now she could hear it. His language was disgusting, using filthy obscenities to berate the poor person at the other end of the phone, albeit delivered with a cut glass, public school accent. She felt sick. She did not dare to tell him what had just taken place between herself and his teenage son. Quickly casting a look around the room, she checked to see if anyone had seen her come down the stairs. There was no one. Perhaps she could just walk out of the front door, leave and never come back. Except that she had no car; Blake had sent a chauffeur to pick her up this morning. She felt all of the life draining out of her limbs. She wanted to run but she didn't have the strength. Feeling dizzy with panic, all she could do was flop down on a black leather Chesterfield, her heart pounding with dread.

By the time that the door to Blake Montague's study opened, Martine had composed herself a little. While gathering herself, she had heard him threaten someone in the vilest way. Clearly, he was going to get angry with her too unless she could somehow take control of the situation and charm him. It was, after all, no more than what she had psyched herself up do when she had arrived here this morning. Unbuttoning the top two buttons of her blouse and easing her skirt away from her knees, she had leaned back as if relaxed, preparing herself for the acting audition of her life.

"Ah, Miss Chalmers. I hope you haven't been waiting long."

Blake was all smiles and charm once more, as if the row in his study had never taken place. He must have known that Martine had overheard at least some of it. She sensed that she was being tested now. She was ready for it.

"Long enough to recognise a man who knows what he wants and how to get it," she responded coolly.

Blake paused, narrowing his eyes slightly as he considered this unexpected answer. The girl was full of surprises. She had seemed like a bit of a mouse when he had talked to her earlier, but this was something altogether different. He was intrigued.

"Indeed?" He raised his eyebrows to signal his approval of her answer. "And how about the man's son?"

Martine threw up her arms in despair. "He's a boy who doesn't know what he wants yet." She tossed Blake a conspiratorial smile. "He actually showed me his collection of gay porn. I think he was hoping to shock me." She shook her head slowly, tutting gently. "He has a lot of growing up to do."

Seeing Blake's features beginning to harden, she responded quickly, her heart fluttering.

"I'm no psychologist, but I think there's a bit of teenage rebellion going on here. Maybe he's gay, maybe he isn't. Frankly, I don't think he's ready for any kind of sex yet. He's just a boy, which is a shame, because I was all ready for a man." As she spoke, Martine wondered where all this was coming from. This was nothing like her. She felt that she sounded like some 1950s movie sirene, Mae West maybe, or Marilyn Monroe. She hoped that Blake would fall for it.

Once again, Blake paused, reappraising this surprising young lady. Despite the nonsense and cliché she was spouting, she was actually rather compelling. Well, she was an actress of course. And rather an attractive one at that. He examined her thoughtfully. Her dark brown hair tumbled around her shoulders and framed a delicate, heart shaped face. Her lips were full and plump. Probably natural he thought, though you couldn't always tell these days. And her eyes. Yes, those were the compelling thing about her; deep, passionate eyes which drew you in and held you. She could have her uses, he considered. She had certainly managed to defuse his anger with Freddie. Not many people could do that. And she was very presentable for when he was entertaining clients. He nodded with satisfaction.

"Well, I wouldn't want you to leave here disappointed. If the son could not oblige you, maybe the father can." He gestured towards his study. "Step inside and we'll see what happens."

Her heart still thudding, Martine rose from the Chesterfield and walked into the room before him, hearing the door close as he entered behind her.

Chapter 8 2019

As the train jolted noisily towards St Pancras Station, Adam rehearsed what he intended to say to Belinda. Her texts had become increasingly angry during the previous evening and she had not responded well to his reply that he was sorry he hadn't been in touch but he was very busy at the moment. He had tried phoning her but it was a very short call. She had barked an ultimatum at him and then slammed the phone down.

"Meet me on Saturday at The Dolphin at 1pm. Do NOT make me wait for you!"

The journey had been a tortuous one. He'd needed to travel in the wrong direction initially to pick up a connection from Rochester. The shabby upholstery of the South Eastern Region train depressed him. It was nearly full, a mixture of commuters, football fans, families and the odd tourist with maps and guide books spread out on their knees. Thankfully, nobody wanted to talk to him, which left him free to consider how he was going to play this.

He'd been dating Belinda for nearly four months now. She had approached him at a party and he had been flattered by her attentions. Now, following a formula he had developed over the years, he weighed her positives and negatives carefully. She was very pretty and lots of fun, a real party girl. She was good in bed, no, very good actually, and she even made breakfast sometimes. Hmmm. She seemed fairly bright but she lacked ambition; most of the time she just used temping agencies to get secretarial work. Her major drawback was that she was very possessive, maybe even a little insecure. If he so much as looked at another girl, she became moody. In fact, now he came to think of it, as time had gone on, he was seeing more of her moody side and less of the party girl. He reflected that Alexis, a previous girlfriend, had gone like that after a few months as well. She had told him, when they broke up, that she had never felt insecure before but that men like him had that effect on women. She wasn't specific what she meant by 'men like him' but he guessed it was connected with her suspicion that he was dating another woman at the same time as her, which, to be fair, he was.

He recalled that his father had spoken to him about his girlfriends once. He smiled at the memory. It had been at Christmas, over a glass of sherry, while his mother was busy making the dinner. Adam had suspected that his mother had put him up to it.

"You need to think about the way that you treat women." He had looked uncomfortable as he had said it.

They didn't sound like his words at all. Much more the sort of thing his mother would have said.

"What do you mean Dad? I think I'm good to them. I mean ... I take them out, I buy them things, I pay for them in restaurants."

His father had smiled indulgently; his heart clearly wasn't in this little father-and-son counselling session.

"The fact is, Adam, you've had more girlfriends in the last six months than I've had in my whole life. You seem to pick them up and put them down again rather casually. That's all I'm saying."

Adam wasn't sure from his father's tone whether there wasn't a little envy mixed in with the disapproval. Generally, he tried to tell his parents as little as possible about his relationships, ever since his mother found out he was dating two girls at the same time, but she seemed to have a sixth sense for these things. Having always wanted a daughter herself, she had naturally gravitated towards his girlfriends, wanting to be protective of them, insisting that Adam be fair and truthful with them. Once he had moved out, it became easier to tell her as little as possible.

By the time that the tired old carriage was trundling slowly through the closely-packed, red brick houses of Stratford, Adam had made his mind up. He would finish the relationship then try to address his recent neglect of Nadia. He was going to tell Belinda that he was living outside of London now in order to research and plan his film project and that, really, he thought that they should go on a break. He was sorry if that wasn't what she wanted but she needed to understand that his career was important to him and it was at a critical stage. He would tell her that he would understand totally if she wanted to date someone else; he might put his hand on her arm at this point, just to show her how sincere he was about this. All the while that he rehearsed this, he was aware that the face of Alice kept reappearing in his thoughts. He sensed that she was in some way involved in this, though he couldn't see how. He wouldn't apply the pros and cons test to her, she would come down heavily on the side of negative with her lack of care for her appearance and her brusque manner with him. And yet, there was something about her that kept finding its way into his thoughts; he felt drawn to her in some way he could not define yet.

There was almost no sign of snow on the busy streets, just a few patches of dark slush left in the corners where nobody walked. He strode briskly, arriving at The Dolphin well ahead of schedule, anxious not to provoke Belinda by making her wait. He chose a table near to the door and sat down in the seat that faced it so that he could see her as soon as she entered and gauge her mood. By the time that his watch showed 1 o'clock, he had been waiting for twenty minutes, nursing a tonic water, a glass of prosecco ready on the table as a peace offering.

Her face, as she entered, was not what he expected. He had anticipated a moody scowl, or else smouldering anger. In fact, she was smiling. This was encouraging. He stood to greet her and smiled back. She was looking gorgeous, her hair coloured a few shades lighter to an ash blonde, her lips red and full. He felt his convictions waver. Maybe this was not the time to end it after all. However, as she drew closer, he sensed it was not a warm expression. In fact, it was more of a sneer. And then he realised why, for, in her wake, Nadia had entered the pub and was bearing down upon him with a similar smirk of contempt on her dark, smooth-skinned face. The two women sat down together on either side of Adam, leaning forward in their chairs so that he felt hemmed in and trapped. His gut lurched sickeningly.

"What, only one glass of prosecco?"

It was Belinda who spoke first, almost theatrical in her sarcasm.

"Which one of us is it for Adam? Or have you got another girlfriend up your sleeve?"

Nadia replied before Adam could overcome his shock and embarrassment.

"I think we're supposed to share it Belinda," she cooed with simulated innocence. "You know, like we're supposed to share Adam."

Both women leaned back in their seats simultaneously, as if to demonstrate their unity against the common enemy, Adam.

"How …?"

Adam was still stunned by their tactical assault, unable to find words to respond. The women were clearly ready for his confusion and had their next phase all prepared.

"Social media, Adam." It was Belinda's turn once more to belittle him. "You know, Facebook, Instagram … You work in the media don't you Adam? So, you know the media is how people connect."

"No Belinda, he's in movies." Nadia's irony was cutting. "It's all one way in Adam's world. He puts on a show and we tell him how wonderful it is."

"Oh, I see." The mock innocence from Belinda this time. "Whereas in **our** world we use the media to find out what other people are doing. You know, our friends … and their friends."

"That's right Belinda. And one of them tells us that this cheating rat is two-timing us." Nadia nodded gravely, like a judge pronouncing sentence.

Adam found himself turning his face from side to side like an umpire in a tennis match, dizzy from the speed and ferocity of this attack. He started to rise from his chair, desperate to escape, but a carefully manicured hand was laid firmly on each arm, one dark and one light, pulling him back into the seat. Long, red, painted nails, pinning him down like an insect on a cork board. He felt the sick rising from his stomach, tasted the bile, bitter in the back of his throat. There was no way out of this. He couldn't run away this time. And anyway, they were right; he was cheating on them both.

He took a deep breath then turned to Nadia, her sweet face framed by long black braids. Her expression of scorn was fading now, replaced by two large tears which tracked from the corners of her huge brown eyes, down her cheeks, towards the corners of her mouth. His stomach heaved once more.

"I'm so sorry," he started. "I never meant to hurt you. It's just that …"

Nadia had raised one palm towards him, shaking her head slowly and miserably to silence him.

"I loved you." It was nearly a sob. "I thought you loved me." She closed her eyes and held them tight shut for a few moments before she continued. When she opened them again, they were wide and fierce. "But now you disgust me, you and men like you. I never want to hear from you again."

She lowered her eyes and sighed deeply as a sign that she had finished with him.

He turned towards Belinda. She was leaning back in her chair, arms crossed, piercing him with her stare. Even now, he was stunned by her beautiful, high cheek bones, her perfect teeth.

"You want it all, don't you Adam? You feel entitled to it. You arrogant, selfish bastard."

Adam had given up trying to speak. He just let the storm of the two women's anger lash down upon him, tearing away his sense of self-worth and leaving him bare and defenceless. They were right. He was a cheat. He was a rat. He wondered why he did it, why he couldn't just date one woman at a time. He'd always done it, he knew that. And it all went horribly wrong every now and then. Well, it would, wouldn't it? As he thought this, it was Alice's voice that he imagined, articulating the statement with that flat, factual intonation she used. Was it exciting? Was it flattering? Again, her face appeared, trying to understand him. Well, no, he couldn't honestly say that it was, not really. It was just like having a drink in front of you and being offered another one. It was just so easy to say yes. But really, he had to stop doing this.

When Belinda's fury finally abated and she lapsed into an emotionally exhausted silence, Adam stood slowly and took a step backwards so that he could address both women at the same time.

"You deserve better." His voice was soft and grave. "You're both lovely people and you both deserve better. I'm sorry."

He turned and slunk away. Neither woman looked up to see him go.

Chapter 9 1979

"Do you know where he is Tabitha?"

Audrey was looking dreadful. The dark rings around her eyes were a clear sign that she wasn't sleeping and Tabitha understood why. She was concerned about Winston; he had quite simply disappeared. Audrey had ushered her into the wrought iron conservatory, while Blake was meeting with a client in his study, in order to confide in her. She seemed to regard Tabitha as an ally. It was not a role she felt comfortable with.

Tabitha sat very upright in the rattan chair, looked out upon the broad sweep of lawn leading to the lake and considered how to answer the question. She felt sorry for Audrey but her behaviour was increasingly self-destructive. Tabitha felt that she needed to maintain a safe distance from her while still acknowledging that she was the wife of her employer and a fellow woman in need of support.

"I'm hoping that Mr Shaw has run away for his own safety, Lady Montague." Her delivery was tight-lipped and formal. "He looked quite worried at the party when Sir Blake asked you to join in that game and go behind the screen. I think perhaps he thought that Sir Blake was angry with you and that it had something to do with him."

Her expression impassive, Tabitha studied Audrey's face to see how she responded. She really did hope that Winston had run. That was what she had advised him to do once she had witnessed the savagery of Blake's humiliation of his wife. She had been very aware that there was personal risk involved in cheating Blake of any revenge he might be planning upon his wife's lover, so she had spoken to him confidentially; a terse interchange, later that evening, while pretending to offer him some recreational drugs.

"Mr Shaw, Sir Blake is very angry with you. You are likely to get hurt. Badly hurt. It would be better for everyone, including Audrey, if you disappeared for a while."

He had looked terrified. Tabitha had felt sorry for him, lured into a world which was clearly way beyond anything he had experienced in his privileged life. These were people who were capable of monstrous cruelty. She felt that he was beginning to understand this now.

"But why, Tabitha? He knows that I love him." Audrey was distraught. Clearly, she really was in love, or thought that she was. Tabitha was beginning to lose sympathy though. Yet again, this sense of entitlement. She had paraded Winston at the party as an attempt to snub Blake and now she was more upset by her own loss than she was concerned about the welfare of her lover.

"I'm sure he does, Lady Montague. I don't know any more than you do where he might have gone, but I think if I was him, I would just disappear for a while until Sir Blake cools down a little. I'm sure it would be your welfare he would be considering."

And if he hasn't, Tabitha reflected, then he's been disappeared by one of Blake's men. She hoped not; he seemed a nice enough man, though rather too gullible and easily influenced for his own good. She hoped he'd had the sense to heed her advice.

"Tabitha. Get your pretty little arse over here will you darling."

It was Blake, shouting from the open doorway of his study.

Tabitha raised her eyebrows to Audrey, excused herself and moved quickly across the house, anxious not to get caught by Blake in conference with his wife. His use of language was clearly designed to impress his client with the nature of his relationship with his PA. As so often was the case with Blake, the jocular tone barely masked his intention to dominate and repress. 'Where else, in this day and age, could you talk to a female employee like that?' she reflected.

Inside the room, she discovered that the client was DI Karen Turner. She was surprised. She knew exactly what the meeting was about but not why she had been invited into it. Karen gave her a shrug, to indicate that she didn't know either. Tabitha had done all of the groundwork with Karen a week ago, setting up a complicated business arrangement which would enable Blake to import significant quantities of Class A drugs into the country without attracting the attention of the police force. Karen would be paid a substantial sum of money to ensure that her officers looked the other way at key moments and did not investigate any leads which pointed towards Blake. She was also getting a cut from the casino which would launder the money. Tabitha looked to Blake to allow him to explain what he wanted her for. As far as she was concerned, the deal was set up and ready to go. Why had he called Karen in today?

"I've just been going over the details of our deal with Karen," he offered by way of explanation, "and I wanted to call you over so that we could both congratulate you on the splendid job you've done here."

Tabitha was wary. This was not how Blake operated. What was he up to? She flicked a glance at Karen, but she too looked a little rattled. What was going on here?

Tabitha responded smoothly. "Thank you, Sir Blake. I appreciate your confidence in me and I will, of course, continue to do my very best to advance your business concerns."

She turned to the bewildered policewoman.

"Very nice to see you again DI Turner. Don't hesitate to contact me if you have any future concerns."

She turned back to Blake, waiting to be dismissed. He nodded, smiling benignly.

"Well, if you will excuse us, Karen and I have some business of a rather more ***personal*** nature to conduct." The word personal was articulated with sardonic emphasis.

One glance at Karen was enough for Tabitha to confirm the intent of that word. There was a look of barely concealed panic on her face. Both women instantly knew that Blake intended to seal Karen's loyalty and underline his dominant role in the relationship by seducing her, right here in his study. He had invited Tabitha over so that both women could bear witness to what was about to transpire. Feeling the blood rush to her cheeks, she nodded to Blake, unable to make eye contact with Karen again, and walked out of the room, shutting the door firmly and ominously.

As she walked quickly away, she closed her mind to what was taking place behind her. Karen was a bent copper. She would waste no sympathy on her.

Chapter 10 2019

"Rough night Adam?"

Alice stood by the open door, attractive in tight jeans and a chunky grey sweater, inspecting his face. He found her expressions hard to read, but the set of her mouth looked more like amusement than anything. He could see that she had taken some care with her hair, letting it fall across her shoulders with just a black band to hold it away from her face. And was that mascara on her eyes? He couldn't be sure through those thick, black rimmed glasses. He looked past her and noted that the hallway too had been tidied up. The carpets had been put back down and the piles of books and clothes had gone. He had only gone round to Alice's house because he couldn't think what else to do. He wasn't in the mood for more discussion about the time capsule but, then again, he didn't want to be on his own either. After yesterday's mauling, he really wasn't sure he liked himself that much.

He shrugged. "Just a few personal problems." He wrinkled his nose. "Sorted now. I didn't sleep so well though."

He wasn't surprised that she had commented. He had groaned when he had looked at himself in the mirror while he was shaving. There were dark rings under his eyes and his face was pale and drawn. He had done the best he could, but he still wasn't feeling good about himself.

"I thought I'd come and see how you were progressing with the documents. Any luck with the code?"

In truth, amateur sleuthing was the last thing that Adam wanted to be doing this morning, but he had come to recognise that he needed a reason to come and see Alice. She just wasn't a drop round and hang out kind of person.

She smiled and nodded. "Yes. There's quite a lot to tell you. Come on through." She stood aside to let him pass, locking the door behind him before she followed him to the kitchen. As he passed the living room, Adam glanced through the half open door. This room too seemed to have been tidied up. She had clearly been working on the house as well as the documents. He was puzzled. He had heard lots of noise over the last few weeks and she had clearly been moving things around, but there was no sign of any actual decoration. She appeared to have moved it all around then moved it all back.

He spoke over his shoulder as he heard her catching him up in the hallway. "Have you finished working on the house?"

"Yes, for now." It was a simple statement. If she understood why he was puzzled, she wasn't letting on.

As he entered the kitchen, he saw that a number of documents had been laid out on the kitchen table as if for inspection. Had she been expecting him? Was the extra care with her appearance for his benefit? He shook his head almost imperceptibly. If it was, she was wasting her time. He was still licking his wounds from yesterday.

"Something wrong?" she queried. The slight head shake had not gone unnoticed.

Adam covered up quickly. "Not at all. Just amazed at how quickly you work. All these documents on the table and the house all tidied up. I don't know how you do it." It was a well-worn routine; flattery to conceal that she had caught him out. His delivery was a little tired, but it never failed, he reflected.

"I do it by keeping my life simple and concentrating on one thing at a time," she responded. There was no edge in her voice, it was delivered in the tone of a teacher giving tips on how to succeed in life, but it was almost as though she knew more than she was letting on. Was she laughing at him? He just couldn't tell.

"Sit down." She gestured at the seat she wanted him to occupy. "I'll make you a coffee while you make a start on the documents I've gathered together. They're in what I consider to be a coherent order. Start at the top left."

"Right away miss," his voice loaded with ironic meekness.

He caught a glimpse of her perplexed expression out of the corner of his eye and smiled to himself. It was an odd kind of flirtation, but kind of fun too.

The document she had indicated was an old, slightly yellowing newspaper clipping. He picked up the faded, wrinkled paper and placed it in the empty space in front of him. The headline was in large, bold letters, taking up nearly as much space as the article itself.

MP's Wife Stabbed In Her Own Bed.

As he read the article, Adam could feel his former excitement begin to mount. This was perfect. As a screenplay, it would virtually write itself. The reporter was barely constraining herself in describing the lavish lifestyle of the family, the lurid parties at their country house in Kent and the stabbing of the MP's wife, Audrey Montague. As his grin grew wider and wider, he sensed that Alice was standing over him with the mug of coffee. Glancing up, he recognised disapproval in her expression. She did not share his enthusiasm. He stopped grinning immediately.

"That's absolutely tragic. That's Dora's mother, right?"

Alice nodded gravely.

"The woman in the picture." He picked up the picture of the family from the time capsule, positioned by Alice in the bottom right corner of the table, and held it against the faded picture of Audrey in the newspaper, shaking his head as he did so. "It's unbelievable. They look like a stable, happy family. They're all laughing. What could have happened to lead them all to such tragedy?" He tossed the photograph back onto the table.

Alice frowned. "It's just a photograph Adam. Photographs like this don't tell the truth. The photographer organises the people before photographing them in order to tell the story that he wants, or his client wants. He takes lots then selects the one that tells the desired story. The fact is, that family was far from stable or happy. There was an evil presence there."

Adam leaned back, his fingers laced behind his head. "What, like something supernatural, you mean?"

She grimaced impatiently. "Evil isn't supernatural, Adam. You've been watching too many films and reading too many books. It's people that are evil. That man," she stabbed the man in the photo with her finger, "Blake Montague; he is the evil presence."

Adam stroked his freshly shaven chin while he considered what was happening. Alice was angry. As a rule, he found it difficult to read her moods, but there was no doubt about this one. And there was something she was not telling him; he was sure of it. He looked down at the table thoughtfully.

"Alice?" His tone was uncertain, edged with suspicion. He waved a hand at the newspaper clippings and other papers positioned on the table. "There's a lot of documents on this table. Those newspaper clippings look like originals to me. Did you get all of these in the past twenty-four hours," he fixed her with a stare, "or have you had these for a while?"

A pink blush appeared on Alice's neck and started to rise towards her face. She looked down at the table, as if checking out his statement. After a long pause, she looked at him directly, a fierce determination in her eyes, visible through her thick lenses.

"I've been searching the house." It was a confession, but it was too fiercely expressed to be an apology. "Ever since I found out that it was connected with the Montague family. You see, I knew that something awful had happened within that family." She cocked her head to one side. "I suspected there might be some evidence if I looked hard enough. These documents," she nodded towards the table, "were hidden around the house."

"Hidden?" Adam was puzzled. "Hidden where? And why?"

Alice shook her head. "I don't know. I think that maybe it was Dora who hid them because her grandmother didn't want them in the house. I found most of them under the floorboards of what I think must have been Dora's bedroom."

"So ... when the tree surgeon found the time capsule, you had already found these documents?" It was an accusation.

Alice nodded. "Some of them, yes."

"But ... you didn't think to mention that at the time."

She shook her head. "No."

Adam waited for an explanation, but she simply maintained eye contact with him, her face impassive."

"Why not?" The softness of his voice belied the mounting anger inside him.

She looked away to gather her thoughts then locked eyes with him again.

"Because I didn't want you involved."

Adam raised his eyebrows, his eyes widening. "But why ever not?"

She screwed her face up a little, breathing out heavily. She seemed reluctant to respond.

"Come on," Adam was growing impatient now, "why would you want to keep this to yourself?"

She took a step forward and laid one hand upon his shoulder, as if to reassure him.

"Because I didn't think you were tough enough." This time the confession was spoken more tenderly. "I'm sorry. When I first met you, I thought you were, well, a bit light-weight really. You see, the more I learned about what had happened in the Montague family, the more it scared me. And I felt like I'd been given a responsibility to do something about it. You just," she paused, "you didn't seem like the sort of person who should get involved in something like that." She sighed, as if happy to relieve herself of what had been weighing heavily upon her.

There was a long silence while Adam considered this. He placed his hands on the table and looked down at them. He had never been spoken to like this before. It came as a shock. His parents had always made it crystal clear that they expected him to be a high achiever; that's when he saw them, of course. They always seemed to be busy. His teachers had told him that he was destined for great things. They had said it to all of the boys; it was practically a school mantra. Girls had always been drawn to him; he flirted with them and they flirted back. But this! This felt like a slap in the face.

"Light weight? Is that how you see me?" The label felt like a cruel assault on his self-esteem. He hadn't been very fond of himself since the meeting with Belinda and Nadia. This was yet another blow to his ego. "Not tough enough?" That was a bitter pill to swallow too. Did he deserve this?

"It's not your fault," she began. "It's just your upbringing."

He laughed bitterly. "Is that supposed to make me feel better? Who are you to judge me like this?"

Alice blinked, as if surprised by his reaction. "Oh, come on Adam. You know what I mean. You were brought up in a wealthy middle-class family, sent to a posh public school. A privileged upbringing isn't the best preparation for dealing with the ugly things in life. Surely you can see that." She shrugged. "I just thought you weren't ready for the kinds of challenges that might be thrown in our path if we continued to investigate together."

Seeing how crestfallen he remained, she added, "I was wrong. I'm sorry. I can see that now."

He looked up into her anxious face. "What made you change your mind?

She smiled. It was a warm smile. She squeezed his shoulder gently. "I got to know you. And there's more to you than I realised. Actually, I'd really like to share what I know with you now … if that's okay with you that is."

Adam found himself smiling back. He had been judged and found to be … merely adequate. And yet … and yet, that felt like a more real and substantial reward than anything he had received before.

He put both thumbs up theatrically. "That's okay with me."

Chapter 11 1979

Tabitha had expected to find Freddie and Gabriel in the library. Ever since he had been expelled from Millfield, Freddie had been tutored at home, much to Blake's disgust. Audrey, having decided that her son was too sensitive to thrive in a school environment, had set about organising for him to be educated in a context that she could control. Most of the tutors didn't last very long; the toxic atmosphere at Montague House soon grew too much for them to bear. Gabriel was the exception. He had stayed for nearly six months now and seemed to have an affinity with Freddie. Tabitha's only concern was where that affinity might be leading them.

She found them in the conservatory. As she approached, she was pleased to see that they were relaxed in each other's company; life had not been easy for Freddie recently. Gabriel looked the epitome of an old school scholar. Dressed in tweed jacket and brown brogues, despite only being in his early twenties, he was lecturing Freddie on something, sweeping the mop of untidy blond hair out of his widely spaced eyes to gaze more closely at his pupil and check that he was listening. Freddie, neatly groomed and dressed in smart jeans and a check shirt was nodding enthusiastically and smiling. He spotted Tabitha first.

"Hi Tabitha. Checking up on us?"

Freddie's question was delivered with good humour, he and Tabitha got on well, but there was a hint of petulance there as well. Freddie was not a boy who responded well to discipline. Tabitha sometimes wondered how he would have been different if he had been brought up in the South London estate where she had spent her childhood. She had encountered plenty of children who had kicked out at any attempt to impose discipline upon them. Such children existed in all levels of society, she reflected. Some of them had been expelled and passed from school to school before they even reached high school age. But, where she came from, they didn't get offered home schooling when there was finally nowhere left that would take them. Their education continued on the streets.

Tabitha supposed that, whether you were a rich kid or a poor kid, it was ultimately all about family, or the lack of it. She loved her mother. She phoned her every week and sent money home frequently. But she had felt like she was the adult in the relationship for as long as she could remember. As a child, she would arrive home from school sometimes to find that her mother had gone out and left no word of when she would be back. It might be soon, or it might be the next day if she had gone out on a bender or was out working the streets for one of the many pimps that operated in the area. She would eat whatever she could find. If there was nothing, she would go out and lift something from a local shop or see if there was anyone out on the streets with something to share in return for picking up or delivering some package for them. And so, it was to the gangs that she had turned. They provided a sense of family for children like her, who had no such sense of family at home. The leaders were parent figures in some ways, stern and punitive on the whole, but also conferring a sense of self-worth and belonging on youngsters who did as they were told and showed loyalty. Tabitha wondered if Gabriel fulfilled that role in some way for Freddie, the sense of self-worth part of it anyway.

"Someone needs to keep you on the straight and narrow," Tabitha responded with mock sternness. It occurred to her that, if Gabriel was a substitute father, she was the nearest thing he had to a substitute mother. Moreover, her relationship with Freddie was, she reflected bitterly, looking likely to be the nearest she would ever get to having a child of her own. Her work for Blake was all consuming. She had begun to realise that the chance that she would meet someone with whom she could develop a stable relationship, stable enough for children, was increasingly unlikely. Audrey wanted to be his mother, but alternated between smothering him with love and ignoring him completely while she battled with her own overwhelming sense of anxiety and insecurity. Tabitha was the only person who provided any stability and structure to his life, encouraging him to eat properly and tidy his room, talking to him about what he might do with his life. There was his sister, Dora, of course, but she was too young to understand what Freddie was going through and largely kept to herself.

"Never mind the straight and narrow, how about the gay and wide?" Freddie gave Tabitha a comical wink and then looked across to Gabriel. The poor man's eyes widened in horror.

"I … oh, come now Freddie." He was clearly flustered. "I'm sorry you had to come searching for us Tabitha. We …" He faltered.

"I asked Gabriel if we could have our lesson here rather than the library," Freddie offered, concerned that he had offended his tutor. "He said we could concentrate better there but I persuaded him that it was a lovely sunny day and we would feel more like learning if we could look out upon the garden and feel the warmth through the glass."

Tabitha shook her head slowly to show Freddie that she did not approve of how he manipulated Gabriel. He was such a pushover.

"I'd like to talk to Freddie on his own please Gabriel." Her tone made it clear that this was not open to negotiation. His eyes widened once more. Was that fear she could see in his face? He definitely didn't look happy. She had been right in thinking that a serious conversation with the two of them was long overdue.

"Oh, yes, right …" Gabriel became flustered once more. The colour was draining from his face now. "I … I'll be in the library if you want me."

"I think I **will** want to speak with you later," Tabitha assented, "once I've talked to Freddie."

She waited for Gabriel to be well out of earshot before sitting opposite Freddie, her hands folded across her lap. She stared into his eyes thoughtfully, deliberately waiting to see if he opened the conversation. He didn't. He just stared defiantly back. Clearly, he was expecting a telling off.

"Freddie, I'm worried," Tabitha began. She waited for the defiance to fade from his expression. An angry Freddie would not open up to her as she needed him to.

"Som' deep shit going down in dis house right now. Me worry 'bout you."

Freddie grinned. He loved it when Tabitha used the language she had grown up with. She had told him tales of the gangs of her youth and of her mother and of her determination to make something of her life. When his own mother or father were nearby, she was always professional and distant, but, when it was just the two of them, she sometimes revealed the hidden part of her character.

"I'm okay," he responded amicably. He shrugged. "It's no worse than it normally is. Well, a bit maybe, but I'm used to it."

Tabitha blew out a jet of air theatrically to show her impatience with his answer then cocked her head slightly towards him. It was a gesture he recognised only too well. She was not satisfied with this answer.

"Okay then," he snapped irritably. "If you must know, everything is beastly. Dad keeps sending prostitutes to my room because he says he thinks I'm a virgin while at the same time he's telling everyone who'll listen that I'm having sex with my mother." He threw both hands up in a gesture of despair. "What the hell am I supposed to do?"

Tabitha sighed. "So, you heard about that then. I'm so sorry. I think he says things like that to upset your mother but he doesn't seem to realise the impact it will have on you."

Freddie shook his head defiantly. "Oh, he knows all right. He takes great delight in humiliating everyone who's in his circle of influence. It's all part of his power trip. You must know that Tabitha. It's because we know enough to have him put in prison if we speak out, so he keeps reminding us of what happens to people who cross him."

Tabitha winced. "You're right Freddie. Look, I'm sorry; I didn't mean to patronise you. It's just that I hate to see you suffering like this."

Freddie softened his angry expression and rewarded Tabitha with a resigned grin. "It's okay. It's all part of being a Montague. I'm coping, all right? I'll be old enough to leave home in two years. I can go somewhere where he can't touch me. And then he'd better look out. The newspapers would pay a lot to know what I know about him."

Tabitha's eyes widened in horror. "Freddie. Don't say things like that. There is no place where he can't touch you. You know that. And if he finds out you're threatening to expose him ..." She did not finish the sentence. There was no need.

"And I don't think you are coping," she continued. She lowered her voice. "I've seen you staggering and slurring your words a few times recently. What are you taking?"

Freddie smiled sheepishly. "Just a little acid from time to time."

Tabitha was not won over by the smile. "LSD? Where are you getting that from Freddie?"

"From him, my dad."

She shook her head vehemently. "I control all of his supply at his parties. It's locked in a safe the rest of the time. Where are you getting it from?"

Freddie smirked. "From his safe."

Tabitha cocked her head towards him once more. "Oh, come on Freddie. You don't have the combination to his safe. In fact, you don't even know where it's hidden."

Freddie was put out by this response. He stared back sardonically. "It's in his bedroom. You just have to slide the picture of the Montague crest to one side. And the combination is 84-77-38. It's the ages at which his father, mother and brother died," he added darkly.

"And you know this how?" Tabitha's suspicions were aroused.

"He once asked me to get something for him. Years ago. He gave me the combination then."

Tabitha paused to consider this. Blake did not leave things to chance. He must know that Freddie was helping himself. She resolved to take this up later with Blake. She had a more pressing issue she needed to discuss with Freddie now.

"Okay then. I'm sorry I didn't believe you. But go easy. I've seen too many people totally screwed up by LSD. I'd really prefer it if you didn't use it at all. But that's not what I wanted to talk about with you today."

"Oh?"

Tabitha took a deep breath. "You can't be making jokes about you and Gabriel being gay Freddie. If your dad hears about that it will be big trouble for him. You too."

"But I am gay, "Freddie protested. "And so is Gabriel." He paused for effect. "We're in love!"

Tabitha's jaw dropped. "What! Do you mean ...?" She searched for the right words. "Do you mean like a physical relationship?"

Freddie sniggered, amused by Tabitha's discomfort.

"I mean like sex, Tabitha."

Tabitha swiftly readjusted her image of Gabriel as father figure to one of student and teacher sharing a bed. It was a horrifying picture; worse than she had imagined. It would be, she realised, pointless to tell Freddie to end the relationship. Gabriel was clearly the closest friend he had. It was down to her to put a stop to it.

"Okay. That's come as a bit of a surprise to me Freddie." She hoped she didn't sound too shocked. She hoped that Freddie wouldn't realise she was about to wreck the one source of happiness in his twisted life. "Just be careful okay. Your father must never know about this."

Freddie smiled happily. "Don't worry. We're careful."

Tabitha nodded, standing as a sign that the discussion was over. "You wait here and I'll send Gabriel back once I've had a word with him."

As soon as she was out of Freddie's hearing, she took out her phone and ordered a taxi. Walking briskly up the wide, thickly carpeted stairway to her bedroom, she listened carefully for any sounds of movement from Blake or Audrey. She prayed they would stay out of the way. In her bedroom, she removed the drawer from the dark oak, bedside table, inverting it over the bed so that all of the contents fell out. She unpeeled the tape that secured a wad of banknotes to the bottom of the drawer, slipped it into the inside pocket of her jacket, then reinserted the drawer into the table and replaced all of its contents. Leaving her room to descend the staircase, she listened once more. Still quiet.

She found Gabriel in the library, waiting for her with an apprehensive expression. Clearly, he had guessed what she had been talking about with Freddie. Good, she did not need to explain anything. Sitting herself as close to Gabriel as she could, she held up her phone to his face.

"There's a taxi arriving in five minutes. It's for you." She lowered her voice and hissed with angry urgency, "If Blake finds out that you have been shagging his only son and heir, he will have you taken outside where they will cut off your cock and balls. I cannot tell you how much danger you are in right now." She paused to restore her composure. "Go now. Take nothing with you as if you are just going out on an errand." She held up her hand when it appeared that Gabriel might speak. "Get far away from here. Never speak to anyone about what has happened here. When you have found somewhere, text me an address where I can send your things. I'll make up some excuse for Audrey and Freddie about why you had to go so suddenly."

She reached into the inside pocket of her jacket and pulled out the wad of bank notes. "Please understand," she stressed, "that I do this because I care about you and I care about Freddie."

Gabriel, face drained of blood, nodded without speaking, took the money, stood on shaky legs and stumbled towards the door.

Chapter 12 2019

Alice sat down opposite Adam and set a glass of water in front of her. He thought she seemed more relaxed than usual. It was as if there had been an unseen barrier which had only become evident after its removal. In any case, he liked this new version of his neighbour. Using the documents as visual aids, she proceeded to present him with the evidence she had gathered, piecing together the story of what had happened years earlier.

"So," she started, "we know from the article you just read that Lady Montague, Audrey, was found dead in her bed. The autopsy confirmed the initial findings of the investigating detectives that she'd been stabbed to death while she was in the bed, possibly as she was sleeping; there was no sign of a struggle."

Adam nodded thoughtfully. "And we know from Freddie's letter to Dora that he was prosecuted for committing the murder, but he denied that it was him."

Alice smiled her agreement. "That's right. These articles here," she pointed at three more newspaper cuttings, "follow Freddie's trial and conviction."

Adam shrugged. "What do you think? Did he do it?"

Alice sat back in her chair and took off her glasses to clean them with a tissue while she considered his question. She was indeed wearing mascara, Adam noted and eyeliner too. They made her intense, blue eyes look very striking, beautiful even. The image stayed with him when she replaced the thick, black rimmed spectacles.

"The evidence in court hinged upon the discovery of the murder weapon. It was found in Freddie's bed with Freddie holding on to it. He was apparently out of his head on LSD at the time, out cold and covered in blood."

Adam shook his head in disbelief. "It's straight out of Macbeth."

"As in Shakespeare you mean?" She sent him an inquiring look.

Adam nodded his assent. "Well, don't you think so?"

Alice shrugged. "I've never actually seen it or read it. It's just fiction isn't it? I mean, it never really happened."

Adam looked mystified. "Are you saying that you place no value on fiction? You're not seriously going to dismiss the works of the greatest writer of all time as 'made up stories.'"

She tilted her head forwards to look at him over the rim of her glasses. Those piercing eyes again, admonishing him like a disapproving school teacher. "I'm not dismissing anything, Adam. I'm just saying that I value reality and truth; fiction holds no interest for me. So, tell me why it's straight out of Macbeth."

Adam took a deep breath, letting it out slowly through pursed lips before he spoke. "Well, Macbeth murders the king, Duncan, but forgets to leave the blood covered knives in the room of the king's attendants in order to implicate them. Lady Macbeth tells him off then takes the knives, goes back upstairs, smears the attendants with blood and leaves the knives next to them. They don't wake up until Duncan's murder has been discovered because Lady Macbeth drugged them at a feast the night before."

Alice looked interested. "Did they get away with it, Macbeth and his wife?"

Adam laughed. "It's complicated. They sort of do to begin with but then justice catches up with them." He paused. "The thing is," he pressed his lips together in thought, "it's not really very plausible, is it? I mean, it's literally straight out of fiction, just like you said. It's like," he held up both hands in front of him as he sought an explanation, "it's like the classic frame up. It's just too obvious."

He glanced across at Alice who was smiling as if enjoying his rather imaginative response to the evidence. Encouraged, he continued enthusiastically. "In Macbeth, it's a dude called Macduff who discovers the dead king. Once he wakes everyone up with the news, Macbeth makes sure he's the next person to go up. He sees the attendants with the knives, covered with blood, just as his wife left them, so he kills them straight off. He says he was too angry to do anything else but I reckon he's just embarrassed. I mean, it was his wife's plan really, not his, and I think when he sees them lying there, drugged, covered with blood, murder weapons in their hands, he figures that it's not a very good plan." Adam shrugged. "Nobody is going to believe that they committed the foul deed then took the knife back to bed with them, are they? So, anyway, he kills them before anyone else comes upstairs so they can't claim to be innocent."

He paused to take a breath then let out a short, explosive laugh. "So that's it. Whoever found Audrey is innocent and whoever found Freddie with the knife is guilty. We've cracked it." He grinned comically at Alice.

Alice smiled back indulgently. "Except it was Tabitha Watts, Blake's Personal Assistant who found them both," she responded with amusement. "And as far as the evidence goes, she doesn't seem to have any motive for wishing harm to either of them." She pointed to one of the newspaper cuttings. "In fact, at the trial she testified that she was convinced that it could not be Freddie. She says that she saw him staggering up to his room that evening under the influence of what she presumed to be drugs and that he was quite incapable of doing any harm to anyone. She also says that he and his mother both loved each other in their way and had no reason to wish each other harm."

Adam sighed melodramatically. "Ah well, back to the drawing board then. Any other suspects? How about the husband? It's usually the husband isn't it?"

Alice pointed to the newspaper cuttings again. "The problem with that theory is that Blake had a cast iron alibi. He testified that he was with his mistress, one Martine Richards, on his yacht sailing off the coast of Cannes when the murder took place. There was confirmation from the yacht's GPS record and from port authority records that his yacht was where he said it was. His crew and his mistress all testified that he was on the boat."

Adam sighed deeply, leaned his elbows on the table and rested his head in his hands. "So, not guilty then."

Alice raised one eyebrow. "You would think that wouldn't you? And that was what the jury believed. However, there was one witness who contradicted the alibi."

"Oh?" Adam responded quizzically. "And why did the jury decide to disregard that witness?"

"Because her evidence was never presented in court." There was a bitter resentment in Alice's voice. "It looks like Blake got to her first and hid her away."

Adam studied her features. Through the thick glass of her spectacles, he could see that her eyes had narrowed. The corners of her mouth were turned down acrimoniously. This was clearly very personal for her; he wondered why.

"How do you know that this evidence exists then?"

Alice picked up the sheet of paper on which Dora had written groups of numbers. "Because Dora says so."

Adam threw his head back and laughed. "You cracked the code. Well done you."

She tilted her head to acknowledge the compliment. "Technically, it's a book cipher. Once I saw that the numbers were in groups of three, I suspected that straight away."

Adam waited a few seconds for the explanation to follow, but none came. Alice seemed unusually comfortable with silences. Adam was not.

"Okay Alan Turing. You know how you're not big on fiction? Well, I'm much the same on cryptography."

He gave her a sardonic smile but it was clearly lost on her. There was no recognition of his humour in her answer.

"A book cipher is an algorithm which encodes a message according to words within a specified book." She pointed at the page. "The numbers are grouped in threes. Each group gives the location of a word within the book. So, for example, the first group on the page is 15, 8, 4. That describes the page, line and number of the word within the line that Dora wants to encrypt. All we need is the same book that she used to create the cipher and we can decode the word."

She looked closely at Adam to check for understanding. He nodded to confirm that he understood so far.

"But how did you find what book she had used? I saw piles of books in the hallway when I first came to your house?"

Alice nodded agreement. "I thought I might have to check them all till I found a match. It occurred to me that she might even have taken the book away from the house, in which case the job would have become so much more difficult. However," she smiled, more to herself than to

Adam, "I worked on the hunch that she might have hidden the book somewhere."

Reaching down to a box by her feet that Adam had not noticed, she pulled out a well-worn, blue, hardbacked book and placed it on the table. Adam turned it round so that the title faced him. The Holy Bible, King James Version.

"Wow, that's a serious read for a young girl."

"This young girl had already lived through quite a lot." Alice's tone was disparaging. She was clearly displeased by the levity Adam was maintaining. "I think you'd like her though. She has a strong sense of the power of metaphor."

"Because she used the bible?"

Alice smiled indulgently. "Specifically, the beginning of the book of Genesis."

Adam paused, then struck his forehead theatrically with the heel of his palm. "Of course. The Garden of Eden, The tree of knowledge of good and evil, the snake, Adam and Eve. Clever girl. Should have been a novelist with that sense of symbolism," he paused, "or a film maker. Where had she hidden the book?"

"Dora was young but cunning." There was real admiration in Alice's tone. "She had created a cut-out in the wall at the back of her closet. I almost didn't find it but I knocked the bottom of it when I was emptying the closet and it just toppled over."

Adam opened his mouth to speak, then thought the better of it. He wanted to say that it was like the time capsule. It was like it wanted to be found. But he sensed that Alice would not entertain this idea. She would accuse him once again of watching too many films."

"So," Alice leaned back in her chair, "now that you understand the principle, try decrypting the first line of the cipher."

"Okay." Adam, pleased that she wanted to involve him in this way, started with the first of four groups on the top line. "So 15, 8 4 is the page, line and word in that line?"

He checked for her nod of assent then proceeded to flick through the pages and run his finger down and across page 15.

The first word is "my."

He looked up and once again received a nod and smile of encouragement. Confident that he understood how it worked, he continued with the other three groups.

Having found the last of the group, he leaned back and regarded Alice gravely.

"My father is evil? Wow, that's what you mean when you say she's lived through a lot isn't it?"

Alice agreed. "She goes on to give her account of the night her mother was killed. She says she heard some sound coming from her parents' room and looked out to see what it was." Alice paused. "She is adamant that she saw her father."

Adam's eyes widened. "Oh my God, then ..."

"Then it was Blake who killed his wife. That's right." That bitter tone again. "He murdered his wife, made his drugged-up son look like he had done it and used his mistress and the crew of his yacht for an alibi."

Adam shook his head in disbelief. "But it's incredible. No jury would believe that. What possible motive could Freddie have had for murdering his mother?"

Alice's face was impassive now but Adam could sense the anger smouldering within her.

"At the trial, a number of witnesses testified that Freddie was having a sexual affair with his mother. It was circumstantial evidence only, nobody had any proof, but the prosecution constructed the story that she had seduced him and he had killed her out of shame and self-loathing." She shrugged. "The jury went for it."

Adam linked his hands behind his head, pursed his lips and expelled air noisily through them. This had moved way beyond providing material for a film. "So, that's it then. We have to do something now. Poor Freddie's been locked up for forty years for a crime he didn't commit. It's monstrous."

Alice shook her head miserably and pointed to another newspaper cutting on the table. "It's much worse than that Adam."

Adam picked up the cutting and read the headline.

MP SIR BLAKE MONTAGUE'S SON COMMITS SUICIDE IN PRISON

"What? Why would he do that if he were innocent?" He shook his head in disbelief.

"He wouldn't. And he didn't!" Alice was bitter once more. "Blake has contacts everywhere, and that includes prison. I've told you already, he's a monster."

"Had his own son murdered?" Adam was incredulous. "Why would he take that risk?"

Alice gave a grim smile. "You said it yourself Adam. He is Macbeth. Once Freddie was dead, all of the loose ends were tied up. There was no one left to point the finger at Blake. And as for risk, take a look at the police officer in charge of the investigation."

Adam looked back at the clipping and saw that Alice had highlighted the investigating officer. "DCI Karen Turner."

"Right. Now check out the investigating officer for Audrey's death."

Adam picked up the clipping from where he had put it down on the table.

"DCI Karen Turner again. Are you suggesting he has a corrupt police officer in his pocket?"

Alice nodded. "I've checked her out on line. She was transferred to the murder investigation team and promoted to DCI 6 months before the death of Audrey. She's suspiciously present whenever there's a hint of trouble for Blake."

Adam's brow furrowed. "Do you think we might be biting off more than we can chew here?"

Alice looked at him quizzically. "Do you mean, are there risks involved in pursuing this?" She looked at him over the top of her glasses. "I've been suggesting that all along Adam." She paused. "And it's still not too late for you to pull out of this, you know."

Adam looked down at his hands, resting upon the table, considering what she had said, then looked intently into her eyes. "But you're not going to pull out, are you?"

She shook her head.

Adam looked down again and sighed deeply. He had a bad feeling about where this was headed. This Blake character sounded like a real piece of work and he clearly had powerful contacts. What could he and Alice do against them? And yet, he didn't want to abandon her, having come this far. He didn't like the idea of her pursuing justice on her own against a powerful politician with influential friends. He reached a decision and looked up brightly.

"I tell you what. How about we try to find Dora? This is her time capsule after all. And we still don't know whether she wanted it to be brought to light or not, do we? We could return it to her and see if she wants us to pursue it. If she wants it put back in the ground then I think we should probably respect that. What do you think?"

Alice considered briefly then nodded. "I think it's a good plan. I'll take responsibility for locating her, shall I?"

Adam smiled gratefully. "I wouldn't know where to start."

Alice shrugged. "Everything is on the internet. It's just a matter of knowing where to look."

Chapter 13 1979

Blake Montague leaned back in his padded, leather chair and smiled across the desk at Tabitha. It was not a comforting smile. She decided that he didn't really have a comforting smile. He had an amused smile, he had a self-satisfied smile, he had a menacing smile, but there was never any arrangement of the muscles in his mouth that communicated anything that could be described as warmth.

And then there were his eyes; they studied, they probed, they pried their way into your very soul. At least, that's how it felt to Tabitha. She had learned to smile back and stay quiet when he was like this. There was no predicting what mood he was in and what might be about to happen.

He lifted his elbows onto the arms of his chair and linked his hands across the front of his sleek black waistcoat, a large red ruby and a gold signet ring coming together in the mesh of his fingers. He was, Tabitha had to acknowledge, a distinguished looking man. Even when ostensibly relaxed he held his head high, his square jaw and aquiline nose marking him out as a man of breeding. It was the eyes that left the lasting impression though; the cold, icy blue of those eyes.

"So, Tabitha. I'm planning to spend some time on the yacht. I'll be flying out to meet up with the crew in Cannes. Martine will be going with me."

She waited respectfully for a moment to see if he would add anything to this before she responded. He hated to be interrupted.

"Very well Sir. When will you be going?"

"Tomorrow." His response was swift and decisive.

Tabitha's eyes widened. He had several appointments in his diary over the next few days; some influential politicians and businessmen. There would be a lot of bruised egos to massage when she cancelled them.

Her recovery was fast. "Of course, Sir. I will cancel your appointments. When are you planning to return?"

He pressed his palms together as if in prayer, bringing the extended fingers to touch his lips while he considered this. He closed his eyes for a few moments, then opened them again and sat up straight in his chair.

"I'm not sure Tabitha. I have some business to conduct out there. Cancel my appointments for the next seven days. I will contact you when I have a clearer idea of when I'll be back."

She inclined her head in assent. "Of course, Sir. Is there anything you wish me to take care of while you're away?"

He shook his head brusquely. "Just keep things ticking over. Anything major can wait until my return."

He turned his gaze back upon her, eyes boring into her head. "I do not wish to be disturbed while I am away Tabitha. Is that clear?" His tone was steely, implacable. "Do not attempt to contact me. I will contact you when I am ready. Is-that-clear?" He left an ominous gap between the last three words.

Despite herself, Tabitha felt her heart beat a little faster. "Clear, Sir Blake." She hated it that he could still unsettle her in this way, but she was very aware that a threat from him, however veiled, was no empty one.

As she waited to be dismissed, Tabitha became increasingly aware of raised voices in the next room. Freddie was raging. She heard Audrey imploring him to calm himself, but it merely stoked his fury.

Blake shook his head testily. "On second thoughts, Tabitha, there is something you can attend to while I'm away." He paused for effect. "You can sort out my fucking family."

Tabitha had to stop herself from smiling. The sound of the aristocracy employing street language with their plummy, upper class accents never failed to amuse her. Judging that his statement constituted a dismissal to go and attend to it now, she stood and walked towards the door but had to stand to one side as an infuriated Freddie came crashing through it, pursued by his distressed mother.

"You bastard. You sick bastard." Freddie's voice sounded a little slurred, as if he had been drinking. His hair was dishevelled. His face was flushed and sweaty. It occurred to Tabitha this might be LSD rather than alcohol. Either way, he was likely to say or do something regrettable if she didn't get him away from his father soon.

"Come on Freddie. This is not the place for this. Come with me and tell me about it."

She tried to take his arm but he shook her off petulantly.

"This sick bastard has been telling everyone that I'm shagging my mother, you know he has."

He was appealing to Tabitha now, looking for her support. And it was true that Blake had made some sly comments at his parties about Freddie and Audrey. But she couldn't afford to come between father and son. That wouldn't help Freddie and it would be very inadvisable for her. Blake expected unswerving loyalty from his employees.

She glanced across at Blake, but his expression gave nothing away. He was waiting to see how Tabitha dealt with this.

"What I know is that you need to go and get some strong, black coffee Freddie. Come with me to the kitchen." Her voice was firm and assured, but inwardly she felt conflicted. The poor boy deserved an explanation for his father's spiteful behaviour and she felt bad that she appeared to be taking Blake's side. She attempted again to steer him towards the door, and this time he allowed himself to be led. His anger was abating now. He looked exhausted and distressed.

As they entered the sitting room, they met Martine walking quickly towards them. Clearly, she had heard the altercation right across the house and had come to investigate. Tabitha had been wondering what status she had assumed since she had recently appeared as a gawky young woman looking for some help with her career in acting. She reflected, cynically, that the news that she would accompany Blake on his yacht for seven days indicated a change in her career path. She took in the expensively tailored silk dress and the delicate gold bracelet on her wrist. No doubt about it then. Blake had taken her as a mistress.

"I heard raised voices," she offered by way of explanation. "Is everything okay? Is there anything I can do?"

Tabitha smiled tartly. "There is. Thank you, Martine. You can take Freddie to his room; he needs to sleep off whatever it is he's taken."

Martine regarded her uncertainly then looked round her to see if she could understand what was going on in Blake's office. Tabitha felt confident that she would not yet be sufficiently sure of her new status to be able to take offence at being given a task by a mere employee. That time would come though. Blake had that effect on people.

"Okay then. Come on Freddie."

He allowed himself to be led meekly towards the stairs.

Turning back towards Blake's office, Tabitha registered that a new confrontation was developing. This time it was Audrey who was raging.

"Well, what do you expect Blake?"

Her husband clearly had no interest in responding to her question. He was leaning back in his chair, all signs of his former irritation gone. Was that a smirk on his face? It was! He was actually enjoying himself. Tabitha decided not to intervene this time. Blake would not respond well to being denied an opportunity to taunt his tempestuous wife.

"You ***have*** been telling people that I've been sleeping with Freddie."

Blake smiled unpleasantly. "The rumour didn't start with me my dear."

She snorted. "It was just a silly comment I made at a party. I was drunk for God's sake." She was working herself into a frenzy now. "Try and understand how upsetting this is for Freddie, to have his own father spreading malicious rumours. He's at a sensitive age." Her voice had risen to a shriek. "Boys of his age don't even want to think about their parents having sex at all. But you're telling people that he's having sex with ***me***. What is wrong with you?"

"He's been at what you call a sensitive age all his life." Blakes voice was thick with irony. "And that, my dear, is your fault. You have never got over the day he stopped sucking your tit."

Audrey gasped with fury but he simply shook his head to underline the folly of her behaviour. "Ever since that day you've smothered him with your frustrated affections. Frankly," he cocked his head to one side as if he were about to deliver an indisputable truth, "the reason the rumour has spread is because everyone sees how the two of you behave together in public and finds it utterly believable."

Tabitha decided this was enough. She took Audrey's arm and tried to lead her towards the door. "Come on Lady Montague. This isn't doing Freddie any good. You're too angry to deal with this now. Come and have a drink with me."

Audrey brushed her off distractedly, stepped up to Blake's desk, put her hands upon it and leaned over him. She was not finished yet.

"I know what goes on in this house." She glared at Blake defiantly. I know about the ***business*** deals you are running." She said the word as if business was a euphemism for something much darker. "And I know about your LSD and where it comes from. And I know about your ***arrangement*** with DI Turner, or DCI, or whatever it is you've turned her into." She was beginning to gabble now, the accusations spilling out of her mouth. Tabitha was horrified, but powerless to prevent what was surely coming.

"I could ruin you." There was a mixture of spite and triumph in her voice now. "Mr oh-so-respectable Member of Parliament. If your colleagues knew about what you get up to you'd be drummed out of The House. You'd be in prison for the rest of your miserable life."

An icy chill descended upon the room. Audrey, exultant in her revelations, towering over her seated husband, seemed immune to it, but Tabitha involuntarily crossed her arms across her breasts and shivered. Blake sat, as still as stone, every muscle stiff with rage. For an agonisingly long time he said nothing. Finally, he turned to his personal assistant. His voice was dangerously calm.

"Tabitha, take Lady Montague outside, give her a drink and explain to her how ruining me would also ruin her and her miserable children."

He turned away, picked up a file from his desk and opened it. They had been dismissed.

Chapter 14 2019

Once again, Adam was impressed with the speed at which Alice worked. In fact, he was so impressed that he wondered, not for the first time, whether she knew more than she was sharing with him. How else could he explain the way that she always seemed several jumps ahead of him, returning after less than an hour with the news that she had located Dora.

She had changed into a smart pair of tight-fitting black jeans and a black sweater. As he followed her from the front door through to his kitchen, he found himself staring at her bottom, unable to understand how he had failed to appreciate how attractive her body was when he had first met her. Or maybe it was an unconventional attractiveness that was just growing on him. Either way, he had to drag his gaze up to her eyes as she reached the kitchen, turned and sat down at the table.

"I've spoken to Dora and she's agreed to meet us." She held up her phone as if to demonstrate how she had done this. "She lives near Cambridge. I've just checked it on my phone. We can be there in less than 90 minutes if we set off now to avoid traffic."

Adam chuckled at her directness. He was gradually getting used to her precision and decisiveness, but it still took him by surprise sometimes. "Well okay then. Do I have time for a wee?"

Even as he said it, he realised that his attempt at banter would fall flat. She stared at him, puzzled. His comment was inappropriate. "Yes Adam. When I said 'now' I meant soon, not this minute."

He nodded earnestly. "Sorry. Course you did. I'll meet you by your car in 5 minutes."

She drove quickly, pushing right up to the speed limit whenever it was possible, but her control and judgement were good; Adam felt very safe. She focused intently on the road ahead and made no attempt to engage him in conversation. The snow had largely cleared by now, but there were still small drifts in places where the sun could not penetrate.

"Do you want me to use Google Maps on my phone?" he asked her, after she had moved onto the motorway and pushed her car up to 70 miles per hour."

She shook her head. "No need. I've pretty much got a photographic memory. Once I've looked up the route somewhere, I seldom need to check it."

There was a long silence while Adam considered what to say next. He still felt that there was something he was missing. Initially she had hidden from him that she had been methodically searching the house and had already found lots of documents and photographs. Okay, she had admitted it later, but the reasons she gave for her secrecy were not entirely convincing. And then she had found Dora's telephone number, phoned her, changed her clothes and come round to his house in less than an hour. Could she have had her details already? If so, what was it that she wasn't telling him? He reflected that a direct question would be what Alice would use if she were in his place, but then again, if he had something to hide a direct question would give him the excuse to seem hurt and accuse her of not trusting him. No, that was not a good strategy. He decided to probe more gently.

"So, how was it talking to Dora on the phone? Did she seem surprised to be contacted? Did you have to talk her into letting us visit."

Alice glanced across at Adam briefly then resumed her determined focus on the road. There was heavier traffic now and an increased number of heavy goods vehicles. Adam waited patiently for her to answer.

"I don't think she was surprised. At least, she never said that she was."

They were approaching the Dartford Crossing at this moment. Alice said nothing more while they funnelled into what she identified to be the shortest queue and passed through into the tunnel. Once they had settled in behind a container lorry with a Scandinavian looking name on it, she spoke again.

"I don't know, but I think that it may be that she expected to be found one day. It was almost as if she had been waiting for my call."

"What made you think that?" Adam was intrigued now.

She shook her head. "Just that she didn't seem surprised at all. When I said I wanted to meet with her she agreed straight away. When I asked her when was convenient, she said I could come today."

Adam nodded thoughtfully. Time to probe a little more.

"You found her pretty quickly. Well, very quickly actually."

She shrugged. "The Internet is like any other place. Once you know your way around, you can get anywhere quickly." She paused as they emerged from the tunnel, pulling across into the right-hand lane to steer around the slower traffic. "The Internet has been my home ever since I started working. Finding my way into the darker corners of The Web was what I got paid for. And, like I said, Dora hasn't really done much to try and hide herself. Apart from changing her name, that is."

"Really. What's her name now?"

"It's Dora Brooke. I suppose she wanted to distance herself from the Montague family after all that happened."

Adam pondered on this. "Couldn't it be her married name?"

"No." Alice's tone was definitive. "No evidence of marriage. Not much evidence of anything really. She seems to have led a very quiet life."

As Adam opened his mouth to ask how she could possibly know this, she anticipated his question.

"We all leave a clear trail of our lives Adam. Electoral roll, bank statements, phone logs, social media, newspaper archives, email accounts; you can even access someone's Google data if you know how."

She took her attention off the road for a moment to flick a glance at his astonished expression.

"And you can access all of those things?" Adam sat up, astonished. "You're like ... an international spy or something."

Alice smiled. "Cyber security is not very glamorous, you know. And there's more than a few people out there who can find their way into your personal life if they want to. That's why people like me are well paid to find the loopholes and stop them up."

Adam leaned back and went very quiet. After a few moments he ventured, "So, you could find out all about my past if you wanted."

She raised her eyebrows. "Certainly could."

He paused again. Finally, he asked, "And have you?"

She smiled, still keeping her gaze on the road. "Only as much as I needed to find out so that I could be sure that I could trust you." There was no apology in her tone.

Adam lapsed into a crestfallen silence. What might she have found out about him? And what must she think of him as a result. Oh my God! The more he pondered, the more he became embarrassed. Some of the things he had done in his life! He had been a dick. Well, some of the time anyway. Did she know about Belinda and Nadia? Wait, hadn't she made some comment about concentrating on one thing at a time? It had been that morning, after she'd commented that he was looking a bit rough. Was that her way of letting him know that she knew what had happened? He closed his eyes and breathed out slowly. Had he really been thinking that there might be some romance between them in the future? Well, he was rapidly re-thinking that now. How could you go out with a girl who knew all of the things that you wanted to forget about yourself?

It was a quiet journey after that.

Chapter 15

Alice found Dora's cottage at the end of a short narrow lane, parking in front of the low wooden fence which separated the tiny front garden from the lane. As Adam unbuckled his seatbelt, she put her hand on his thigh. It was intended to stop him from getting out so that she could speak to him before they met Dora, but its unexpectedness had the effect of sending a sensation like a mild electric shock through his body. The intimacy of the contact initiated a tingling in his crotch which he recognised, with horror, as the beginnings of an erection. He laced his fingers together and rested them on top of his swelling member to hide it from her.

"Don't mention your film." Her tone was sharp and authoritative. "This poor woman has been through a lot.

Telling her that you're going to put it on a screen for everyone to see is likely to make her very defensive."

It occurred to Adam that he had all but forgotten about his plans for a film script. Now that he knew more about the events of 1979, now that he was about to meet the woman who had lived through those awful events, it seemed wrong to want to turn it into entertainment for popcorn munching crowds in a darkened cinema. He nodded his assent, feeling slightly ashamed of himself. The erection was no longer a problem.

From the boot of the car, Alice took out a cardboard box containing the documents, photographs and artifacts that had tumbled from the broken jar. She joined Adam as he stood in front of the neat little gate that led into the garden. The cottage was like something out of an English holiday brochure, all thatched roof and climbing roses around the door. Now that Adam had been reminded of his former plan to make a film of the Montague family tragedy, it occurred to him that this was, ironically enough, a very cinematic moment. The cottage was ideally suited to the scene where the intrepid sleuths track down the wounded heroine who has shut herself away from society. But this was all too real now. He turned to Alice.

"Are we sure about this? I mean, are we sure about reminding Dora of all the terrible things that happened forty years ago?"

Alice shrugged. "She invited us, remember. We've come all this way. Let's see what she has to say."

They walked through the gate, past tall plants that had been flattened a little by the recent snow, to the light-oak front door with a hanging basket on either side, both full of the remnants of last summer's plants and flowers. Alice knocked and they waited.

When the door opened, Adam took a step back, amazed. The beautiful woman in front of them bore a disturbing likeness to Audrey in the family photograph from the jar, albeit she looked somewhat older. She was dressed rather drably in a long grey woollen skirt and matching cardigan. Her bobbed hair was greying too as if the colour were spreading up her body, but there was no doubt at all that she was Audrey's daughter. He glanced across at Alice, who smiled with gentle amusement. Once again, Adam felt that he was two steps behind.

The woman smiled too, holding up her hands as an acknowledgement of Adam's response. "I know, I look just like my mother. I've tried my best to distance myself from the Montague legacy but some things are inescapable." Her voice still bore the unmistakeable tones of an upper-class upbringing.

Adam couldn't help himself. "It's a good job that your mother was so beautiful then." As soon as he said it, he realised that Dora might take this the wrong way. He was relieved when she blushed gratefully. Adam guessed that she probably didn't receive many compliments, tucked away from society as she was. A glimpse from the corner of his eye of Alice giving him a reassuring nod encouraged him further. He had been given a licence to flirt.

Dora took them into a cosy little sitting room furnished with three old armchairs covered in a faded floral fabric. They sat in an awkward silence, dominated by a large carriage clock ticking noisily on the mantelpiece. Dora, noticing that Adam's attention was fixed upon the photograph of a small black cat on top of her well-worn piano, spoke first.

"That's Misty, short for Mr. Mistoffelees. He'll be around somewhere. He's rather shy in company, unlike his namesake. She looked from Adam to Alice, checking to see that they recognised the allusion. Adam was pleased to be a step ahead of Alice for a change.

"The conjuring cat from Old Possum's Book of Practical Cats. It's a great name for a cat. Perhaps he'll pop in later and show us a trick or two."

And this was apparently enough flirting; Alice was keen to get on with what they had come for. "You changed your name Dora, from Montague to Brooke."

Dora smiled shyly. "Another literary joke I am afraid. I've always spent too much time with my head in a book. It's my way of escaping when things get too much."

This time even Adam was stumped. Seeing the incomprehension on both faces, Dora explained. "My mother wanted to call me Dorothea, after Dorothea Brooke in Middlemarch. My father said it was an old lady's name; he would only agree if it was shortened to Dora. So now I am as my mother would have wished, Dorothea Brooke."

"Why Dorothea?" queried Adam. "Not an obvious role model I would have thought."

Dora gave a tight-lipped smile. "Mummy was a great romantic. She liked to see herself as a tragic heroine who sacrificed her ambitions to marry into what she thought would be a life of service to a great man." She pulled a face. "She soon found that the man was not what she thought he was. I don't know what my father was like when she married him but, even as a child, I could see that he was very far from a great man. I think self-deception was Mummy's way of dealing with her disappointments."

Adam nodded to show that he understood. "I had presumed that Dora was short for Theodora or Isadora."

"Or Pandora," interjected Alice, picking up the cardboard box and placing it on the dark oak coffee table. "I'm afraid that the jar broke when we picked it up but all of the contents are here just as you buried them, forty years ago. Perhaps it's more fitting that they're in a box now."

Dora shook her head. "It's a mistranslation. In the original Greek, Pandora opens a 'pithos'. It's a clay storage jar that would have been used for wine or oil. So, you see, my sweetie jar was really quite appropriate. But I was trying to bottle the evil up, not like Pandora. It's you who let the evil out again Alice, you and Adam."

Adam leaned forward, interested. "Do you mean that literally, when you say you bottled the evil up, I mean?"

Dora considered this for some time, looking down as she tried to think how to answer. By the time that she looked up, Adam felt that a deep sadness had descended upon the room.

"I think I felt that it was my responsibility to do something about what had happened. I mean, I was the only one who knew exactly what had happened. It was too much responsibility for a thirteen-year-old girl. I was totally unprepared. Burying it in the garden was," she searched for the words, "it was my way of trying to purge myself of the responsibility to expose the evil actions my father had perpetrated."

Adam was captivated by the beautiful, melancholy woman, moved by her loss of innocence at such a young age. "Tell us about your childhood Dora. What was it like to be a member of the Montague family? That is," he added hastily, "if you don't mind talking about it."

He was aware that Alice shuffled impatiently in her seat. She would be thinking that he was just getting more material for his film, but let her think that. He wanted to understand what Dora had been through and what had led her to bottle everything up and bury it under a tree.

Dora regarded Adam thoughtfully for a while as if she were considering his request. She crossed her arms, a little defensively Adam thought. When she spoke, there was a guarded suspicion in her voice. "What are you going to do with any information I give you?"

Alice interjected before Adam could speak.

"You're right Dora that we're the ones that broke the jar and raked up what you had hidden away as a teenage girl. We feel that maybe we have a responsibility to do something. We're not sure. We don't know if you want the case to be reviewed after all this time."

Dora nodded her understanding. "I've thought about what happened many times over the years. And I've felt bitter that my father got away with murdering Mummy and Freddie."

"Did you ever consider going to the police and telling them what you know?" Adam asked.

She shook her head sadly. "You need to know, if you decide to pursue this, that my father is a very dangerous man with some very powerful friends. I'll tell you what happened, but I won't bear witness to that in a court. Blake made it very clear what he would do to me if I ever crossed him."

She left a few moments for this to sink in before she continued. "I'm going to make us some tea now. It will give you a chance to talk this through with each other and decide whether or not you want me to tell you what I know."

There was a long silence after she had left the room and shut the door to give them some privacy. The clock on the mantelpiece ticked oppressively. Adam broke the silence.

"Realistically, I don't think we can ask the police to re-open the case. If Dora is too frightened to tell them what she saw then there is no evidence. We'd just be putting ourselves in danger for no reason."

Alice screwed her mouth to one side. "Maybe. I still think we should hear what she has to say. When I talked to her on the phone, she seemed keen that we should come."

Adam shrugged. "Okay then. I got the impression that she hasn't told anyone about it since she buried the jar. Too frightened to open her mouth probably. It must have been totally traumatising. If I'd been in her place, I'd have wanted to talk about it. Maybe it would be good for her just to share the responsibility with someone else."

Alice smiled. "You can be quite caring once you forget about yourself for a moment."

Adam screwed his face up. "Are you taking the piss?"

Alice looked distressed. "No, I mean it. You can be a really nice person."

By the time that Dora returned with the tea they were both laughing and smiling. Dora was amused. "I guess that means you want to know more then," she chuckled.

Chapter 16

"Basically, Freddie and I were pretty feral as kids." Dora was staring blankly into the corner of the room as she recalled moments from her childhood. "We were just allowed to run wild most of the time. Mummy was always busy planning parties, buying clothes, having love affairs. Blake was," she frowned and turned to Alice, "doing what Blake does, making himself rich and stamping on anyone who gets in his way."

"Did you get on well with Freddie?" Adam asked.

Dora half smiled. "Yes, when we were younger, we did. When we got older, Freddie got really screwed up by what was going on around us and we drifted apart."

"But you didn't get screwed up?" Adam inquired gently.

"We were really different in character," she responded. "Freddie was a bit of a drama queen, like Mummy. He was always throwing tantrums about what he saw in the house." She shook her head slowly as she remembered. "There were always scary people visiting Blake. We both knew that the business he was doing was illegal, right, but Blake got angry if we ever suggested that to him. Anyway, I was younger than Freddie. Like I told you, I just retreated into books when I couldn't cope. I spent a lot of time on my own in my room once Freddie became angry all the time."

There was a long pause as she remembered the shouting and hysterics that had gone on.

"You mentioned the parties," Alice prompted.

"Oh God yes, the parties," Dora acknowledged. "I was supposed to stay in my room, but I used to creep down and peep into the ballroom sometimes. The parties were wild." Her eyes opened wide with the memory. "I was too young to understand a lot of what was going on, but there were crazy games, sex games I'm sure, and drugs, I think, and men and women going off into bedrooms. I didn't realise it at the time but, looking back at it now, it was all about Blake demonstrating his control over the guests. I mean, there were people there who would have been ruined if it had become public knowledge what they'd been doing at his party."

"Was Freddie at the parties?" Adam asked.

Dora sighed. "When he became older, he seemed to be able to get his hands on drugs and alcohol whenever he wanted. And I think that was his way of coping with his unhappiness."

She caught sight of an inquiring glance from Alice.

"Freddie thought he might be gay. He actually had an affair with his tutor, Gabriel. Did you know that?" She didn't wait for a reply before continuing. "That was a scary moment. Tabitha, Blake's personal assistant, told me about it later. Apparently, Freddie told her he was sleeping with Gabriel. She packed him off on the spot before Blake could find out."

"Did Blake know that Freddie was gay?" Adam queried.

Dora winced. "Blake is a total homophobe. He refused to even consider it. He used to hire prostitutes to take Freddie upstairs to try to seduce him." She laughed sardonically. "That's how Martine became Blake's mistress. She was a budding actress. Blake told her he would get her a role in a West End play if she managed to get Freddie into bed. Poor Freddie. When Freddie told her he was gay, she went and seduced Blake instead." She stared intently at Alice. "She's actually the one who gave him his alibi for the night of the murder."

During the pause that followed, Adam realised that his mouth had fallen open. It was just incredible. He looked across at Alice, but she remained totally impassive.

"Can you tell us what you saw on the night that your mother died Dora?"

Dora nodded once then took a deep breath as she relived the events of the night.

"It was round about midnight. Blake had supposedly gone off to his yacht with Martine a few days before. Our housekeeper had gone home, so there was only Mummy, Freddie, Tabitha and me in the house. There'd been a terrific row between Mummy, Freddie and Blake before he left. I couldn't hear what it was about but I could tell it was awful. So, anyway, it had been a peaceful day without Blake. The four of us had supper together for a change and it was quite nice, except that Freddie had been drinking, or taking drugs maybe, because he became quite slurred as the meal went on and, in the end, Tabitha took him upstairs to bed."

She looked up at Adam, who nodded encouragement for her to continue.

"So, I went to bed just after nine and read for a while then turned off my light and went to sleep. I woke up around midnight because I heard a noise out on the landing. I was a bit frightened so I just lay there listening for a while. All I heard was some whispering, but it was really loud whispering, if you know what I mean, and I thought it sounded like Blake. I knew it couldn't be him, but I couldn't get back to sleep without making sure so I got up, opened my door a little and looked down the corridor."

"And you saw Blake," Alice affirmed.

Dora had tears in her eyes now; the memory was clearly distressing her. "It was him, I saw him. And he saw me, I'm sure of it." She spoke emphatically, dismayed at the memory. "He never spoke of it later and I was too frightened to say anything to him but when the policewoman asked me about it the next day, I told her. She didn't even write it down. She told me that I had dreamt it; he was on his yacht with Martine and his crew."

Alice's eyes narrowed slightly. "Policewoman? Was it DCI Karen Turner by any chance?"

Dora nodded her assent, unable to speak for a moment. She recovered in a few moments but there was a quaver in her voice. "I'm sure that Blake paid her to stay quiet about what I had said. The next day, I was packed off to live with my granny. Nobody ever spoke to me about Mummy's death after that. Granny refused to talk about it. It was like I had been expelled from the family."

She leaned back in her seat as though fatigued by the effort of reliving the events of her mother's death. Adam and Alice exchanged a silent glance.

"And it was your granny's garden where you buried the time capsule," Alice stated, looking to Dora for verification.

"That was some time later," Dora acknowledged. "Blake had murdered Freddie, well, had arranged his murder in prison, by that time."

"Do you have evidence for that?" Alice asked gently.

Dora shook her head emphatically. "Blake is too clever. But I know he did it. Freddie didn't kill Mummy. He had no reason to. Besides, he was too drunk or drugged to be able to even if he wanted to. He was trying to prove his innocence. You've seen his letter in the jar. Blake had him murdered because, unlike me, Freddie wouldn't stop challenging him."

Adam felt sick. This brave woman's account of her ordeals made him just want to go and give her a hug. She was though, he realised, rather stronger than he was. He wasn't sure that he would have been able to cope with what she had endured. He looked across at Alice. Although she still appeared unmoved by the story, when she spoke there was a smouldering anger in her voice.

"Have you ever spoken to Blake since the night of the murder, Dora?"

"Once. On my twenty first birthday he came to visit me at Granny's. Dora sounded calm in comparison. He made me an offer. I would receive a house, this house, and a monthly allowance provided that I agreed never to speak to anyone about what went on during my childhood and about the deaths of Mummy and Freddie of course. As you can see, I agreed."

"And you never told him that you knew that he'd been there on the night of your mother's death?" Alice queried.

Dora's eyes widened. "Never! He murdered my mother and my brother. I'd have been next if I hadn't agreed to his demands."

There was a long pause as Adam and Alice processed the implications of what Dora had just said.

Dora broke the silence. "Thank you for giving me the opportunity to tell you the truth of what happened. I'm glad you found the time capsule. When I buried it, I hoped that it wouldn't be found while I was still alive. I thought the tree would keep it covered. But as time has gone on, I half hoped that it would be found after all. And I'm glad you came to see me. But, understand this, I can never speak of this to anyone else while Blake is alive. The contents of the time capsule are yours now. You can do what you like with them. If you choose to take this any further, you need to know that you're putting yourselves in grave danger. Grave danger," she repeated for emphasis.

Alice nodded. Adam was disturbed by the grim set of her lips. He had a horrible feeling that he was going to be persuaded by Alice, during the journey home, to continue to investigate.

"Just one more thing," Alice said. "On the family tree, you and Freddie are Audrey's only offspring. Is that right?"

Dora regarded Alice keenly for a few moments as she considered her answer. Adam looked between the two women in turn. Once again, there was something happening here that he did not understand. Why had Alice asked that question and why was Dora pausing before answering it?

After a long pause, Dora nodded, as if she had come to a decision. She spoke slowly, her voice a little lower.

"It didn't come out in any of the reports, but Mummy was pregnant when she died. She'd been trying to cover it up. I think it possible that Winston, was the father and she didn't want Blake to know." She looked towards Adam. "Winston was her lover at that time. I don't know if she was sleeping with Blake as well. I doubt it. Anyway, she told Freddie and me when we had supper together, on the night she died, but it was obvious really. I mean, she was huge. Blake must have known, and Tabitha of course, but, like I said, Mummy was very good at self-deception. The thing is, I really don't know if the baby survived or not.

Adam made a wry face. "Babies in the womb die very soon after their mother dies." He caught sight of a surprised glance from Alice. "What? I worked on a documentary about it once," he added by way of explanation.

"But Mummy was still alive when Tabitha found her." Dora asserted. "She didn't die till after the doctor came. I heard Tabitha and the doctor talking together before the police and the ambulance came."

Alice was on the edge of her seat at this news. "None of that was ever reported anywhere. It's like it never happened."

Dora agreed. "The thing about Blake is, he can control the narrative. He has so many people in his pocket, influential people, that he decides what did and didn't happen. Everyone else just has to agree with his version of events." She shrugged. "If they agree, he rewards them. If they don't," she paused, "well, he punishes them, kills them even. It's how he's stayed out of prison all these years."

"But you think the baby might have lived?" Adam asked carefully, looking for verification.

She nodded. "It's possible. I just don't know. If you do decide to go on with this, you should probably go and see Winston. He might know something. Gabriel too, Freddie's tutor. Freddie might have told him something we don't know."

Both Alice and Adam embraced Dora and kissed her on the cheek, as if she were an old friend, as they lingered in her tiny front garden to bid farewell. As Alice reversed down the narrow lane, Adam watched Dora's bravely smiling face receding until she was out of sight. Alice had looped her arm over the back of his seat so that she could turn right round while she reversed. He leaned his head back a little so that it lightly touched her arm. Right now, he felt in need of some reassuring contact.

Once they had turned onto the main road, Alice drove until she found a place where she could park the car safely. Turning to Adam, she gave him an inquiring look. "What are you thinking?"

Adam swallowed hard. He wasn't sure she would like what he was thinking. "I think that, without Dora's testimony in court, we have no evidence. If we take what we have to the police they'll do nothing. How could they? More to the point, there's always the chance that Blake still has people in the police who report back to him. It would be too risky."

Alice nodded once. "I agree."

"Really?" Adam was surprised.

"Absolutely. We need solid evidence. And I have no doubt that Blake's network is as strong as ever. I've been looking at his online profile. He's still very active. And he's still in contact with DCI Karen Turner. She's retired now but I'm betting she still has good contacts on the force."

"So … we drop it, just like that?" Adam countered.

Alice tilted her head slightly forward to look over the rim of her glasses. "No, Adam, we carry on. I think Dora's idea of finding Gabriel and Winston is a good one. If the baby was Winston's, he might well have tried to find out if it lived. And if it did, he might know who the doctor was who delivered it."

There was a steely determination in her voice. Adam made a half-hearted attempt to make her change her mind. "The longer we pursue this, the more likely it is that Blake will get to hear about us and what we're doing."

Alice nodded her assent. "He may already know. If he doesn't, he surely will. We need to find out as much as we can before it gets too dangerous."

Adam smiled weakly. He knew that he was being carried along by Alice's resolve and energy. He knew that he should bale out before things got really frightening. And yet, somehow, he was exhilarated too. Despite what he told people, he had really achieved next to nothing in his life so far. That was the truth of it. All that potential he'd been told that he had, and yet it had yielded precious little that he could be proud of. All the stories, the bluster, the front, it was all just a cover for his disappointment. And Alice, he flicked a glance at her as she waited for his answer, could see through it all. This, on the other hand, this mission to find out the truth about what had happened forty years previously, felt like something, and he didn't want to stop.

He nodded to indicate that he was ready for more and extended his hand, palm upwards above the dashboard, to indicate that he was ready for her to drive on.

Chapter 17

Karen Turner looked around the lounge of her penthouse flat while she considered what Jasmine had just told her. She had always taken care to enjoy her wealth without flaunting it. Most people, she thought, would not realise the true cost of the artwork on display, the bespoke furnishings, the black designer dress she was wearing. Down in the street, her car was a modest 4-year-old Audi. She could easily afford much better than that, but it did not look good for a police officer, not even a retired police officer, to seem too wealthy. It smelt of corruption.

Pushing down on the padded arms of her chair, she rose to her feet and crossed the room to close the curtains. It was dark enough for the streets lights to have come on in the street below and the commuters in their cars, heading home after a day's work, had all switched on their headlights. It frustrated her that she did not fully understand what her much younger ex-colleague had just told her. She had always prided herself on being up to speed with new developments, new technologies, new ways that criminals could break the law. She had stayed in touch as much as she could during her ten years of retirement, but cyber-crime had moved too fast for her and she was at a loss to keep pace. It occurred to her that she could nod, as if she understood, and ask DI Woods to continue with her findings. There was a buff file deposited on the coffee table. She could read it later and research what she did not understand. But that was not her way. Her desire to understand and augment her knowledge was too strong.

She looked back at the young policewoman. Like herself, she had moved up fast, though, of course, it was easier for a woman now than it was back in her day. And a mixed-race woman like Jasmine, well, she would have stood no chance back then. She wondered whether Jasmine had taken any short cuts, as she had. Probably not. But then she didn't have to.

"I'm sorry Jasmine. You're going to have to explain that one to me in plain language. I need to know just what we might be up against here."

"Oh, sorry Ma'am. It's easy to get carried away with the cyber speak."

Settling back into her chair, Karen noted with pleasure that the respect for her position still persisted, despite her long absence from the force.

Jasmine looked away to ponder for a moment then looked back and smiled brightly.

"Think of the hacker as being a house burglar and the computer system as the house. There's a whole bunch of security systems around the house, alarms, cameras, security locks and the like, but there's also a weakness. There's a blind spot around the back of the house which allows the burglar to approach the house unseen and a window which hasn't been alarmed. The burglar can jemmy the window open without being detected and gain entrance to the house. Quite simply, he or she has found a back door into the system."

Karen nodded thoughtfully. "So, they can get what they want and leave without being detected then?"

Jasmine nodded brightly, pleased that her analogy had worked and that Karen didn't feel patronised. "Almost, though, as you know, burglars usually leave some trace of their visit. In this case, it's a bit more than that. The hacker has left a trojan horse behind." Seeing Karen's face cloud over again, she pressed on quickly. "In terms of our burglar, it's a bit like leaving a thin wedge in the window so that it never quite shuts properly. It allows the hacker to get back in easily if they want to come back for something."

"And have they taken something?" Karen was sure that her voice sounded calm and measured, but she was aware that her pulse had quickened. Her instincts told her that there was cause for concern.

"Well, you asked me to alert you if anyone showed an unhealthy interest in the Montague case Ma'am. I.T. are certain that the hacker looked at the old files."

Jasmine hesitated just for a moment. Karen wondered if she had any suspicions about her relationship with Blake Montague. Surely not. Surely, Jasmine would not be here now if she was aware of how she had compromised herself, risked everything, in order to reach DCI and to earn more than a humble policewoman's salary. Unless, she reflected, Jasmine herself had a business relationship with Blake. Interesting thought.

"They're also certain that the hacker looked at some personnel files too Ma'am." She paused again, looking down briefly to regain her composure. "In particular, your file Ma'am." She looked up again, gazing directly at Karen to gauge her response.

Karen nodded slowly, hoping that it looked as if she had been expecting this and had tasked Jasmine to watch out for it. She raised her hand to her face, two fingers resting on her lips, thumb underneath her chin, buying some time by staring out of the window while her pulse steadied.

When she spoke, her voice was cool, composed. "Any idea who the snoopers might be?"

Jasmine smiled brightly. Karen wasn't just an old colleague; Jasmine was aware that she still had good contacts on the force. Here was her chance to shine.

"The hacker was good Ma'am. He or she covered their tracks carefully. However, as it was the Montague case they were interested in, I put a PC on obs. with Dora Montague. She calls herself Dora Brooke these days. Lives on her own in the middle of nowhere. Very few callers. Seldom goes out."

Karen knew all this but said nothing. She could see that Jasmine had more to tell, was building up to demonstrating good police work.

"So, she had visitors yesterday. A young couple. Stayed for a couple of hours."

Karen kept her face impassive, just the faintest of nods to encourage the young DI to continue. She could see the girl had more to tell.

"The car was driven by the young woman. It's registered to an Alice Liddell. There's an address in Kent." Jasmine was enjoying herself now. "We found out what we could about her, but she has a very small digital footprint." She looked across to check that Karen was familiar with this terminology before continuing. "No social media accounts that we could find. Almost no clues about who she is and where she's come from. It's like she just popped out of nowhere." Jasmine raised her hands, palm up, to underline her surprise at this. "However, we do know she's been working for a company that specialises in cyber security. It seems that our mystery girl has all the qualifications to be our hacker and to keep her identity a secret." She raised her eyebrows to underline the enigma of her findings, studying Karen closely to see any signs that she was impressed.

Karen decided that now was the time to deliver that pat on the head. It was restrained in its tone, just enough to keep DI Woods on the hook, but unmistakeable in its affirmation.

"That's good police work Jasmine. I'd heard a whisper that someone was nosing around the Montague case. This confirms it. I can take it from here." She hoped this would be enough to explain her request to monitor interest in the case. She didn't want DI Woods investigating this any further. She was far too bright, too perceptive. Hopefully, she would be bright enough to realise she had been dismissed.

"Any idea what they want?" Apparently, Jasmine was not quite as bright as she had hoped.

Karen waved a hand vaguely. "The media would be my guess. It's 40 years since it all happened. The media love an anniversary." She smiled sardonically. "And they love taking a pop at the aristocracy. But if they've hired a hacker to look at our system then that's a little bit naughty. A sharp rap on the knuckles will convince them of the error of their ways. I can deal with that." She stood to indicate that the interview was at an end.

Jasmine rose uncertainly. An intrusion into a police IT system was a little more than naughty. It was a serious crime. She ought to report this. Sensing her hesitancy, Karen pulled rank, hoping that her historic standing in the force would be enough to carry her through.

"I'll talk to your DCI. I'll tell him what you've discovered and make sure he knows you've done a good job here." She dropped her voice a little. "This is a sensitive matter Jasmine. There were questions left unanswered at the end of the Montague investigation. Keith won't want those being raked up again. It will waste valuable police time and it could give the media a chance to have a pop at us as well. Leave it to me to contact Keith." She shook her head. "I can remember that case like it was yesterday. I'll tell him what you've found out and he can decide how to proceed."

Jasmine smiled thinly. If she pressed any harder, she would undo any kudos she might have won here. There was an authority in Karen's voice that was reassuring, but still, she would check that her DCI had been informed of everything once Karen had spoken to him. She knew only too well that things had been done differently when Karen Turner was DCI. That kind of behaviour was old school. It wasn't how they did things now.

Leaning forward, she pushed the buff file across the coffee table. "I've put it all in here. I'll give a copy to Keith tomorrow afternoon. That will give you a chance to talk to him first."

Karen eased one of the curtains a little to one side in order to watch the young police officer while she climbed into her car and set off home. Weighing what she had heard carefully, she considered the severity of the threat that she was facing. The Montague case had come relatively early in her career. In many ways, it had been a pivotal time in her career. She sighed at the memories that flooded back. For the media, it had been racy, juicy even; murder most foul with an aristocratic twist. Her high-profile success had consolidated her position within the force, afforded her a kudos that many of the other officers, all of them male, had withheld up until that point. It had also, she reflected ruefully, strengthened the bond between herself and Blake Montague. There was, on balance, little that she regretted about the course of her career. Policing was, she reflected, a dirty business. Yes, she had taken money from a businessman involved in illegal dealing in return for doing him favours, but she had also removed a huge number of villains from the streets with the assistance of that same businessman. You couldn't thrive in cleaning up the streets unless you had contacts within the criminal world. And anyway, she had given her life to policing. The least she deserved was a decent wage for her commitment.

The problem was, a relationship with Blake Montague had strings attached.

She crossed the room to the drinks cabinet, poured herself a large glass of a rather expensive single malt whisky that she had recently discovered, and sank back into her chair. Blake Montague. Bloody Blake Montague. It was a relationship that went back forty years and, yes, it had been very profitable for her in so many ways. She took a sip of the whisky, savouring the smoky peat flavour on her tongue then feeling the warming glow in her throat as she swallowed. He had given her access to tiers of society that she could never have accessed on her own. She nodded thoughtfully. And some of her most high-profile convictions would not have been possible without his criminal connections. Oh yes, Blake could usually supply an informant or a witness when one was needed. And then there was the money. She cast her eye around the room once more and took a larger sip of the whisky. She had undoubtedly lived a lifestyle that a police salary could never support. And she deserved that, without a doubt. But the cost had been high. Blake Montague had made sure of that. She swallowed the remainder of the whisky in one mouthful and put the glass down firmly on the coffee table beside her.

Leaning back in her chair, she placed her elbows on the arms and interlinked her fingers, pushing her first fingers together like a church steeple, or, when she tilted them forward, like the barrel of a gun. Blake Montague had raped her. Even the thought of it, after all these years, made the hairs stand up on her arms. The humiliation, after all this time, was still unbearable. There was no physical force involved. Oh no. And she had put up no resistance. She shook her head at the memory. He had referred to it as a sealing of the business arrangement. He had presented it as a celebration for them both, a bonding of two partners in a deal. She felt a chill course through her veins. The arrogant bastard had then invited his PA into the room to act as a witness to what was about to take place, confident that she was powerless to refuse his advances. Her lips tightened across her teeth. It was rape. It was a demonstration that, having entered a pact with the devil, he controlled her destiny.

Karen looked at the empty whisky glass and considered pouring another. She knew that she shouldn't. There were things that needed to be done and she would need a clear head. She closed her eyes for a moment and breathed out heavily, but the feelings of loathing and revulsion continued to crowd in on her in a way that they had not done for many years. This is what happened when you got older, she reflected, when the speed of life slowed down and you had more time to think back and remember what you had done. Opening her eyes, she picked up the glass, crossed to the cabinet and poured herself another large whisky.

He had made her cover up the murder of his wife, and then, later, the murder of his son. And she had been powerless to refuse. By that time, she was so compromised herself that she knew he had the power to ruin her if she did. And at the time she was enjoying the reflected power and lifestyle that Blake's patronage afforded. She shook her head slowly. It was only latterly, since her retirement from the force, that she had begun to experience deep regret over this deception. Audrey Montague was a silly bitch but she didn't deserve to die for that. More importantly, there was Freddie. Poor screwed up kid. He was a complete innocent, he was Blake's own flesh and blood for Christ's sake, but he had him silenced with no sign of any compassion.

Returning to the window, she pulled one of the curtains right back so that she could look down on the street. The traffic was even heavier now, moving at a crawl most of the time. Part of her wanted to see Blake punished for what he had done. Business was one thing but the man was a cruel sadist, a monster. At the same time, she knew, as she had always known, that he would take her and many others down with him if she told the authorities what she knew. She considered again what Jasmine had told her.

It was doubtful that this Alice Liddell woman could harm a reputation as strong as Blake's. However, it would be prudent to investigate further. And she would need to ensure that Jasmine's DCI was on side so that he could keep his DI away from any more digging into what had happened forty years ago. She had, she realised, been delaying the inevitable, but she could not put it off any longer. Suitably fortified by the whisky, she picked up her phone and dialled Blake Montague.

"Karen, darling, how good to hear from you. It's been ages." The very sound of his voice made her feel sick. He was smooth and charming, the public front that most people experienced, but she could sense the edge in his voice too. He was wondering why she had contacted him.

She was not in the mood to keep up any semblance of friendship with him. This was purely business.

"Blake, do you have any influence with DCI Keith Saunders?"

Blake was non-committal, unsure where this inquiry was going. "Is there a problem darling?"

"I'm not sure. It could just be the media nosing around, but some hacker has been into the police records to look at the deaths of Audrey and Freddie." She wanted to say murders but knew that would not be helpful. "Keith's DI, Jasmine Woods, came to tell me about it. Bright girl. Ambitious. I need you to tell Keith to delay any investigations and to get his DI to back off. We don't want her digging up anything from that old case."

"Mmmm." As always, Blake was unruffled on the surface, though, Karen reflected, you never knew what was going on behind that façade. "Someone needs to look into it though. We don't want anyone else digging anything up either."

"Agreed." Karen was firm and officious. She wanted as little contact with Blake as possible. "I have an ex-colleague, Gordon. Completely trustworthy. I'll put him on the case. It might be nothing. We don't want to go in mob handed if there's no need. If there's a problem, Gordon will find it and then we'll decide how to deal with it. I'll report back to you as soon as I have anything. In the meantime," she paused meaningfully, "I need Keith Saunders and Jasmine Woods to stay away from it."

Blake was reassured. Years of working with Karen had afforded him complete confidence in her judgement. "You can rely on me darling," he purred, resuming the smooth and charming persona. "Keith owes me a few favours. Consider it done."

Karen put the phone down and heaved a sigh of relief. She would phone Gordon later and instruct him to follow this Alice Liddell woman and find out what she was up to. In the meantime, she needed another drink.

Chapter 18

Animated chatter flooded the room. Adam surveyed the people seated at the groups of tables and chairs then allowed his gaze to travel up to the people standing at the bar. He had met gay people before, of course; there had been plenty at Uni, and the film world had its fair share too, but never this many at one time, particularly in the context of an evening out. He had felt a little nervous when Alice had told him that Gabriel wanted to meet in a gay bar, but, now that he was here, it felt much like any other bar. He looked across at Alice and was surprised to see a smile of amusement on her face. It made her look almost beautiful.

"What?"

She shrugged. "You!"

"I what?" Adam was intrigued now.

Alice gave him a knowing look. "Come on. Even though you're not interested in gay men, you're still looking around to see how many of them fancy you. You know you are."

Adam snorted with impatience. "You really think I'm that shallow? Really?"

She shrugged again. "I think we both know you are." She raised her eyebrows when Adam snorted again. "Come on then. Tell me I'm wrong. Tell me you haven't been looking out for admiring glances."

Adam hesitated. Actually, he had noticed that a few heads had turned when he'd entered the bar. And yes, he had presumed that they were giving him the once over. And, okay then, it gave him pleasure to feel that some of them might fancy him. Damn the woman. He shrugged back.

"There are a lot of gay men in here and I'm a very attractive young guy. It's just chemistry. No big deal."

She smiled again, a bewitching, seductive smile. "Okay then attractive young guy, you can go to the bar and buy me a Perrier water with ice," she tilted her head towards him in the parody of a stern look, "but no tapping off with any of the locals. I know what you're like."

He shook his head as he rose from his seat. "Tapping off?" He shook his head in a parody of sadness. "Who ***says*** that anymore?"

As he stood at the bar, separated from Alice's chaperoning, Adam became aware of a more overtly sexual signalling from the men around him. There was a strong scent of expensive male cologne mixed with pheromones. The haircuts were smart, distinctive. As he ordered the Perrier for Alice and a gin and tonic for himself, he felt a hand massage his bottom then gently spank it a few times. Turning sharply, he found he had to look up to lock eyes with the man who stood directly behind him. He wore tight jeans, and a carefully ironed white vest, clearly chosen to allow a good view of his toned biceps, both sporting tattoos of elaborate geometric designs. The man was smiling down at Adam with perfect teeth.

"If you get tired of the lady, I'll be waiting up here for you at the bar," he purred.

Adam smiled back nervously. "Thanks, but we're meeting someone. Another time perhaps."

Walking back to the table with the drinks, he felt sure that eyes were on him from the group at the bar. Did they fancy him or were they just enjoying his discomfort? Certainly, he had caused a bit of a stir, he was sure about that. And, on the whole, it felt better to be garnering attention than to be ignored, even by gay men. Oh God, he groaned inwardly. Maybe I really am that shallow. Fortunately, a man had joined Alice at their table now, presumably Gabriel. With a bit of luck, she hadn't witnessed the scene at the bar.

"Ah. And you will be Adam." The man had the same upper-class accent as Dora, delivered with just a hint of campness. He was in his sixties, Adam knew, but he looked younger. Clearly, he took care of himself. He rose and held out his hand. He was wearing the same tight jeans as many of the occupants of the bar, but had a dark blue blazer over an open necked check shirt. Once again, Adam couldn't help feeling that he was being checked out as the man looked him up and down with eyes which were spaced just a little too far apart.

"I'm Gabriel."

The handshake was firm, accompanied by a welcoming smile. Adam liked him immediately.

"I'm sorry about insisting on meeting you here, but talking about Blake still makes me nervous and I feel safe here". He waved a hand towards the men at the bar as he sat down. "We all know each other here. If a stranger entered, he'd be spotted immediately." He gave a sly wink. "You've probably noticed that you've both attracted a lot of attention since you came in. You'll be fine now that they've seen you with me."

Alice smiled knowingly and gave Adam an ironic glance, causing him to look down, embarrassed. Gabriel picked up the communication instantly.

"What ... am I missing something here?" he ventured.

Alice shook her head with a smile. "Sorry. Private joke," she responded smoothly. "And thank you for agreeing to meet us. Dora said that you might be able to help."

Gabriel's brow furrowed. His eyes narrowed slightly. "Yes, but help with what exactly? Why are you bringing all this back up again after forty years?" His gaze flicked back and forth between Alice and Adam, but they had both looked down. Adam realised that he did not have an answer that would be likely to satisfy Freddie's old tutor. In fact, he wasn't at all sure himself why he was pursuing this investigation. There was a certain excitement in behaving like a sleuth, but really it was just that he didn't want to let Alice down.

It was Alice who caught Gabriel's gaze, her jaw firmly set with determination.

"Justice for Freddie." There was conviction and strength in her voice. "Blake Montague has ruined so many lives. And he is still active." There was a bitterness in her tone now. "He needs to be stopped."

Gabriel gazed at her thoughtfully, glanced across at Adam, then looked back at Alice. There was a keen intelligence in his eyes.

"But why you? There's great risk involved in crossing Blake Montague, you know. What's your interest in this?"

She held his gaze. "I can't tell you exactly. I'm sorry, but it would be dangerous for both of us if I told you everything." She paused, looking down for inspiration, then refixed her gaze on his. "Let's just say that I too have been hurt by Blake Montague. I hope that's enough to convince you that I realise what the dangers are and that I'm willing to risk them."

They were all distracted for a moment by a shriek from the bar followed by laughter. They looked across. It appeared that the tall muscular man in the white vest had tried his introduction technique once more with another newcomer and elicited a more positive response. Gabriel smiled knowingly then turned back to Adam and Alice. He raised his eyebrows, considered carefully, then nodded slowly. "Very well then. I'm not sure how useful I can be after all these years, but ask away and I'll tell you what little I know."

As usual, Alice took the lead. "Dora told us a lot about the months leading up to Audrey's murder. We know that you had gone by then, but we were hoping you stayed in touch with someone, Tabitha maybe, or Freddie. Can you shed any light on Freddie's death in prison?"

Gabriel shook his head sadly. "Certainly not Freddie. Tabitha made it very clear to me that our relationship was putting us both in danger. It's why I left so suddenly." He winced slightly. "She made me realise how foolish I had been." He blinked rapidly several times as he recalled his flight from the house. "I was terrified at the time. When Freddie was put in prison I wanted to go and visit him, of course I did, but I didn't dare."

"Terrified of Blake?" Adam chipped in.

Even the name made Gabriel flinch. Adam felt sorry for this gentle, timid man.

"You'll think me naïve, no doubt." Gabriel looked from Adam to Alice and back again, as if daring them to contradict him. "They say there's no fool like an old fool. And while I was, admittedly, still in my twenties, I was much older than Freddie." He paused and stared above their heads while he considered this. "But I felt such love for that poor boy." He shook his head sorrowfully. "He was so messed up by his malevolent father and feckless mother you know." He threw his hands up in the air, helplessly. "They call it rescue fantasy, the psychologists I mean. I wanted to deliver him from the awful pressures being heaped upon him." An angry edge came into his voice. "Did you know that his father regularly sent prostitutes up to his room to try and seduce him?"

Adam and Alice both nodded sympathetically.

"The poor boy. No wonder he was going off the rails. He was drinking far more than was good for him. And taking drugs too, Blake saw to that." Gabriel's tone was bitter now. "That boy was systematically set up by his father to take the blame for his mother's death. As if Freddie could have murdered Audrey …" He shook his head in disbelief, sighing deeply.

Alice gave him a moment to recover his self-control before she pressed on. "Dora thought that Audrey lived long enough for her baby to be born."

Gabriel examined her closely while considering his response; he appraised her earnest face, the hint of sadness that hid behind the business-like façade. He liked this young lady; she was direct and incisive. He decided that he trusted her.

"I have been in contact with Tabitha twice since I left the house. She told me that Audrey delivered a baby girl before she died," he confirmed. "Apparently, the baby had been sent away somewhere. I'm not at all sure if Blake knew about this. I hope not but …" He trailed off into thought. "He must have known that Audrey was pregnant, of course, she would have been clearly showing in the weeks before her death, but the baby wasn't mentioned at Freddie's trial." He shook his head to indicate his lack of understanding of why this should be. "Anyway, Tabitha seemed to think that someone had intervened to protect the poor little thing. As to whether she lived," he shrugged, "who knows."

Alice leaned forward in her seat. "Do you know who the father was?" She looked at Gabriel keenly.

He shook his head. "There was the new lover-boy, Winston of course. It could have been him. If you could find him, he might be able to shed some light on that. Of course, Blake would have wanted everyone to think it was Freddie's." He snorted in disgust. "Ridiculous idea, but it's why I fear that the little one didn't make it. If Blake knew that she had been born, she might represent a threat. A DNA test could be most unhelpful for his testimony against Freddie. If he had known that she had survived, he would almost certainly have ordered his paid thugs to dispose of her."

Alice leaned back in her seat, visibly disappointed.

"There was a second time after Freddie was murdered in prison, a phone call with Tabitha, I mean," Gabriel continued.

With Alice buried in her own thoughts, Adam took over the role of encouraging Gabriel to continue. "Why do you think she contacted you?"

Gabriel flashed him a friendly smile. "I think she wanted someone she could share her grief with. Tabitha was as close to Freddie as I was in her way, something between a mother substitute and a big sister really. She was very upset, very angry with Blake. She had a suspicion that he might have ordered Freddie's murder, but she had no proof." He shrugged his shoulders. "She talked to me about wanting to hand in her notice to Blake and leave the house. She didn't dare to though, not after she had got over that initial rage. You see, she was as wary of him as the rest of us. Not frightened, you understand." He held up his hand for emphasis. "She's a tough cookie; she'd seen plenty of violence before she came to work for Blake. Smart though. Smart enough to realise that she couldn't just leave. He paid her well and provided a wonderful career for her, but she was also his prisoner. Ultimately, she knew too much for him to ever let her go."

Alice had re-joined the conversation now. She nodded at Gabriel's comment. "She's still working for him, still living in the house." She cocked her head to one side thoughtfully. "Do you think she still bears a grudge against Blake after all these years?"

Gabriel considered this, rubbing his hand thoughtfully over the incipient grey stubble around his jaw. "I know that **I** do. And Tabitha?" He swayed his head from left to right as if weighing the pros and cons. "Yes, I think that Tabitha probably does too. She never had children of her own, you know. Freddie was the closest to a child that she ever had. His death hit her hard."

Alice nodded. Adam noticed a grim smile pass fleetingly across her lips. He wasn't sure why Alice had asked the question, but he could see that the answer was what she wanted to hear. He didn't know why, but something in her mood since she had heard about the birth of the baby unsettled him. He would ask her about it later but he wasn't confident that she would share her thoughts with him. There was a darkness there which was unnerving.

The bar was filling up by now. The men at the bar were having to raise their voices to be heard over the general chatter. Gabriel looked up, caught the eye of a couple of men and smiled at them to let them know that all was well.

Alice started to gather her things together to signal that it was time to leave.

"I'm sorry I couldn't be more help," he apologised, turning back to Adam and Alice. "It was forty years ago now and I was long gone by the time that the murders took place."

Alice shook her head emphatically. "You've been more help than you know Gabriel. Thank you for meeting with us. And I'm sorry to have stirred up some old memories." She gave Adam a sardonic look. "Time to take you away from your admirers. There's gonna be some broken hearts when you've gone."

Outside the bar, it had grown dark and the streetlights were on. Adam shivered in the cold, damp air, pulling his coat more tightly around himself. Small groups of young people were moving quickly from one bar to another, the girls tottering on high heels with bare arms and bare legs; the boys too were mainly in short sleeves or T shirts, gym-toned muscles or tattoos on display. Despite the miserable weather, there was a party atmosphere. The alcohol was doing its job, with much banter being thrown from one group to another as they hurried past each other to get to the warmth of the next bar.

Adam gave Alice a sidelong glance as she strode with him towards the car. She seemed, somehow, to be changing. It could just be that he was getting to know her better, but he didn't think so. She seemed, he struggled to put his finger on it, less … well, less geeky really. Her sarcasm just now in the bar! He was sure that she would not have done that just a few days ago. In fact, she'd seemed incapable of understanding that kind of humour. Could it be his influence that was promoting this metamorphosis? She was certainly more vivacious, more attractive even. He smiled at the idea of being responsible for her transformation.

"What?"

Alice had sensed that he was studying her and had looked across to see him smiling. Her expression was impassive apart from a slight furrowing of her brow.

Adam shrugged. "I don't know really. I just feel oddly happy. Her eyes flashed and she opened her mouth to speak, but Adam hurried on to prevent her from interjecting. "I mean," he paused while he searched for the words, "I understand that what we're doing is dangerous ... and obviously we are uncovering things that are ugly and nasty ... and yet, I really like being with you and feeling that I can be of some use in helping you to ..." He trailed off as he realised that he still didn't really understand what it was they were doing.

The muscles in Alice's face relaxed, to be replaced by an indulgent smile.

"I'm glad you're happy," she responded. "And I'm glad we're doing this together."

Adam was encouraged by her words, but disappointed by what he perceived as a slight lack of warmth behind them. Still, it was early days yet. He would need to work on that with her.

Chapter 19

Gordon King rolled the scotch around appreciatively on his tongue before he swallowed. It was good scotch. It was some years since he had been in Karen Turner's apartment. He looked around with a critical eye at the changes she had made, nodding thoughtfully. She had done well for herself.

"Been a while Gordon," she said, reading his thoughts.

He caught her eye, continuing to nod. "It has."

Both of them were thinking of a brief but intense relationship many years ago. That was the last time he had been in this room. Neither of them was prepared to refer to it; that was ancient history. And yet, reflected Gordon, it had been quite something. Karen had become the benchmark for the three wives that he'd married and divorced since that time. Somehow, they had never quite seemed to measure up to her.

"You've done the place up nice," he pronounced. "Very nice indeed. But then, you always did have good taste."

Karen gave him an amused smile. They both knew that he meant expensive taste. Even if he didn't recognise the brands of the furnishings and artwork, he would know that they could not be funded from a police salary alone.

"We've both done well, as far as that's concerned," she replied. She was keen to remind him that she had put a lot of money his way over the years. If he hadn't spent it on acquiring nice things, well, it wasn't her fault that he'd been through three expensive divorces.

"Oh yes," he assented. "I'm not complaining, not at all." He shot her a conspiratorial smile. "We've both done very well out of upholding the law."

Karen considered that Gordon had aged rather well considering that he was a man who had always liked to drink. There were a few broken veins in his nose and he'd put on a few pounds, but he was still an attractive man. His wiry hair had gone grey, but it rather suited his craggy features and deep, resonant voice. Ah yes, that voice, with its soft Edinburgh tones. She could still almost fancy him really, except that she was done with all that now. She'd never been very successful in her relationships. A bit like Gordon really, except that she hadn't made the mistake of marrying any of them. And anyway, she was happier on her own these days. No need to compromise.

"So," she uttered with a touch of authority, to clarify that niceties were over and they were getting down to business, "what do you have to report?"

He leaned forward to pull a folder from the table in front of him and opened it on his knees. He'd been pleased when Karen had contacted him. Not only would the money be a useful supplement to his pension, but he also missed the buzz of working in that no-man's land between the law and the criminal fraternity. He'd done a thorough job in the hope that there might be future prospects.

"Okay, so there's a detailed account of activity over the last 36 hours. Not a great deal to report there apart from one very significant outing." Gordon took two photographs from the file and placed them on the table for Karen to view. "This first one is of Alice Liddell and Adam Parkinson entering a gay bar in Greenwich. And this one here," he pointed to the second photograph, "is the man they met there."

Karen picked up the photo and stared hard at the man across the table from the couple. The picture had clearly been taken through the window of the bar with a high-powered lens but it was clear enough for her to make out a strangely familiar face. It had been a long time. The blond hair was now grey, the skin a little more wrinkled, but there was no mistaking those widely spaced eyes.

"Is that who I think it is?" she checked, looking at Gordon quizzically.

"It is if you think it's Gabriel Williams," he assented. "He was Freddie's tutor, right?"

Karen nodded to confirm this. "He left rather suddenly, shortly before Audrey Montague was murdered. We checked him out, but he was never a suspect in the case. He told us that he was unhappy about the tensions in the house and Blake Montague's PA, Tabitha Watts, corroborated that." She tapped one finger on her cheek thoughtfully. "Mind you, seeing him in a gay bar puts a different complexion on it." She flashed a sharp look at Gordon. "Blake hates gays. Always has done. Between you and me, I've sometimes wondered whether something happened to Blake when he was younger; maybe when he was at boarding school. Homophobia is one thing but Blake is very extreme. He seems to have a pathological hatred of all gay people." She shrugged. "Anyway, it might explain why Gabriel made such a hasty exit from Montague Hall."

Gordon remained impassive. His job was to report facts, not make judgements. He would not allow himself to be drawn into speculation on the people he was investigating. He waited for Karen to raise one eyebrow to check what else he had before he continued.

"So, the address in Kent of Miss Liddell is interesting."

He pulled out a photograph of the house with Alice's Renault Clio parked on the front drive.

"The house used to belong to Grace De Lacy. It was ..."

Karen held up her hand to interrupt. "Wait. I know that surname." She searched her memory for a moment, shook her head impatiently, then looked across to Gordon for a clue.

"You probably remember it as Audrey Montague's maiden name," he continued smoothly. Grace De Lacy was her mother, Dora and Freddie's grandmother."

Karen frowned, cross with herself for being unable to recall this detail. "That's right. Dora went to live with her for a few years after Audrey's death." She frowned again. "So, Alice Liddell becomes the owner of the house where Dora used to live and then starts investigating the Montague case?" She raised one eyebrow at Gordon as a way of asking if he had any explanation of this.

He responded to the cue. "So, Alice Liddell inherited the house from her mother, Evie Reynolds." He registered the puzzled look on Karen's face. "That's right, our Miss Liddell is actually Emma Reynolds. But there's no evidence of an official name change; it just that she's been calling herself Alice Liddell since the death of her mother."

Gordon was enjoying himself now. This case had turned out to be much more interesting than he had been expecting. "So, you're wondering now what the connection is between Evie Reynolds and Grace De Lacy."

Karen shrugged in assent.

Gordon smiled. "And we don't know the answer to that." He waited for Karen to assimilate this before continuing. "Evie Reynolds was the adopted child of Reginald and Mary Reynolds. She lived her whole life in Leeds. Grace De Lacy bequeathed the house to her in 1995 but Evie never took up residence there. The house became Emma Reynolds's when Evie died a year ago."

Karen posed a question with her eyes to which Gordon shook his head. "Nothing suspicious. She died of breast cancer two years after her diagnosis."

"Father?" Karen asked.

Gordon shook his head. "No father on the birth certificate. No evidence of him in Evie or Emma's life. Maybe just a one-night stand or maybe a married man who wouldn't leave his wife. Either way, Evie clearly didn't want him to have any rights over her daughter. I'm pretty sure Emma never knew who he was."

Karen sank back in her chair, laced her hands under her chin and pondered what Gordon had told her. He waited patiently, watching the changing expressions on her face as she considered the evidence. After several minutes, she sighed heavily, sat up straight and held her left hand out in front of her, fingers spread. She used the first finger of her right hand to tick off the key points on her left.

"So, Emma Reynolds discovers that she is the owner of a house that she has never been to and possibly knew nothing about. She decides to take up residence there and discovers that the house has history. She starts investigating that history and makes contact with Dora Montague and Gabriel Williams. Why would she be going to all that effort?"

Gordon, reached into the folder and pulled out another document with a small photograph attached and allowed himself the luxury of conjecture. "She might not be the main driver in this. Her side kick and next-door neighbour is Adam Parkinson." Gordon glanced at the photograph. "Our good-looking boy, apart from being something of a hit with the ladies, is also a film editor."

Karen screwed up her features. "You think Alice has shared what she knows with him and he's persuaded her to help him make a film out of the Montague case?"

Gordon stayed impassive. "He's been with her for the visits to Dora and Gabriel. He seems to spend a lot of time round at her house. She's not the kind of girl he normally dates; his taste is for the gorgeous and the glamorous and our girl doesn't really fit the bill. So … it could be that he has other reasons for wanting her company."

Karen nodded. "Okay. Worth bearing in mind anyway." She smiled gratefully at her former colleague and erstwhile lover. "Thanks Gordon. You've done good work there."

Gordon smiled back, hopeful that this wasn't an end to his involvement. "How do you want me to proceed, Karen?"

She flicked a look into the corner of the room while she considered this then looked back at him. "Just keep them under surveillance until I've had a chance to speak to Blake. He'll want to know what you've discovered." She paused, then nodded. "I'll be in touch."

Gordon nodded back. He would have liked to ask her out for a drink, but he didn't want to do anything that might endanger his role in this case. Maybe, when this was all over, he might drop a hint or two to see if she was still interested.

Once Gordon had left, Karen poured herself another whisky, selected Chopin's Etudes on her hi fi, then sat back on the sofa. Closing her eyes, she allowed the dazzling arpeggios to cascade over her as she considered what she had just heard. Gordon was losing his touch. That was for certain. He seemed unconcerned about several loose ends that he had not tied up. In his prime, he would have pursued them with a dogged determination until he had accounted for them all.

Firstly, there was the connection between the Emma Reynolds girl and the Montague case. Gordon's suggestion that she was simply pandering to the handsome, young film editor didn't fit with all of the evidence. For a start off, the girl had hacked into the police computer system. She must have known that was a serious crime. It was too big a risk to take just to attract the attentions of this Adam Parkinson man. She must have more compelling reasons of her own to pursue this. And then there was the change of name. She mused upon this for a moment. Dora Montague had changed her name to try to hide her connection to her family. What was Emma Reynolds trying to hide? Alice Liddell. Her eyes snapped open as she struggled to understand why the name was troubling her. There was something, but it just wouldn't come to her. What had Jasmine said? Something about it being like it she had just popped up out of nowhere. Hmm. Putting the glass down on the table, she stood up and walked through the lounge to the room she used as a study and opened up her laptop. Alice Liddell. Why was that name ringing alarm bells? And then she found it.

Back in the lounge, she turned the music down until it was only just audible and settled back down on the sofa to think. Emma Reynold's change of name to Alice Liddell was a signal, she was sure of it. But who was it intended for? Karen massaged her temples with her fingers as she considered this. Could it be that the signal was intended for her? That's if it was a signal. If it wasn't then it was a very odd coincidence. But if it was, then who else could have identified it apart from her? She nodded slowly. She wasn't sure what it meant, but it made her want to proceed with extreme caution. It also made her want to meet this Emma Reynolds - Alice Liddell - girl very much indeed.

"If you're trying to get my attention, Miss Reynolds, then you have it." She spoke out loud to herself, as if Alice were in the room with her, nodding thoughtfully. "The question is, why do you want my attention?"

She considered soberly what she should tell Blake. If she was going to keep things from him, she would need to tread very carefully. If he even suspected … well, she shuddered, forty years of collaboration would count for nothing.

After rehearsing the conversation several times, Karen picked up her phone and dialled Blake.

"What have you found out?" He was more direct this time, more business-like.

Was there an undercurrent of concern? She hoped not. She took a deep breath and focussed on keeping her voice calm and controlled.

"Gordon's done a thorough investigation, Blake. Looks like it's a media stunt." She kept her language as vague as she dared, her tone leaning towards the casual, with just a hint of irritation. "This Alice Liddell, her boyfriend is a film editor. There's no other connection between them and the Montague case that Gordon could find."

She was covering herself as best she could, making it clear that Gordon had conducted the investigation not her. She prayed that Blake would not register her reluctance to take responsibility.

"So, what's your strategy?" Blake was blunt, brusque even. Karen shut her eyes in celebration of her lucky timing; Blake was clearly engaged in something and resented the intrusion.

"Well, I thought it would be best to go in gently for now, get a good look at the pair of them, find out if there was anything that Gordon missed, then make it clear that stirring up unhappy memories will make them a lot of enemies. I'll let them know what the penalty is for the hacking of the police computer system then offer to forget about it if they drop the project immediately. Hopefully that should do it."

"Perfect darling." Blake sounded pleased. Which meant that she still had his trust, thank God.

"And if not ...?"

"And if not, you can send a couple of messengers round to demonstrate what happens to nosy parkers," she responded quickly. "But hopefully it won't come to that."

But secretly, she wasn't so sure. Her instincts told her there was trouble ahead. The question was, trouble for whom?

Chapter 20

While he waited for Alice to come round, Adam tidied up his kitchen and washed up the dishes from the previous night's supper. He had been pleased that she had agreed to his invitation. He had pushed the boat out with a lasagne and a salad from the shop in the village, hoping to show her that there was more to him than she had realised. And it had gone well. He smiled as he looked out across the garden, bathed in winter sunshine. The tree was gone now, but the smashed fence panels had been left as they were and there was a clear mark of the tree's impact remaining in the lawns on either side. It was the bridge that had first connected them just a week ago, he reflected. And what a lot had happened in that time. He shook his head as he considered how unattractive he had found her on their first meeting, her scraped back hair, her thick, geeky glasses, her unflattering clothes. How wrong he had been.

She was beautiful, he could see that now. And smart; smarter than him probably. He shrugged. He could deal with that. This had been a crazy week, he knew that, and he had no idea where events were taking him, but he had no intention of backing out now. He would show Alice that he could be her rock, someone she could depend on.

A toot from Alice's car horn was his signal that she was ready. He pulled on a jacket and hurried out to join her, flashing a smile at her as he bent down to open the passenger door.

"I enjoyed yesterday evening," he said, as he fastened his seat belt.

He looked across at her for affirmation, but she had turned her attention to a route atlas, plotting the course to Winston's house. Satisfied that she had mastered it, she turned to toss the atlas onto the back seat, started the car and set off.

"Where are we going?" Adam asked, once they were out on the main road. He found that he was getting used to Alice controlling the agenda, and that he was fine with it.

"Hythe," she replied without taking her eyes off the road. "It's a little town outside of Folkstone. Should take about an hour."

Adam nodded. "And we're going to see Winston, Audrey's old lover." He knew that they were, but he just wanted to start a conversation.

"Yes Adam, as I said." There was a note of impatience in her voice. He had thought she might be a little more relaxed after their late-night supper the previous evening, but apparently not. He left it for a few more minutes, then tried another tack.

"You said to Gabriel that Blake had hurt you too. Is that true?"

She shot him a sidelong look of curiosity then returned her gaze to the road.

"How could it be? I've never met him." She shook her head, as though in disbelief at the stupidity of the question.

Hurt by the brusqueness of the response, Adam remained silent. After a few moments, she shot him another glance, then continued. "I felt that he needed a reason for telling us what he knew. He was suspicious of us. I thought that telling him that I was a victim too might help him to open up."

Adam nodded his understanding of the strategy. In the silence that ensued, he considered it. So, Alice was happy to tell lies to get what she wanted. Not that he was in any position to criticise. He'd lied to girls all of his life when it had suited him. Actually, not just to girls. When he thought about it, he had been quite happy to tell lies whenever he'd screwed up or needed to get himself out of a mess. He hadn't really considered them as lies really, now that he thought about it; more a convenient way to reconstrue the truth so that things fell out in a way that suited him. It was just that, well, he'd thought that Alice might be better than that. It was yet another thing to consider as he learned more about this extraordinary woman.

The rest of the journey largely passed in silence. Adam thought that Alice seemed distracted; once or twice, she seemed to mutter something to herself. She was upset or angry about something, he sensed, maybe both. He wanted to broach the subject but he knew from experience that she was best left alone at such times. Instead, he looked out of the window and watched the scenes that flashed by. Much of the journey was taken up with high-speed driving down the M20, with flat green countryside on either side of the road. There was a lot of freight traffic, Adam noticed; on its way to and from the Channel Tunnel he supposed.

Winston's house was a grand affair on the edge of a small housing estate just outside of Hythe. It had the look of a holiday house, with large windows and a picture-book garden. A balcony, supported on grand pillars, stretched along the entire length of the back of the house, overlooking the pebbled beach which led down to the sea. When he answered Alice's knock on the door, Winston himself seemed less than happy to see them. It seemed that, this time, Alice had not contacted him in advance.

"Hello. What can I do for you?"

"We're here to talk about Blake Montague." Alice's direct approach seemed designed to shock Winston into a response. If that was her intention, she was not disappointed.

"What? Who the hell are you?"

He looked nervously up and down the street. "Are you alone? Does anyone else know that you're here?"

Alice coolly took control; she seemed to instinctively know how to manage the highly-strung man. "I think you'd better invite us in Mr Shaw. If you're worried about attracting attention then it would be better if we were all inside, don't you think?"

He paused for a moment, scanned the street again, then stood aside to let Alice and Adam enter. Closing the door firmly, he locked it, then ushered them through into the back of the house. While Adam and Alice settled themselves in a black, leather sofa, he switched on an ornate brass standard lamp then closed the beige curtains, looking left and right through the window as he did so. Apparently aware that Alice's attention was upon him the whole time, he avoided looking in her direction, retreating to an armchair in the gloomiest corner of the room before he looked up to meet her stare.

"What's this all about?" There was arrogance and anger in his voice, but even Adam could tell it was all bluster. The man looked very shaken by their visit.

"Blake Montague, Mr Shaw. We know that you were once Audrey Montague's lover. We think you might have some information that might help us." Alice's voice was cool, neutral in its tone. Adam thought it was probably her way of trying to calm him.

"What damn business is it of yours? Who the hell are you, anyway?" Winston was not calmed.

"We're friends of Dora Montague, Mr Shaw. We're carrying out investigations on her behalf."

Adam shot her a look, but she kept her attention firmly on the frightened man in the armchair. That wasn't strictly true, he reflected. In fact, come to think of it, it wasn't true at all. He no longer understood quite why they were putting themselves in danger to investigate this most dangerous of men, but it was definitely not on Dora's behalf. In fact, she'd made it very clear that she wished them well but wanted no part in it. Adam marvelled at the way the lies slipped so easily from Alice's tongue. He couldn't decide whether it was just that he was learning more about her or whether she was actually changing as they delved deeper and deeper into this murky world of corruption and murder.

"Dora Montague. Good God. I haven't heard that name in years." Winston looked like he'd seen a ghost. "In fact, I thought that she had probably died. She just seemed to disappear after all that business with Audrey and then Freddie."

Alice nodded and gave a reassuring smile. "Very much alive Mr Shaw." Her voice was brisk and business-like. "And keen to set the record straight; to get justice for Audrey and Freddie."

Winston's eyes widened in horror. He opened his mouth to speak but only emitted a strangled croak. Closing his mouth, he shook his head in disbelief then lowered it into his hands. Adam watched Alice carefully, waiting for her to break the silence she had created, but she sat still and impassive, allowing the silence to stretch out until Adam could hardly bear it. He wanted to intervene, to say something, anything, but he felt powerless. He didn't recognise the narrative Alice had delivered to Winston and he didn't know how to contribute to it. Finally, she spoke.

"I promise you that anything you tell us will be in strictest confidence Mr Shaw." Alice seemed unmoved by the man's obvious distress. "We just want to know what you can remember about the events immediately before and after the death of Audrey."

Winston lifted his head from his hands and fixed Alice with a manic stare. "Do **not** pursue this." The intonation upon ***not*** was emphatic. "Blake Montague is a dangerous man with powerful friends. He is utterly ruthless." Once again, his tone was bleak, bitter. "If he finds out that you are investigating what happened …" he trailed off, shaking his head unhappily.

Alice smiled brightly, completely unmoved by his discomfort. "Don't worry about us, Mr Shaw. We too have power and influence. More to the point, it's high time that people stopped allowing degenerates like Blake Montague to intimidate and bully them into submission. Times are changing Mr Shaw. The Blake Montagues of this world will be answering for their crimes."

Adam shot her another look which, once again, she ignored. What was she talking about? Power and influence? For someone who professed no interest in fiction, she seemed well equipped to fabricate fictions of her own. And yet, there was something about the confidence with which she spoke, the belief she expressed, that made her seem entirely credible. Looking at Winston, Adam could see that he had been considerably calmed by her self-composure.

As the old man gathered his thoughts, Adam wondered what Audrey had seen in the younger man that had inspired her to take him as a lover. Had he been a stronger man back then? Adam didn't think so. He seemed to be a vain man, even in his seventies. He wore a blue velvet jacket with a yellow cravat arranged loosely around his neck. His thinning hair, dyed an extremely unlikely shade of dark brown, was carefully combed forwards to try to hide the bald patches. He was, Adam concluded, pale and uninteresting. Perhaps that was it. Perhaps he had been the complete antithesis of her powerful husband.

"You need to understand," Winston commenced, "that everything that Blake Montague did was designed to give him power over other people. The parties, the drugs, the sex, it was all just a game for him." He paused, looking up into the corner of the room as he reflected. "He understood, you see. He understood the darkness we all harbour within ourselves - the lust, the desire for pleasure and money. He used the weakness of people to exploit them for his own ends."

Alice smiled and nodded, waiting for him to continue.

Winson shook his head thoughtfully. "The odd thing is that, despite the way he abused and manipulated people, many of them still wanted to be loved by him. He had charisma, you see; it gave him so much power over them. Even Audrey, after all that he had done to her, still loved him." He smiled grimly. "Her increasing wildness, her affaires, they were all borne out of her fear of losing him."

"Including her affaire with you?" Alice suggested.

He smiled at her candidness. "If you could call it that. Audrey told everyone that I was her lover as an act of revenge. It was when Blake had started an affaire with another MP. She hated it that the woman was much younger than her. And he used to bring her to the house, supposedly for meetings, but it was clear to everyone what was going on; he even had sex with her in his study once, while Audrey was at home. You see, Blake took pleasure in taunting Audrey. It made him feel powerful to know that he could humiliate her and she would still come back for more."

Adam smiled to himself. He had been right then. This was no grand passion. Winston had just been a convenient passer-by who had been swept up into the perverse carnage of Audrey and Blake's marriage. He was glad, really. He had begun to form an odd kind of affection for the long-deceased lady and didn't like to think of her throwing her affections away on this inconsequential dandy.

"With Freddie it was something else though." He was pensive now, remembering the many slights and injustices that Blake had inflicted upon his only son. "Many people are homophobic," he said after a long pause, "but Blake seemed to be repelled by homosexuality, afraid of it even." He nodded with conviction. "His anger at Freddie's sexuality was unnaturally strong. Once his attempts to turn him into a heterosexual failed, he used to send call girls up to his room, you know ... he seemed intent on, well, destroying him really. He could never resist an opportunity to belittle Freddie publicly. And I'm certain that Blake encouraged Freddie to take LSD and other drugs."

"Are you suggesting that Blake was a repressed homosexual himself?" Alice offered.

Winston shrugged. "Who knows. He was a complicated man when I knew him. Maybe an experience at school. Public schools can be cruel, confusing places you know."

Alice nodded that she understood before she continued with her investigation. "Audrey was pregnant. We have evidence that the baby was born by Caesarean section before she died and that it survived."

Winston narrowed his eyes a little and observed her for a moment while he considered his response. "That's true ... but I'm surprised that you found that out. There can't be many people who know about the baby. How did you…?"

Alice shook her head even as he started his question. "Sorry. We can't answer that. As I said, everything you tell us is in strictest confidence. That goes for anyone else we've been talking to as well."

Winston nodded. "Of course. On reflection, I don't wish to know."

Alice smiled charmingly. "Do you know anything else about the baby? Do you know if it was a boy or a girl? Do you know where it was taken?"

Winston rubbed his chin thoughtfully. "I only know what Tabitha told me, and she knew very little. I believe that it was a little girl. And, as far as I know, she was placed with foster parents. I think it most likely that Dora's grandmother organised it. She took care of Dora, of course, after Audrey's death, and I think she would have stepped in to protect the baby."

Adam waited for Alice to ask her next question, but she seemed deep in thought. He stepped in. "Any idea where the foster parents lived?" he asked.

Winston started a little, as if he had forgotten that Adam was there. "Somewhere in Yorkshire I believe. I heard that the grandmother had some connections there."

Adam looked across at Alice. She was avoiding his gaze, increasingly upset. Winston seemed not to have noticed; his attention was fixed firmly on Adam now.

"How has this been kept so secret?" Adam asked. "I mean, an aristocrat's baby. How could it just disappear into darkest Yorkshire? Why hasn't this come to light before now?"

Winston gave him a knowing look. "Think about it. What would Blake have done if he'd known that the baby was still alive?" He paused, waiting for an answer, concluded that Adam wasn't very bright, then continued. "A DNA test of the baby would have proven that it wasn't Freddie's. The case for the prosecution rested upon the fiction that Audrey had slept with Freddie, and that he had murdered her out of guilt. The grandmother must have done the only thing she could have done to protect the baby. She made it disappear then swore everyone who knew about it to secrecy."

"Was it yours?" Alice cut in suddenly. There was a wild look in her eyes.

Winston looked up in surprise. "What, the baby, mine?" He laughed.

Alice's composure was gone now. She looked back sharply. "What's so funny?" she hissed. There was fury in her trembling voice.

"Sorry." Winston looked crestfallen at having upset her. "It's just that ... well, Audrey and I never slept together. Tabitha only contacted me because, like you, she thought it could be mine, but I told her that was impossible."

Adam and Alice exchanged astonished looks.

Winston shrugged. "As far as I know, Audrey never slept with any of her so-called lovers. We were all just for show. All she wanted to do was to make Blake jealous." He smiled ruefully. "The fact is that Audrey never stopped loving Blake, despite all of the abuse and fighting. She just wanted him to love her back."

Adam looked across at Alice. She looked too upset to speak. He turned back to Winston.

"So, who was the father of the baby then?"

Winston shrugged. "It can only have been Blake."

Chapter 21

The journey home was largely spent in silence. Adam attempted light hearted conversation once or twice, but Alice barely responded. She drove more quickly than she usually did, eyes fierce and fiery. Adam risked a glance across at her, concerned by her refusal to engage with him. She was gripping the steering wheel hard. Was that a slight tremor in her hands that she was trying to hide? He thought it might be. What could have made her so upset? He ran the meeting with Winston back in his thoughts, trying to identify the moment when she had become enraged. Why had she snapped at Winston when he had laughed at the idea that he could be the father of Audrey's baby? Was she angry with herself for getting it wrong or was it just a contempt for people like Winston who messed up other people's lives?

By the time that they had arrived home, the sun was already low on the horizon. As Alice opened the door of the car, a dank chill rushed into the car making Adam shiver. She climbed out and stalked towards her house without a word. Disturbed by what, even for Alice, was strange behaviour, he hurried after her.

"I think we should talk about what happened this afternoon."

She turned and shot him a look that stopped him in his tracks.

"Adam, I'm cold and I'm tired. I want a warm bath and a glass of wine."

He would have liked to say that he would love to share a warm bath and a glass of wine with her, but he sensed that this was not the moment for flirtation. Instead, he decided to be candid.

"The thing is Alice, I'm not sure why we're doing this anymore." He watched her closely to gauge her reaction. The slight narrowing of her eyes indicated that she had not been expecting this.

"I mean, it was fun to begin with," he continued. "But you seem to be upset by what we discovered today and I don't know why. You're not sharing your feelings with me anymore. It feels like I've been shut out."

He watched carefully as she continued to regard him thoughtfully, as if waiting to see if he had any more to say. Well, he did, didn't he?

"And you keep saying stuff that we haven't talked about and … well, that isn't true really. All that stuff about our power and influence. And you said that we were acting on behalf of Dora. That just isn't true, is it?"

Alice's gaze softened. She nodded as if to acknowledge the truth of what he had said and motioned with her hand for him to follow her.

"You're right," she agreed. "We should talk. Come on in. We can have a glass of wine and clear the air."

By the time that they were seated across the table from each other with a glass of red wine each, the mood between them had changed completely. There was a warmth in her voice, a note of apology.

"You're right Adam, and I'm sorry. It's a weakness of mine. I get so absorbed in something that I neglect the people around me." She smiled gently; it was the old smile and it worked its magic on him once again. He loved that smile.

"It's the injustice of it all … that's what drives me," she continued. "That's why I make things up sometimes." She smiled wryly. "That's why I seem to be shutting you out." She reached across the table and squeezed his hand. "I am really glad that you're coming with me to meet all of these people." She looked down at their entwined hands then looked deep into his eyes. "I don't think I could carry on if I didn't have your support."

Adam found himself transfixed by her eyes. She hadn't removed her hands after the squeeze and he could feel the warmth of her palms on the back of his hands. Turning them over so that they were palm to palm, he grasped her hands a little more firmly, encouraged by her sudden tenderness.

"The thing is," he began, "the thing is, I really care for you. I'm not entirely sure what we're doing with this investigation but, well, if it matters to you then it matters to me too." He looked down at their hands. He usually found it easy to talk with women, flirt with them, ask them out, but he found himself feeling unusually shy. "The thing is, I thought that maybe you might care for me too, and that we might, you know, be more than just friends."

He wanted to look up to gauge her reaction, but he dared not. It felt like being a kid again, talking to a girl for the first time.

There was a long pause. He looked up to see Alice smiling at him ruefully.

"I care for you too Adam, I do, but I know too much about your history with women to ever become your girlfriend."

Adam gave her a bewildered look. "My history?"

She shrugged gently. "You lack commitment Adam. If you ever kissed me, I would be constantly worried that you were looking over my shoulder to spot someone better, someone prettier." She smiled softly. "When you picked up your phone, I would always be thinking that you were lining up your next conquest."

Adam spluttered in protest. "But, but, that's not fair, it's not true ..."

"It **is** true Adam. We both know it is." She shook her head sadly. "Your problem is FOMO, a fear of missing out. Until you are able to value what you have you will never be satisfied. That's why you constantly let your girlfriends down."

His mouth fell open in shock. Had she been …?

She nodded. "I know about your cheating with Belinda and Nadia, Adam. Those poor girls really cared for you and you let them both down.

Adam felt the blood rush to his cheeks. "You had no right to check up on me like that." He paused as he remembered a prior conversation. "You said you only looked at my online data to check that you could trust me. This is stalking. It's outrageous."

She shrugged. "I did check up on you to see if I could trust you. And I concluded that I could, as far as the investigation was concerned. And as a friend," she added. "But as a boyfriend?" She gave him a knowing look. "No, I can't trust you with that Adam."

Chapter 22

As the warm water from the shower cascaded off Adam's hair and ran, steaming, down his body, he ran the events of the previous evening through his head again and again. He had hardly slept. Alice's response to his advances had jolted him badly.

What the hell had happened there? The knowledge that she had accessed such intimate information about his relationships was shocking, despicable. It was an unacceptable intrusion into his privacy. He wanted to be angry with her. He ***was*** angry with her … but it was, well, it was all mixed up with other emotions too. He couldn't very well take the moral high ground with her when he himself had behaved so despicably, could he? And she had told him, after he had calmed down, that she had been badly hurt by a cheating boyfriend in a previous relationship. She left him feeling that he had let her down almost as much as that boyfriend. Damn it. He felt more guilt about his behaviour now than when Belinda and Nadia had ambushed him in the pub. And then there was another emotion mixed in with all this anger, regret and guilt. He had fallen in love.

As he towelled himself dry in front of the steamed-up bathroom mirror, he gazed through the condensation to the hazy reflection of his face, considering what he should do next. He wiped the mirror with the towel but it steamed up again instantly. Standing, naked, in front of the misty representation of himself, he wondered what she saw when she looked at him. Could she ever develop trust in him? Probably not. Was that it then? Should he move out and never see her again? He didn't think he could bear to continue living next door, knowing that she would never allow herself to develop any romantic feelings for him. Damn it. It was all such a mess.

He had resolved that he would not go round and see her today. Let her come to him if she wanted any help. He would decide then if he wanted to continue with her obsessional pursuit of justice for Audrey and Freddie. It was, he reflected, feeling more and more dangerous to continue to provoke Blake Montague by digging up what had happened all those years ago. He had only continued this far because he wanted to be with Alice. He could see that now. If she didn't want to be anything more than friends, then what was the point of continuing to put himself in harm's way?

His thoughts were interrupted by the swishing of a car down the rain-soaked lane, slowing to pull up outside. Wrapping the towel around himself, he stepped through to the bedroom so that he could look out at the road. Through the grey, drizzly, morning light he could see a blue Audi parked across the entrance to Alice's driveway. A woman in a dark blue raincoat with the collar turned up was making her way down the path to Alice's door. It was difficult to tell in the dim light, but she looked quite old, maybe in her seventies, he thought. Alice opened the door and invited her in just a few moments after she had knocked on it, almost as if she was expecting her. Still, Adam had concerns. She was, he considered, the right age to be a friend of Blake Montague. He needed to go round and check that everything was all right. Throwing the damp towel onto the bed, he dressed quickly.

Karen Turner sat in a wooden kitchen chair across the table from Alice Liddell and watched her carefully.

"So, you are Alice," she began thoughtfully, almost as if speaking to herself.

Alice nodded but said nothing. She noted the short but artfully cut hair, the expensively tailored raincoat with the discreet Ted Baker logo on the buttons, the intelligence in the eyes that were studying her. She was impressed.

"Alice Liddell," she continued, with extra emphasis upon the surname, searching for some sign that the name had a meaning that was intended for her.

There was none. Alice's face remained impassive. Or, was that just the suggestion of smile on her lips? Her limpid blue eyes behind the thick lenses of her spectacles gave nothing away. Alice Liddell was, Karen decided, a very cool customer. She was clearly testing her out as much as she was testing Alice. Under the circumstances, that was entirely understandable.

Alice had not missed the emphasis put upon her surname. As she had suspected, Karen was a very sharp woman. After all, no one else had ever queried her name. But that didn't necessarily mean that she would be an ally. She would have to tread very carefully. After all, Karen had worked with Blake Montague for many years; she was a corrupt police officer, no doubt about that. Her only chance was that Karen might want to be free from Blake's influence, now that her career was over, but lacked the opportunity to achieve it; a slim chance, Alice realised, but one worthy of investigation. At the very least, she needed to convince her to stay out of the way while she put her plans into action. If she could convince Karen that she could bring down Blake Montague without compromising her, she might have a chance.

Karen decided it was time to put a little pressure on this guarded young lady, just to see if any cracks appeared.

"You hacked the police computer system," she stated assertively. "Clever, but very dangerous." She cocked her head on one side. "Do you realise the potential penalties for what you've done?"

Alice was a little taken aback by the speed and directness of the assault, but she was ready with her response. She was just about to deliver her explanation when the doorbell rang, followed by three heavy knocks. She sighed inwardly. Adam. She had been hoping that he had not noticed the visit from Karen; she had wanted to probe her relationship with Blake without him. However, there was no ignoring him now. She needed him still to assist in the execution of her plan and, anyway, he would not give up if she didn't answer the door. She was very aware that he had fallen in love with her.

"I'm sorry but I need to get that," she said apologetically, rising from her chair and walking to the door. As she moved, she reflected upon Karen's very incisive statement. It was designed to put her on the back foot, clearly, but there was the compliment of "clever" and the very slight mitigation of "potential" rather than the simple threat of a penalty. It was almost as if Karen was offering her a way out if it was to her advantage. At least, that was what she hoped it meant.

Alice opened the door to see a damp, dishevelled Adam. He looked concerned. Alice put a finger to her lips to signal that he should not speak then ushered him into the kitchen.

"Adam, this is DCI Karen Turner."

Karen smiled politely. "Not a DCI any more though. Plain Karen will suffice. Nice to meet you Adam."

Adam's eyes widened, his mouth gaping wide. He looked towards Alice to see if the request to stay silent still applied. She smiled back reassuringly and signalled for him to sit down. She was encouraged by Karen's preference to drop her police title. Was this an olive branch that was being offered?

"DCI … Karen has just been ticking me off for my little indiscretions in making use of the police database to pursue our story," she started. Adam nodded dumbly. He had no idea where this was going.

Karen nodded too and smiled to herself. This woman really was smooth. She was attempting to turn the barely veiled threat about prosecution into a simple confession of indiscretion, as if that was all it was. She leaned back in her chair and waited expectantly. She was looking forward to hearing her talk her way out of the crimes she had committed.

"So," Alice began, smiling at Adam as she sat down, "you'll remember from our research that Karen was the investigating officer in the Montague case." She flicked a wary look at Karen then resumed her fixed eye contact with Adam.

Adam tried to read her expression. He hoped she had a plan.

"I did warn you that the police might spot that we'd been using their databases for our research," she continued, shaking her head as if recalling the discussion. Switching her attention to Karen, she spread her hands as a signal of contrition. "It's unfortunate because we had hoped you might be willing to give us some help with the project. I hope we haven't jeopardised that."

Her tone was friendly, open, but Karen sensed the intelligence at work behind the false front. This woman was playing a dangerous game. She was sounding her out to see if she would take sides with her against Blake Montague. The stakes must be high for her to take such risks. She raised one eyebrow. "Project?"

Alice nodded and gave out a girlish giggle, except that she was far from girlish, Karen was certain of that.

"Oh, yes, it's a film project. Sorry, I should have explained. Adam is a film director." She looked towards him, waiting for him to make some signal of assent. Adam, blushing slightly at the sudden promotion to director, obliged with a smile and a nod. "Yeah," she continued, "he's planning a film about the Montague case." When Karen's eyes narrowed with suspicion she added, "I'm his researcher. And yeah, sorry about looking on your database without permission. That was a mistake. We got a bit carried away there."

The woman was good, Karen had to give her that. Her fake disingenuousness was being extended towards her as a signal that she had much darker designs than a documentary film. Clearly the girl had powerful reasons for pursuing Blake Montague, but what could those be? Karen considered the possibilities, but could not find a compelling explanation. For now, the question was, what did she intend to do and, more importantly, was she up to the challenge of taking on Blake Montague and the full might of his empire? It might very well depend upon her motives for taking such a risk. She would need to be absolutely certain before acknowledging that she understood what was being asked of her. At this time, she was far from certain.

Alice waited, watching the retired police officer's impassive face for any sign of recognition of her strategy. Outwardly she was calm, but she could feel her heart thumping against her ribs. Would Karen understand that she wanted her as an ally? She didn't dare to be any clearer, for fear of compromising herself. For God's sake! When was the woman going to give her a reaction? The silence seemed to hang in the air for an eternity.

Karen broke the silence finally, nodding slowly as if thinking the matter through as she spoke. "Clearly, your breech of the police security systems is a criminal act." She pouted, then expelled air slowly. "But you claim that your intentions are good. Hmmm, well, I might be able to put in a word for you; I still have a little bit of pull in the force." She cocked her head on one side and put her fingers across her mouth to signal that she was choosing her words carefully and should not be interrupted. Removing her hand, she continued, "I would need to be confident that you are who you say you are and that you are fully qualified to carry out this project." There was a slight emphasis upon the word ***project***. Alice dared to hope that it was a sign from Karen that she understood that the project was nothing to do with film making. "As it is, I have no idea of your abilities or experience. You just seem to have," she paused for effect, "popped out of nowhere. You understand what I'm saying?"

Alice felt a weight lift off her shoulders. She understood. Thank God for that. Karen had decoded the encrypted signals she had been sending her; she was sure of it. And, more than that, she was considering standing aside to let her get to Blake Montague. She could not hope for a better outcome at this stage. As she nodded at Karen, she felt a warmth and an energy flow through her.

Looking across at Adam, she smiled at the look of blank incomprehension on his face. He took it as a sign of affection and smiled back. Good old Adam; he had played his part well. She would reward him later.

Rising from her chair, Karen straightened her raincoat and gave Alice a frank stare. "Blake Montague is a powerful man, I don't have to tell you that, I'm sure." She narrowed her eyes in warning. "I will try to reassure him that you were just researching for a film and that I have instructed you to stop. I'll tell him that the threat of legal proceedings was enough to scare you." She gave her a stern look. "In the meantime, don't do anything rash."

So, she had guessed right then. Karen Turner had no love for Blake Montague and, while there was no direct offer of assistance, she had signalled that she was at least willing to keep quiet about Alice's darker intentions. It would be up to her to inspire confidence if she wanted any more help than that. She would need to reassure her that she would keep her knowledge of the crimes that Karen had committed to herself. She would need to convince her that she had the resources to bring Blake Montague to justice.

At the front door, Karen turned to face Alice, looked intently into her eyes then held out her hand. Alice took it and felt the strength of her grip.

"Don't fuck this up," Karen whispered, so that only Alice could hear it. And with that, she turned and walked out of the door.

Chapter 23

Alice returned to the kitchen to find Adam still sitting in the wooden chair, looking down at his hands clasped upon his lap. After a few moments, he looked up and gave her a bewildered shrug.

"What the hell just happened?" He paused, then gave a deep sigh. "We're in deep trouble, aren't we?"

She shook her head, smiling gently.

"That went well. Karen isn't going to get in our way. She has more reason than most people to hate Blake. She just needs reassurances that we aren't going to compromise her."

Adam stood up abruptly and took a step towards her. "Alice, we need to stop, like Karen said. We need to stop provoking Blake Montague. What you said to Karen, just now, about the film I mean, well, I abandoned the idea of a film a long time ago. I thought you knew that." There was fear in his voice now, desperation even. "And we can't bring a man like that to justice. You know we can't. He's too powerful. We've been fooling ourselves that we could get justice for Freddie and Audrey. It's ridiculous." He paused, seemingly exhausted by this rush of emotion, then continued wearily. "We're just going to get hurt Alice, both of us. And I know that you don't care for me in the way that I care for you, but you must understand that I don't want to see you get hurt."

Alice took Adam by the hand and led him into the sitting room. Easing him gently down onto the aged sofa, she sat close to him and slipped her arm around his back. Startled, he turned and stared at her. What was she doing? He opened his mouth to speak, but she touched her fingers to his lips to silence him.

"I've been thinking a lot about what you said yesterday Adam," she began. She smiled warmly and squeezed him gently with the arm around his back. "About, being more than just friends," she clarified. "And you're right. We are more than just friends." She stroked his hair gently with her free hand then kissed him lightly on the mouth. "We've been through a lot together. And you've stood by me the whole time. You've been my rock." She grinned. "I couldn't have got this far without you, I really couldn't."

Adam blushed slightly. He wasn't sure where this was going but he had no desire to interrupt her. He smiled back and willed her to continue.

"The thing is," she continued, her eyes lowered, "when you told me you wanted to be more than friends yesterday, I froze. I'm sorry, I didn't mean to be so hard on you. Its's just, well, like I said, I've been cheated on before. I guess I overreacted. I'm sorry."

She looked up to check that her performance was being received as she would wish. It was. Adam still looked a little confused, but she definitely had his attention.

"The thing is," she explained, "we come from such different worlds." Adam started to speak but she touched his lips again to quieten him.

"You've had so many girlfriends, such pretty girls too. And I've only had one boyfriend. And the truth is ..." she lowered her voice a little as if confiding a secret ... "the truth is I'm not really girlfriend material. I'm a computer geek, a loner; I'm not very good at sharing my space with other people."

She put her free hand around his tummy so that she could give him a firmer squeeze, and lay her head upon his shoulder. Adam felt dazed. Her body language and her words didn't match, and yet he felt as if he were under her spell. The warmth of her body soaked into him; her arms around him made him feel safe and cherished.

"I can't be your girlfriend Adam," she spoke with her head still on his shoulder, her arms still tightly wound around him, "but I think we should go to bed together."

She waited a few moments for this to sink in, then lifted her head and stared deep into his eyes. "No commitment, you understand. I'm not making any promises for the future. I just think, well, we are more than just friends and, well, I'd like us to make love."

She giggled a little, then stopped herself as she realised it was the same giggle she had used when pretending to Karen that they were just a couple of young innocents planning a film. She hoped that Adam hadn't noticed. Looking across to check his expression, she needn't have worried. There was a dreamy smile upon his face.

Taking him by the hand, Alice led Adam out of the room and upstairs to the bedroom. It occurred to him, as he walked up the stairs, that he had never seen the upper floor. He was intrigued by the spartan nature of her bedroom. There were no pictures on the wall, no ornaments on the windowsill or the dark-veneered dressing table. There was just a hairbrush and a few tubes and pots of cosmetics. Catching sight of the closed doors on the wardrobe, a thought occurred to him. "Was this Dora's room?"

Alice nodded, amused. "I don't suppose that a man has been into this room for a very long time. You should feel honoured."

Crossing the room to the window, Alice glanced momentarily at the garden. The window wasn't overlooked by anyone, but she still felt the need to draw the curtains, shutting out not only the light but also the connection with the fallen tree and the time capsule. When she stood here, she couldn't help imagining Dora herself, watching the progress of the tree from seed to sapling and remembering the dark secrets below it.

She turned back to Adam. The room was gloomy now but there was still enough light seeping through the threadbare curtains to reveal the cheeky grin on his face. That was a relief. A few minutes earlier he had been looking scared and panicky. She had been right to think that this was the right moment to re-engage his support by giving him some glimmer of hope for their future.

Returning to Adam, she noted that he hadn't moved. He seemed to be waiting for her to take the initiative, as if he was worried that she would change her mind. Well, that suited her fine. It had served her purpose to present herself, up until now, as inexperienced in relationships, but that would not serve now. And anyway, he had, she felt, already started to notice that there was more to her than she had presented to him at the outset. Well, he was about to learn that she knew her way around a bedroom at least as well as he did. More to the point, she was about to move their relationship onto an entirely different footing.

Stroking his face with one hand, she started to undo the buttons on his shirt. As she reached the bottom, she used both hands to undo his belt, unzip his trousers and pull them down to his feet, along with his briefs. Adam stood, as if in a trance, dazed by the speed and competence of her hands, stripping him almost naked in just a few moments. Easing the shirt off his shoulders and helping him slip his pants over his feet, she pushed him gently down onto the bed. Within a few more moments, she too was completely naked, standing at the side of the bed, unbearably beautiful, her skin so white and soft, her small breasts perfectly formed, her narrow waist flaring gently out to the smooth curve of her hips.

"Alice...," Adam began, but she silenced him by kneeling on the bed, her knees straddling his waist, placing her palm on his cheek and inserting her thumb into his mouth to moisten it. Withdrawing it, she ran it lasciviously around his lips, reinserting it and burnishing them repeatedly until they seared. Then bending over him she kissed him long and hard, chafing his inflamed mouth with her lips and tongue. Breathless, he stared at her in astonishment as she lifted her head and fixed him with a forceful stare, compelling in its intensity, her lips slightly parted in a sensual smile. Without moving her head, she reached behind her and started to stroke his burgeoning erection, gripping it more and more tightly until its stiffness ached exquisitely.

Just when he thought he could stand no more, she lifted herself on her knees, moving her hips back, guiding his erection inside her. Adam gasped at the suddenness of it as she sank down on his erection and let it push deep within her. All this while, Alice kept her stare fixed on Adam, smiling serenely at the reaction his face was registering. Without warning, she brought both hands up to his neck and laced them loosely round it, her thumbs lightly resting on his windpipe. Leaning forward a little, she whispered huskily, "Trust me, trust me, trust me …" repeated like some mantra as she began to rise and sink slowly on his erection. As she increased the speed of her movement, her thumbs began to exert light pressure on his throat. Adam brought one hand up in alarm, but she shook her head gently and smiled warmly. "Trust me, trust me, trust me …," she continued, increasing the speed of her movement, increasing the pressure on his throat until the blood pounded in his ears. He felt himself drowning in her gaze, falling into the deep wells of her eyes. He was dazed by her beauty, dazzled by the pure, white light that radiated from her.

His orgasm burst over him like a wave over a rock, drenching every part of his body, jangling through every nerve. The waves came again and again, pounding him, lifting him up like a ragdoll with their power. Even as they subsided, the throbbing motion continued to course through his body like some echo of a shock wave. He slumped back upon the sheets, panting for air, his heart thumping.

Alice was lying beside him now. He opened his eyes to see that she was grinning widely into his face. She tried to rub her hand over his chest, but his skin was so sensitive that it sent him back into spasms and he had to clamp her hand down on his torso to stop her.

"Wow," he sighed. It was all he could manage.

"Good eh?" she responded with friendly enthusiasm.

He shook his head, still unable to fully comprehend what had just happened. "And you've only had one boyfriend?" he queried playfully.

She shrugged. "You don't need to have a boyfriend to have sex Adam. Surely you know that?"

He laughed. "There's a lot about you I still don't know isn't there?"

She winked back at him. "There surely is Adam."

Chapter 24

Karen Turner sat very upright in her chair and looked around her. It had been some considerable time since she had last been in Blake Montague's house. It was not a comfortable feeling. She looked at the ancient portraits upon the wall, the antique furniture, the huge, sweeping staircase. It was in this room that she had first seen how Blake could humiliate people for his own entertainment. It was in the office next to this room that she too had been humiliated, just so that he could demonstrate his utter control over all things within his empire. She shuddered involuntarily at the memory. Up that staircase was the bedroom where Blake Montague had murdered his wife Audrey, a murder which she had helped to cover up. She sighed gloomily. She had done well out of her relationship with Blake, but the price had been a heavy one. How she loathed that man.

"Can I get you some refreshment?"

Tabitha Watts stood in the doorway, watching her. She had aged well, Karen reflected. She must be in her sixties now, but she was still a very attractive woman. Her braided hair was still dark. Karen wondered if that colour came out of a bottle. Perhaps not, she concluded. Her skin glowed youthfully; she moved with supple grace. She thought that it must take a very special kind of resilience to live this long in the presence of a man like Blake Montague and still retain that sense of her own dignity. Did Tabitha loathe Blake as she did? Surely she must do. Surely it could not be loyalty that had kept her here as Blake's assistant all these years.

"No, I'm fine thank you." She paused, then added, "It's good to see you. It's been a while. You look good."

Tabitha did not like her, Karen knew that. Despite their common association with Blake, they inhabited very different worlds. And Tabitha must have her suspicions about the part she had played in helping Blake to prove himself innocent of Audrey's murder and the investigations into Freddie's death. Still, Karen reflected, they both had good reason to hate Blake. She wondered whether he had forced himself upon Tabitha as he had done with her, just to underline the power he held over their lives. Probably. The need to be in control, the drive to dominate, it was in his very DNA. He probably wouldn't have been able to resist.

"Won't you sit with me while I wait for Blake?" Karen asked. She smiled warmly and leaned forwards to pat the arm of the chair opposite her.

Tabitha smiled back and crossed the room to sit in the chair. There was something very feline about her,

Karen reflected. She moved with lithe detachment through this awful house as if she was not really part of it, owed no allegiances to its master, mistress of her own destiny.

"You've been a loyal assistant to Blake for a very long time now," Karen started.

Tabitha stared at her quizzically for a few moments, then smiled sardonically.

"We both know that loyalty is the only option," she responded with a hint of bitterness.

Karen was taken aback by the candidness of the response; she had expected something more guarded. She decided to probe gently.

"I sometimes wonder," she mused, "how different my life would have been if I had never met Blake."

"It would have been both richer and poorer, much like my own," Tabitha responded with disarming simplicity.

Karen nodded thoughtfully. Was Tabitha offering herself as a potential ally? As she was considering how to proceed, the door opened and Blake strutted into the room.

"Well, well, well," he began, as if it was a surprise to see Tabitha and Karen there, despite the fact that that they had both been summoned. "My two favourite ladies together in one room." The fraudulence of the statement was deliberate; it was designed to remind them of their subservience.

It had been some time since Karen had seen Blake in person. His charcoal grey suit still expressed wealth and success, but the years had not been kind to him, she reflected. The fine head of dark hair was now thin and wispy, more white than grey really. His formerly imposing jaw line was now hidden beneath folds of loose skin that hung down to his jowls. It was, she considered, as if all those years of deception and savagery had allowed his inner corruption to seep to the surface. It was only the eyes that reminded her of the man he had once been, those icy blue, cruel eyes

There was another chair available for Blake to sit in, but Tabitha stood and motioned to him to take her seat. He slumped heavily into the chair.

"I'll be nearby if you need anything from me," she said to her employer.

Blake shook his head. "No, no. I'd like you to stay. You know I value your counsel in delicate matters such as this one."

Tabitha knew no such thing, but she nodded and continued to stand by the side of Blake's chair. It allowed her, thought Karen, to make eye contact without Blake seeing it. Was that intentional?

"So, to business," Blake continued. He turned his icy stare on Karen. "You talked to our two young nosy parkers. What did you learn?"

Karen gave a terse smile and launched into the narrative she had prepared.

" As you know, Blake, Gordon's conclusion from his investigations was that Adam Chalmers is planning a film on the murder of Audrey and possibly the death of Freddie too."

She looked at Blake to give him the opportunity to ask a question, but he gave her a single nod and waited for her to continue.

Karen shrugged. "So, that was pretty much the story they gave me. He's made a few low budget films but he's looking for something more sensational to cut his teeth on. She's the computer geek next door who can do his research for him and do a little hacking when required. Their story was that, when she inherited the house and moved in, she discovered some documents left behind by Dora, your daughter, and thought it might interest her new neighbour."

Blake narrowed his eyes a little and gave Karen a searching stare. "And what do YOU think Karen?"

Karen felt her heart begin to beat a little faster. She would need to weigh her words carefully. She wanted to protect Alice and Adam if she could, but not at the expense of her own safety. She noticed that, unseen by Blake, Tabitha's attention was fully focused on her and there was some tension showing on her face.

"I think it's possible, Blake." Karen cocked her head slightly to one side to indicate that she had given this serious thought. "I was doubtful when Gordon told me his theory because of the seriousness of hacking a police database. I wasn't convinced that anyone would take that risk just to write a film script. However, they do look like a very ill matched couple. Mr Chalmers is a very good-looking boy; public school, full of charm, but not a lot between his ears. He probably isn't fully aware of the risks that Miss Liddell has taken. She on the other hand is a sharp cookie, proper computer geek, but very, very plain. I'm guessing that she's not his usual romantic interest. So

…" she paused to allow Blake to digest this … "it's possible that he's stringing her along because she can access the information he wants and she's prepared to take big risks to gain the attentions of her handsome neighbour."

She paused again to allow Blake to give a reaction. She wasn't prepared to go any further than this until she was sure that Blake trusted her narrative.

Blake turned in his chair and looked towards Tabitha. "What do you think Tabitha?"

Karen felt the fear flash through her; they were both being tested. He was unconvinced by her account of her meeting with Adam and Alice. She glanced across at Tabitha. The tension was no longer there in her expression though she too must be aware that she was being tested. Karen admired her control. Her voice was even and professional.

"It's plausible Sir," she began, "but by no means certain. The question would be what other explanations there could be. Why would this young couple be digging this up now after all these years?" She paused as if considering this. "Whatever the reason," she stated coldly, "there is a possible risk of damage to your reputation."

Blake nodded grimly and turned his attention back to Karen. She could see a tense expression of warning on Karen's face. She was instructing her to stop protecting Adam and Alice. She was signalling that Blake had already made his mind up and this was just a test of their loyalties.

"And where did you leave it with our intrepid young reporters?" Blake inquired mildly.

"Well, I instructed them to stop. I made it clear that legal proceedings would be taken against them if they continued. I did my best to scare them off."

"And?" Blake raised his eyebrows.

Karen could feel Tabitha's fierce attention without even looking in her direction. She swallowed hard.

"I don't know," she responded, shaking her head sadly. "They looked scared. They told me they would stop but ..." she trailed off, unable to finish the sentence.

"...you're not entirely convinced." Blake finished the sentence for her.

She took a deep breath and blew it out slowly. It was time to protect herself. "No, I'm not entirely convinced." As she said the words, she felt her heart sink. She had just thrown the young couple under the bus. She looked up to see Tabitha smiling grimly at her and nodding almost imperceptibly. She had passed the test.

Blake pushed himself up out of his chair and straightened his jacket. "I am not convinced either," he stated evenly, "which is why I have borrowed Gordon for the evening. I hope you don't mind."

Karen smiled obediently at his false humility. Inside, she felt cold.

"He will give them a more physical demonstration of our demands. That should make sure they really ***do*** stop their snooping." Beneath the calm politeness of his voice lurked a savage ferocity. Karen could imagine exactly what Gordon's instructions for a more physical demonstration would be. Her heart sank. This was surely the end of all this. Even Alice Liddell would not be able to continue after what Gordon King would do to her and Adam.

Chapter 25

When Adam opened the door, he found Alice standing under the dim porch light dressed in a tight-fitting white blouse and a pleated grey skirt; he thought it looked like office wear, except that the skirt was a little short for that. She continued to be full of surprises. Her hands were behind her back, as if she were hiding something.

She shivered. "Can I come in? It's freezing out here." She raised her shoulders to illustrate how cold she was feeling, but without revealing her hands.

Adam nodded amicably and stood aside to let her enter, noting that she edged around him, still concealing something from him.

"What have you got behind your back Alice?" He was puzzled; it was as if she had multiple personalities. When they had first met, she had seemed geeky, bookish. She had seemed to lack humour or empathy. Now she was so very different. He considered her behaviour over the last few days; she could be vivacious, flirty, girlish even. To begin with he had thought that it was his influence which was changing her, but now he wasn't so sure. It was quite unsettling really.

She gave him a mischievous grin and edged towards the staircase. Dashing up the steps, she leaned over the landing rail and gave him an exaggerated wink. "If you want to know, you have to come up here." Then she disappeared into his bedroom.

Adam found her sitting on his bed, legs crossed to reveal her soft, pale thighs, arms crossed over her tiny bust, a loop of fluffy cord resting on her lap. The grin was still fixed to her face.

"I thought you might like to try something a bit different," she suggested, glancing down at the cord momentarily then back at Adam to gauge his reaction.

Adam screwed up his face, perplexed. "Different as in ...?" He tailed off, unsure what question to ask.

"As in, you are my prisoner," she answered simply. "I put this loop of rope over your hands so that you can't escape then I have my wicked way with you." She raised her shoulders to express that it was all very simple really.

Adam raised his hands, baffled. "But why would I want to escape?"

She sighed with mock frustration. "Oh, come on Adam, it's roleplay. The cord doesn't really prevent you from escaping, does it? It's symbolic. It's just a game."

Adam scratched his head while he considered. It all seemed a bit odd to him, perverse even. This was definitely outside his comfort zone. On the other hand, she did look very enticing, sitting on his bed in her prim, but at the same time revealing, skirt and blouse.

"Well, okay then, but I rather fancy that you should be my prisoner." He pondered for a moment. "Baron Chalmers," he continued, "the very wicked Baron Chalmers. But you must call me Milord."

"That's the spirit. Very well Milord," she giggled. Placing the loop around her wrists, she rotated one wrist in a complete circle to secure the cord. Then she leaned back onto the bed and wriggled on her back up towards the pillows.

Adam leaned over her and paused. It just didn't feel right. He wanted her to reach up and pull him towards her, but her bound hands rested motionless on her midriff and her eyes were closed. Taking a deep breath, he unbuttoned her blouse slowly and peeled it back to reveal a black lacy bra with a front fastening. He nodded. Ingenious. He unfastened it and pulled it away from her svelte, creamy breasts. Then, placing his hands on either side of her torso and one knee next to her thigh, he leaned over and began to nuzzle her nipples, one at a time, feeling them stiffen and swell, feeling her shiver at the flickering touch of his tongue. He heard a faint sigh from her lips and then a gasp as he took one nipple between his teeth and gently nipped it.

Feeling Adam move away from her, Alice opened her eyes to find him sitting on the bed by her feet. He looked troubled.

"What is it?" she asked.

He shrugged. "I don't know. It just feels wrong. I know it's just a game, but it still feels wrong."

She smiled patiently and raised herself to a sitting position, unlooping the cord from her wrists. After refastening her bra and buttoning up her blouse, she looked up at him, her eyes appraising him shrewdly.

"Okay then. How about we go back to plan A? You have the cord and I show you how it's done." She raised her eyebrows as she waited for him to consider this. Extending her arms, she offered him the cord. "We can stop whenever you like." Adam nodded his assent and held out his hands to have them bound.

Gordon King paused outside the front door while he removed the small pack from his back and placed it carefully on the floor in front of him. Opening the pocket at the front, he withdrew a slim torch and a flat leather case secured with a zip. Holding the torch in his mouth, he directed its beam at the case, unzipped it and opened it out to reveal a row of thin steel implements. He selected a suitably sized tensioner tool and a smaller pick, rested the case on top of the pack, then inserted the tensioner into the bottom of the lock, twisting it gently until it was under tension. Holding it in position with his left hand, he grunted with satisfaction; this would prevent the pins from falling back after he had lifted them above the shear line. Directing the light from the torch upon the lock, he probed the opening with the pick in his right hand, feeling for the first of the pins, then lifting it into position and holding it there with the tensioner tool. With practised ease, he worked his way along the row of pins until they were all lifted and the steel tensioner slackened a little. With a gentle twist, he rotated the lock. He was in. Checking over both shoulders, he confirmed that he had not been observed. The street was silent. Perfect. He replaced the steel implements in the case, zipped it up and placed it back in the pocket. Then, picking the pack up, he eased the door open, stepped inside and shut it gently.

The hall was dimly lit by the light from the landing. None of the downstairs lights were on. Gordon smiled. From his car, he had watched the young lady as she had dashed round to visit her neighbour and, as he had hoped, the light had quickly been switched on upstairs. If his suspicions were correct, he had left them more than enough time to get into bed together. The light was still on, but with a bit of luck, they might be asleep by now; that would serve his purposes perfectly. He moved towards the stairs.

Bound and helpless upon the bed, Adam wanted to beg Alice to let him come. For what seemed an eternity, she had teased his erection with her fingers and her lips, always stopping just before he reached his climax. She seemed to have a sixth sense that enabled her to take him to the very brink of orgasm without ever allowing him to dive over the edge. Initially he had raised his tethered hands to try to touch her, but she had pushed them back. Then, gradually, he had come to feel the power of handing over all control to Alice, granting her dominion over his destiny. When she finally allowed him to reach his orgasm, it wasn't the jarring explosion that it had been the last time. Instead, it was like slipping gently into a bubbling spring of warm water; it was like a gigantic sigh of release. Alice tenderly removed the bonds from his wrists, lay down next to him and wrapped her arms around him, holding him tightly. Neither of them spoke.

Outside the bedroom door, Gordon silently placed the pack on the floor and withdrew a cosh. He felt its reassuring weight in his hand, the black, braided leather that covered it. It had been a present from a colleague from the Singapore policeman who had been visiting the UK and had befriended Gordon. He had rarely had the opportunity to use it, but it would be perfect for this job. It wasn't a job that he savoured. Roughing up villains was one thing but he had reservations about intimidating a couple of youngsters who had strayed into Blake Montague's territory. Still, Blake paid well and it didn't do to let him down. He used the cosh to push the door open gently then he silently stepped inside.

Alice heard him first. Opening her eyes to see the stocky dark figure moving towards them, she leapt from the bed and threw herself at him. Poised on the balls of his feet, Gordon stepped to one side, raised the cosh over his left shoulder and slashed down diagonally to the side of her head. Alice collapsed like a rag doll. Adam was still struggling to raise himself from the bed when Gordon was upon him. He raised his hands to parry the anticipated blow to his head but Gordon had already anticipated that, stabbing him in the solar plexus to make him bring his arms down then striking him across the head, just above his ear.

Alice was the first to recover from the blow. She opened her eyes with a start to find herself leaning against the headboard, her arms pinned behind her back. Her head throbbed oppressively; her vision was slightly blurred. She tried to move and felt a sharp pain in her wrists. Looking over her shoulder, she could see that they had been pinned to the headboard with cable ties. Screaming in pain and frustration through the gag that had been placed across her mouth, she glared at the intruder with wild eyes, but he was busy securing Adams's wrists and ankles with cable ties, tying a gag across his mouth, then dragging him into a sitting position, leaning against the wall opposite her. Once he was satisfied, he turned to face her.

"I represent a party that resents your interference in his affairs," Gordon began in his soft Edinburgh brogue. "You have been warned to stop, but you have ignored that warning." He shook his head sadly. "Regrettably, it has become necessary for me to give you a taste of what is to come if you continue to interfere."

Alice's eyes widened in horror as the realisation sank in. She thrashed her legs on the bed and emitted a muffled shriek of anger, but she was helpless.

"I'm sorry I had to strike you," Gordon continued. "I don't like having to hit women. I just needed to incapacitate you long enough to tie you to the bed. But as for your boyfriend … well … I'm afraid that he is going to have to suffer for your disobedience."

He turned to look at Adam, folded against the wall. He was just beginning to stir. "He is a pretty boy isn't he?" He rubbed his thumb and fingers over his chin. "I think I'm going to spare his good looks on this occasion. However," he turned to Alice and raised the cosh like a wagging finger, "if you don't take heed of ***this*** warning, then I'm afraid it will get very ugly next time."

Without further warning he crossed to Adam, just starting to try to push himself up against the wall, and struck him hard across the thigh. Adam collapsed with a muffled cry. Gordon proceeded to strike at Adam's arms, legs and ribs. The sound of the cosh as it struck was sickening, punctuated by stifled howls of agony. Alice wailed through the gag, flailing her body across the bed, but to no avail. The cable ties bit deeper into her wrists, causing her to cry out with pain.

Gordon turned his attention to Adam's solar plexus. He stabbed repeatedly into his midriff, grunting a little with the effort of it. Adam, groaning with each blow, doubled over with pain, then vomited violently. Standing back, breathing heavily, Gordon nodded then turned to Alice. She was lying still now, sobbing uncontrollably.

"Right then Lassie. This is your final warning." He tilted his head towards her and raised his eyebrows to emphasise the point. "You need to back off. If my employer asks me to visit you again, we'll be looking at a life changing injury for your boyfriend. Do you understand what I'm saying to you?"

Alice cursed violently through her gag. Gordon couldn't distinguish the words but the sentiment was clear. He held the cosh in the air and sighed. "Do I have to hit him again?" he asked. Alice's body went slack on the bed, finally realising the futility of her resistance. She shook her head slowly. Gordon nodded with grim satisfaction. "Sensible. Put it down to experience. You had a good run, but it stops now. Try to understand the power of the man you are up against. You're well out of your league, believe me."

He crossed to Adam's inert body. Took a small knife from his pocket and turned to Alice meaningfully. Her eyes widened. Surely he didn't intend to …

Unfolding the blade, Gordon cut the cable ties on Adam's wrists and feet. "He'll be able to free you once he feels a bit better. You can explain to him what I've just said. I don't know who the main driver in this investigation is but I'm getting the feeling that it might be you. Just persuade him that it's all over." He nodded. "I'll let myself out," he added, chuckling at his own joke as he opened the bedroom door, picked up his pack and walked down the stairs.

Chapter 26

For two days, Adam lay in bed, sleeping fitfully, waking periodically to find Alice's anxious face peering down at him. She had wanted to get medical help, but concerns about how a doctor might react to Adam's injuries had prevented her. The last thing they needed right now was to call attention to themselves. She hoped that Adam would understand. She stayed right next to him in a battered old armchair, sleeping when she could, going over and over the plans in her head while she was awake.

On the third day, she was able to gingerly sit him up a little, a pillow behind his head, so that she could more easily help him to drink some water. She spooned a little soup into his mouth until he signalled that he'd had enough. Alice wanted to cuddle him, to reassure him that everything would be okay, but he shied away from her, eyes wide with panic, when she moved her hands towards him. Instead, she kissed him lightly on the top of his head.

"I'm so sorry this has happened, Adam," she began. She shook her head slowly; Adam couldn't tell whether it was from sadness or anger.

"Right from the start, I didn't want you involved in all this," she continued. There was a new air about Alice that Adam had never sensed before. She seemed older, detached, dispassionate.

"I always knew that Blake would try to hurt us," she sighed, pulling her lips tight across her mouth. "And I never wanted you to get all tangled up in what I was doing…" She tailed off, looking down as she thought back to the discovery of Dora's jar and Adam's excitement about what it might all mean. "It's just that …" she looked back into his eyes once more … "it's been wonderful." Her eyes were shining now; it was the old Alice back with him once more. "I don't know how I would have got this far without you. Really!" She nodded for emphasis. Then, taking a deep breath, she withdrew from him once more.

"But I have to finish this on my own now Adam." Her voice was icy cold.

He looked deep into her limpid eyes, shocked by the distance he could feel between them. He hardly recognised her.

"Look, Alice," he interjected. "I know that I'm less than useless at the moment, but I'll be well again soon." He shrugged, then winced with the pain of the movement. "He gave me a good beating, that's true, but nothing's broken, I'm sure it isn't. We need to be sensible about this. Blake is too powerful for us. I don't want you to do anything until I'm ready to help you again."

She shook her head resolutely. "It's too late to pull out now. We're in too deep." She paused, choosing her words carefully. "I need to deal with Blake."

Adam's eyes widened. "What do you mean? Deal with him? We need to get as far as possible away from him. You've *seen* what he can do!" His voice was raised now, his fear overriding the pain that wracked his body.

Alice flashed a pair of cold blue eyes at him. Her voice was chilling. "I mean, I'm going to kill him."

There was a long silence while Adam tried to assimilate what she had just said. He stared at her, astounded. Finally, he spoke. He too was measured now, shocked into sobriety. "Alice, you can't kill Blake Montague."

She blinked at him. "Why not?"

He gave a gasp of exasperation. "Because, even if you can get close to him, which you can't, and even if you could try to hurt him, which you couldn't," he paused and took a breath, "you're just not someone who could kill another person."

Alice smiled gently, touched by Adam's candour. "Yes, I am, Adam. I can kill Blake Montague. It's been my plan all along." She looked down momentarily then fixed him with a cold, blue gaze. "It's what I have to do."

Adam was horrified. Sinking back into the pillow, he closed his eyes, exhausted by the exchange, descending into a deep, troubled sleep. When he awoke, Alice wasn't there. Panic gripped him. Where had she gone? What was she doing?

"Alice? Where are you?"

She appeared quickly with a mug of hot sweet tea and some biscuits.

"Sorry. I just took the opportunity to get you something to cheer you up. You've barely eaten anything in three days." She placed them on the bedside table then sat down carefully on the edge of the bed.

"I'll just let the tea cool down a little. I need to explain to you why I have to kill Blake."

Adam opened his mouth to speak, then thought better of it. Let her explain what was on her mind.

"Blake Montague is evil, Adam." Alice's voice was calm and even but Adam could sense the tension beneath it. She was maintaining control for his benefit. "And evil perverts everyone and everything it touches. Blake Montague needs to be stopped before he does any more damage."

Adam shook his head, then winced at the movement. "You don't recognise the damage he's done to you, though, Alice. You've become obsessed with him. The act you are considering is ... well ... it's just as evil as Blake's behaviour. You need to rise above it. You're better than him. We both are."

Alice exhaled heavily, then nodded as she reconsidered her explanation. "Okay then, let's imagine that Blake was running at you with a knife and you were holding a gun. Would you stop yourself from shooting him because it's evil?"

Adam scoffed at the idea. "Obviously not. He's going to kill me if I do, isn't he? I'm not an idiot Alice. I can stand up for myself if I have to. The thing is, your analogy is flawed. We're the ones who are running towards Blake Montague, not the other way around. We're a threat to ***him***. If we run away from him, he'll leave us alone. He'll have no reason to come after us if we're no longer a threat. And anyway, he's an old man now. He can't have that much longer to live. How much more damage can he do at his age?"

Alice shook her head vehemently. "He'll never leave us alone Adam. And he's doing more and more damage every day, spreading more and more evil. And evil thrives on people looking away or running away. That's the problem. We'll never be safe while Blake is alive and nor will anyone else."

She reached across to the bedside table and picked up the tea. She tried to hold it to Adam's mouth, but he raised his hands and grasped it himself, ignoring the pain that shot through his arms and shoulders. He drained the mug quickly then held it out to Alice to replace on the table. She picked up the plate of biscuits but he made a face to indicate that he was not ready for solid food yet.

Alice continued. "There are very few objective truths or values in life, Adam. Truth is controlled, mediated by those who have the power. They create the narrative to suit their own ends and then convince everyone that it's the truth, whether it is or not." She shrugged. "We all do it to some extent. Like the teenager with acne and an eating disorder who puts her carefully airbrushed pictures of herself onto a social media platform and describes to the world how perfect her life is. Then there's the more extreme ones. Like the High Court Judge who spends his day passing down sentences to miscreants than spends his evening paying a middle-aged woman to spank his bottom and help him pretend he's back at school. But neither of them is doing too much damage to anyone except maybe themselves."

Adam gave her a sardonic look. He wasn't about to be lectured by a computer geek on the mechanisms of the media. "I understand all about representation and mediation, Alice, probably better than you do, in fact. It's how I make my living."

Alice smiled. "Of course it is. I wasn't trying to patronise you. But it goes so much deeper than just a TV programme or a propaganda pamphlet. It underpins the way we see the world. It defines what we see as true or false. Take the bible, for example, written centuries after the death of Christ to represent the complete narrative of existence; where we came from, why we are here, how we should behave while we are here, where we go after this life. We revere this book so much that we name people after its characters. Like you Adam," she smiled, "and Eve, or Evie, like my mother. The narrative of the book is embedded deep in our psyche. It's part of who we are and how we see the world. But the thing is, people use it to justify laws and values which suit their own purposes. In the 1950s, the narrative from that book was reinterpreted by narrow minded bigots to justify the persecution of Alan Turing for his sexuality; a man who had saved millions of lives during the Second World War. It's a national disgrace; the man credited with the development of the first computer was hounded until he took his own life. The irony is that today he would be ***allowed*** to get married to another man. The narrative has changed even though the bible is still the same document.

Adam pulled his lips tight across his teeth in an expression of scepticism. "That suicide verdict is in some doubt, you know. There is a distinct possibility it was accidental."

Alice nodded enthusiastically. "Exactly. We cannot countenance that we killed a national hero, so we rewrite history. We find a way of suggesting that it wasn't a result of our harassment. The narrative has changed. Homosexuality has become normal. So, The Queen pardons him, we build a statue in Manchester and put him on a first-class stamp and a £50 note. We are not guilty. We're off the hook. Except that one of the greatest geniuses of all time is taken from us at the age of 41, when he had potential for so much more."

Adam sighed. Where was all this leading? "So, what are you saying, Alice? That there are no truths and no values, only stories? That makes no sense. There must be good and evil. There must be right and wrong."

Alice took a deep breath to hide her frustration. She needed to stay calm. She needed Adam to understand. "Okay then, let's take the example of Joseph Goebbels's wife, Magda. The narrative that Hitler has given her about the evils of communism, the supremacy of the Aryan race and the disgrace of losing the war, are so convincing that she turns down the opportunity to rescue her six children and fly them to safety. Instead, she has them injected with morphine to make them sleep then administers cyanide to them, one by one. The youngest, Heidrun was four years old. There is forensic evidence that at least one of the children woke up while the cyanide was being administered and had to have her mouth held shut so that she couldn't spit it out. Was Magda Goebbels a good person for protecting her children from the awful things that were going to happen or a bad person for murdering them? Was Alan Turing a pervert or a national hero? Was the judge who found him guilty of gross indecency and ordered chemical castration right or wrong?"

Adam cocked his head to one side. He was beginning to understand. "So, how do we tell right from wrong, true from false? You're saying it just depends upon whose story we listen to, right?"

"No." She shook her head again. "We have to believe that there is a true story, a right story … and we have to find it. We need to remove all of the evil people who take control of the true story and subvert it for their own profit."

Adam shrugged. "And how can we recognise who are the evil ones if we're brainwashed by their stories?"

Alice smiled mysteriously. "It takes an outsider - an innocent - someone who has formed their view of what is right and wrong in a different place, someone who hasn't been influenced by the stories that evil people have used to trick those around them."

"An outsider?"

"An Alice!"

"You mean you?"

She smiled again, amused this time. "No, I mean ***an*** Alice. Like Lewis Carroll's Alice. Think about it. She falls down a rabbit hole into a different world where things have been turned upside down; where the values she cherishes do not apply. She encounters the Queen of Hearts, a cruel and vindictive ruler who uses flamingos as mallets to hit hedgehogs as balls and keeps changing the rules of the game so that only she can win. If anyone disagrees with her, she shouts, 'Off with his head'. And yet she has no actual substance. Everyone else is frightened of her except Alice, the outsider. She alone recognises that she is just a playing card. She also meets Humpty Dumpty, who decides that words have no objective meaning. They can mean whatever he wants them to mean. Lewis Carroll realised how dangerous this could be to those who are taken in by it, but only an outsider, like Alice, can recognise that it's really just nonsense."

"Okay, so it's just a coincidence that your name is Alice then."

Alice made a face. "It isn't Alice, not really. It just appealed to my sense of irony to call myself that. It was part of my cover story. It was also a signal to anyone who knows about Lewis Carroll. Alice Liddell was the name of the little girl that he based his story on." Reaching across, she took one of Adam's hands, sandwiching it gently between her own. "The name on my birth certificate is actually Emma Reynolds. You see, I too have created a narrative, but mine is to hide my identity while I gather the evidence that I need to rid the world of Blake Montague."

Adam stared at her, incredulous. "Oh my God. So you've been feeding me a pack of lies right from the start." He paused as realisation struck him. "Of course, it all makes sense now. Like, for example, you've been pretending to be some kind of geek – someone who doesn't read fiction, who doesn't understand banter or sarcasm. But that's not you at all really is it? I mean, you've named yourself after a character in literature, haven't you. And you just said that it appealed to your sense of irony."

He shut his eyes and breathed out slowly. It was a lot to take in. He'd been thinking, well, hoping at least, that it had been his influence which had been changing her, making her more sociable. He winced inwardly. Idiot! She'd been playing him all along. He opened his eyes. Her cold blue stare was fixed on him.

"I'm sorry Adam. I wanted to tell you earlier, but the geek character was a good cover for me. Less threatening. And, once I'd assumed her identity, I couldn't keep switching back to my real character every time I was with you. It was just easier to stay in character."

Adam snarled angrily. "Anything else I should know, Alice, or should that be Emma now?"

Alice gave a conciliatory smile. "Let's stick to Alice for now. It will be easier for both of us. And yes, there's a lot more you need to know. But try not to judge me so harshly. We all create stories to hide what we want to keep secret." She paused. "Like you Adam. You tell stories to your girlfriends so that they don't find out about each other. You exaggerate how many films you've made and how successful they've been." She shrugged. "It's how we get through our lives. It's how we shape our lives so that we can make them the lives that we want them to be."

Adam reeled as she lay bare his lies and deceptions. It was delivered with a gentle tone, but the revelations were savage."

"Wow. You really have done your research on me haven't you?" The bitterness in his voice hid the embarrassment he was feeling. She was right. He had been a fraud. And he'd been a shit. She'd seen right through him from the start.

"Don't you see that I needed to, Adam. I am tracking a dangerous man. I needed to know who I could trust and who was a danger to me. And the thing is, despite all your infidelities and exaggerations, you have an innocence and a purity of heart which means I ***can*** trust you. And care for you," she added.

She leaned forward and kissed Adam again. Her lips lingered on his, this time. She caressed his cheek gently with her palm and leaned down to kiss his hands. Then she sat very upright on the bed and raised her eyebrows a little.

"Okay. Better buckle up your seat belt. It's revelation time."

Adam nodded his readiness. Alice leaned back and relaxed her features.

"So, I've thought of myself as Emma Reynolds for most of my life. I never knew my father." She shrugged. "My mother told me it was a one-night stand. That's all I've ever known about him. And that's why I have my mother's surname," she added. "Anyway, from when I was very young, I've always known that my mother had been adopted when she herself was very young and that Reynolds was Nanny and Grandad's name. I always presumed that they chose the name Evie for her." She shrugged. "We never actually talked about that. We never talked about who her real parents were either. I asked Nanny once. I was too young to see the signs then, but … now I think back to it …," a cloud passed across Alice's features, "she was too quick with her answer, too dismissive. She just said that Mum had been left in the waiting room of the local hospital and that her mother had never been traced." Alice shook her head. "I understand why she said that now. I don't approve, but I do understand."

Adam raised an eyebrow as a signal that he needed clarification, but Alice raised her palms towards him. "Sorry, getting ahead of myself. We'll get to that in a minute." She looked down while she gathered the next stage of her narrative.

"So, the first time that I realised that something wasn't right was when I was contacted by a firm of solicitors. This was about three months after Mum had died," she added. "They told me that I had been left a house as part of my inheritance. Apparently, they had been holding onto the deeds for some considerable time; since the death of its owner, Grace De Lacy, in fact. They told me that Grace had left it to Mum but that she had never wanted to take possession of it and had told them to keep the deeds."

"That's really odd. Had you ever heard of her as a relative?" Adam asked.

Alice shook her head. "She'd never been mentioned. As far as I knew, Mum had no idea who any of her relatives were. Now I wonder if that's right. She must have realised that there was some connection with Grace, otherwise why would she leave her the house? But, then again, why wouldn't she want it?"

"It makes no sense." Adam had forgotten the pain in his body now, and his anger with Alice. He was fully engaged with the mystery of it all. "If she didn't want to live in it, she could have just sold it."

"You're right." Alice responded. "It didn't seem to make any sense at the time. It was only later that I came to understand it all."

Adam's eyes begged her to continue.

"So, are you ready for this?" Alice couldn't help teasing Adam by delaying the revelation a moment longer. She found that she was enjoying the moment.

He sighed. "For God's sake," he gasped in exasperation.

Alice relented. "Grace De Lacy was Audrey Montague's mother. It's why Dora Montague came to stay with her after Audrey's death. It was a safe haven, away from Blake."

A puzzled look passed across Adam's face as he struggled to assimilate all this. "So, Grace De Lacy was Audrey's mother and Dora's grandmother, but ..." a thought struck him, "you think she was also related to your mother and therefore to you too, don't you?"

"She was my great grandmother," Alice answered brightly.

"Whaaat!" Adam sat forward in the bed, gasped with pain and sank back into the pillows. He breathed heavily for a few moments, his eyes closed, until the pain subsided, then opened his eyes again. Alice had taken his hand and was squeezing it gently in sympathy.

"How can you be sure of that? What ... what evidence do you have?"

Alice smiled. "I'll tell you if you promise not to try and sit up again."

He smiled back ruefully and nodded.

"At first, I was as confused as you are now," Alice continued. "How could the old lady be related to me? At the time, remember, I'm still buying the story that Mum had been abandoned by some poor mother in the hospital. But, since Grace has left Mum a house, I figure there's some link I don't know about. That's when I start doing my research and that's when I learn about the connection between Grace De Lacy and the Montague family and then about the deaths of Audrey and Freddie."

Adam had another flash of inspiration. "So, you changed your name, moved into the old lady's house and started searching for any clues that could explain how you were connected to all this."

"Clever boy," Alice agreed. "And I was just about to make contact with Dora when the tree fell down and you came round."

Adam examined her face thoughtfully. "So, you've only recently come to this conclusion that Grace was your great grandmother."

She nodded. "It was Dora's account of the delivery of Audrey's baby by caesarean section which got me thinking. And I started wondering. What if that baby was my mother?"

Adam gave her a doubtful look. "Well, that's a big if, isn't it?"

"Of course. It was just a starting point. But, once we started investigating, it just all fitted together really."

Adam opened his mouth to say that he was still not convinced, but Alice anticipated his comment and continued. "So, you're going to say that we need more concrete proof than that."

Adam nodded. That was exactly what he was going to say.

"Okay, so remember the locket? As well as the picture of Audrey there was a lock of hair in it, wasn't there?" She flashed him a winning smile. "I figured that hair had to either belong to Audrey or Dora herself. And if my hypothesis was right then that would mean the hair would have come from either my grandmother or my aunt. Luckily, there were follicles on some of the hairs, it must have come from a hairbrush or comb, so I had it DNA tested and matched against mine. I also found a hairbrush here in Dora's room, so I had that tested as well. And guess what?"

"You got a match?" Adam responded compliantly.

"I got two matches." There was a note of triumph in Alice's voice. "Audrey was my grandmother and Dora is my aunt."

"Have you told Dora?"

Alice shook her head. "Not yet. She might have had her suspicions about how I had gained ownership of her grandmother's old house but I think she didn't really want to know any more than we told her. I might tell her at a later date, but not till I've done what I need to do."

Adam's face darkened at this reference back to her plan to kill Blake, but Alice chose to ignore it and press on with her explanation.

"That still left me with the question of who my mother's father could be," she continued. "Dora thought it was probably Winston, but he told us that he'd never slept with her and he didn't think she'd ever slept with anyone but Blake."

"You think that Blake is your grandfather?" Adam was incredulous.

"Almost certainly. Actually, if you check out photos of him, you'll see that I have his eyes." She made a face as she said this. "All the more reason why I have to kill him. It's personal now. He murdered my grandmother and my uncle."

"How long have you known this?" Adam wanted to know.

"I've been pretty sure ever since I saw Dora's family tree," Alice replied, "but I wanted to wait for the DNA results before I told you, just so I could be certain. Anyway, you're up to date with everything now. I'm being completely open with you. You deserve that, after all the loyalty you've shown me."

Adam sank back into the pillows. It was a lot to take in. Alice was really Emma who was really Blake and Audrey's granddaughter. He was exhausted from the effort of listening.

"I've told you that I didn't want you involved at the beginning Adam. I thought you were too naïve and too innocent. But actually, what I didn't see was that your innocence is also your strength." Alice's voice was soft, in his ear as he lay back in the bed. "I've told you that I couldn't have got this far without you. I really mean that." Her voice took on a more serious, faraway tone. "I know that you've fallen in love with me, Adam." He snapped his eyes open but she was looking away from him as she spoke. "I never intended that to happen. But I'm not sorry that it did." She paused, looking down towards her hand, holding onto his, then looked into his face with her glacial blue eyes. "I'm not sure I've ever been in love with anyone, or even if I'm capable of it. But I'd like to try with you. I think that maybe I could come to love you in time." She gave him a hopeful smile. Then her face changed and she released his hand and stood next to the bed.

"But in the meantime, I need to kill Blake."

"Alice, I don't want you to," Adam pleaded. "There must be another way."

Alice's face was hard and unyielding.

"I'm going to do it Adam and I'm going to do it now. You need to stay here and get better. I'll bring you up provisions for a few days."

"But Alice, you can't kill a man like Blake Montague. How are you going to do it?"

She puckered her face up as if thinking then pronounced theatrically, "Be innocent of the knowledge, dearest chuck, till thou applaud the deed."

"You're quoting Macbeth at me? Really?"

"Of course. It's only the computer geek, Alice, who doesn't read Shakespeare. Emma is actually rather well read, as you'll find out later."

She leaned across to kiss him then went down to the kitchen to assemble drinks and food for a few days.

Chapter 27

Alice didn't start working until 2 am. She had very few callers on the whole, just the postman and the odd cold caller really, but she needed to be sure that she was working at a time when there was no chance of interruption. She had identified the back bedroom as the best venue for her workshop. It faced the back garden and wasn't overlooked. Even so, she closed the curtains once she had opened up the windows for maximum ventilation. The weather had warmed up a little during the day but was still just a few degrees above zero at night. She wore thermal underwear under a thick jumper and fleece. A steady hand with no risk of shivering was essential.

On a table in the centre of the room, she had organised the equipment that she had been carefully collecting from a variety of different sources. Each one had been purchased from a different internet supplier, hiding her identity through a series of anonymous proxy servers. They had been delivered to a range of PO boxes that she had set up using fake identities. It was, unfortunately, necessary to collect the items in person from the various sorting offices where the PO boxes were sited, but once again she had spread her purchases across several sites and always wore heavy disguise when going to collect them. She was satisfied that, even if Blake Montague's death was subject to a murder investigation, her part in all this could never be traced.

She started by putting on closed-circuit breathing apparatus. She wasn't sure exactly how long the operation would take and she didn't want to place her trust in the use of an external air supply. This would be perfect. Sliding her arms through the straps of the filtering apparatus, she settled it upon her back like a rucksack. She fitted the mask to her face and connected the tubes which would carry the scrubbed air from the filters to the mask. It was a little claustrophobic but it was highly portable, being based upon the design used by fire officers in smoke filled buildings. She had practised putting it on several times now. At first, she had breathed too fast, misting up the visor of the mask. It had made her feel decidedly odd, like an observer in a laboratory, watching someone else controlling an experimentation process. Except that this was no experiment. She had researched the process carefully, always using the anonymous proxy servers to hide her identity. She was confident in her actions. This would work.

Slipping on a pair of clear latex gloves, Alice counted out the ten castor beans. She nodded grimly; like the beans that Jack had exchanged for his mother's cow, they would enable her to slay the giant. She placed them in the electric coffee grinder and replaced the lid, smiling in amusement at the repurposing of the household item. Looking through the visor of the mask, she watched as the beans turned to granules, then to powder, registering the change in pitch of the muffled whir of the grinder's electric motor, until it was a fine as dust. Perfect. She opened the grinder and emptied the contents into a glass flask, pleased with the steadiness of her hands as she did so. Once she had added a small quantity of solvent, she pushed a rubber bung firmly into the top and gave the contents a vigorous shake. It was from this point onwards that the contents of the flask were dangerous, she knew that for sure. And they would become more deadly as she refined them further.

As she worked, Alice hummed to herself, inside the mask. At first, she hummed out loud but the mask started to mist up so she hummed inside her head.

"Oranges and lemons, say the bells of St Clement's

You owe me five farthings, say the bells of St Martin's."

It was a rhyme that her mother had sung to her when she was little. She had always finished on, "I do not know, says the great bell at Bow." It was only when she was at school, studying George Orwell's 1984, that she had discovered that there were extra lines that her mother had missed off.

"Here comes a candle to light you to bed

Here comes a chopper to chop off your head!

Chip, chop, chip, chop, the last man is dead."

When she had asked her mother, she had told her that she thought it was too scary for a little girl who was about to go to sleep. It might give her nightmares.

Her English teacher had told her that the original meaning was that the poem was about debt and the execution of debtors. Alice had researched it herself. There was no reference for anyone being executed for debt; they simply died in prison if they never paid. She put this to the teacher but he shook his head, puzzled by this grave and intense young student. No one had ever questioned his interpretation before.

"The important thing, Emma," he had said, "is what it means to Winston Smith in 1984. For him, it is about the insincerity of authority and of those who use it to subjugate the proletariat. It is about the way in which authority is dressed up as something benevolent and for support of the people, a big brother, when it is truly only designed to keep all of the power in the hands of the ruling elite."

She'd had a brief affaire with him when she was in sixth form. It was during what her mother had referred to as her promiscuous phase. And it was true, she did sleep with a lot of boys, and older men too for that matter. She hadn't really understood it at the time but, looking back, it seemed as though she was just trying to understand what all the other girls meant when they talked about falling in love. Her teacher, Michael, had told her it was a relatively modern idea, created from works of fiction. He would talk to her in bed, or lecture to her really, after they had just had sex, about how writers had conspired over the years to fabricate this idea of falling in love, as if it was something simultaneously wonderful and awful which just happened to you and which you could not control.

"The thing is, Emma," she remembered him saying, "the great love affairs of literature are embedded deep within our cultural history; Romeo and Juliet, Heathcliffe and Cathy, Gatsby and Daisy, Rick and Ilsa in Casablanca. We're brought up to believe that this is the height of human existence, the pinnacle of emotional fulfilment. We're made to feel that we're missing out if we can't feel what they felt."

She had been dubious of his assertions at first. She had pointed out that hardly anybody read books like that or watched films like that anymore. But he had scoffed, told her that the tradition was so deeply ingrained that modern writers simply built upon the tradition.

"If you've watched that Titanic film with Leonardo DiCaprio and Kate Winslett then you've imbibed the spirit of Romeo and Juliet. If you've read Fifty Shades of Grey then you've met Heathcliffe, only now he's called Christian Grey."

Michael had ultimately convinced her that we all end up by either fooling ourselves into believing that we have truly fallen in love or else by being disappointed at the failure of our lives.

A few months after their affaire ended, Michael disappeared from the school. The rumour was that he'd been sacked but the official version was that he had left for personal reasons. Either way, he had never returned her calls and she had never heard from him again. She'd checked him out on line later and discovered that he was older than he had claimed to be, married with two children.

She wondered what stories he had told his wife about what he had been doing when he was actually in bed with her.

Alice's thoughts drifted back to her mother. She wondered whether she had known that she was part of the Montague family. She had never mentioned it. The story that she was abandoned in a hospital waiting room was all that she would tell her. Nanny and Grandad must have known the truth; they were part of the deception; they must have been. Had they maintained the fiction of her origins for Evie's whole life, just to protect her from Blake? It was just possible that her mother had died never knowing that she was the daughter of Blake Montague, one of the richest and most powerful men in England? Or maybe she did know. After all, she knew about the house that Grace De Lacy had left her in her will. And something had caused her to reject the house. Perhaps she wanted to deny that connection, to seal herself and her daughter off from it. Maybe she was just protecting her, like she protected her from the scary ending to the rhyme.

Whatever her mother and her adoptive parents had known or had not known, Alice felt that she was warming to the interpretation Michael had put upon the original rhyme. Blake Montague had run up a debt, an enormous debt, through his lifelong exploitation of the weakness of the people around him. It was time for him to pay that debt. The chopper was coming to chop off his head.

After thirty minutes, shaking the flask every five, she removed the bung and poured the contents into a flask with a filtering device fitted to the neck. The liquid dripping through the filter was almost colourless. And that was the beauty of it; odourless, virtually colourless and very difficult to detect. Alice nodded with satisfaction as the dripping ceased. She removed the filter, poured the liquid into a ceramic crucible positioned upon a tripod, slid a tiny camping gas burner beneath it, turned on the gas to its minimum setting and lit it with a cigarette lighter.

Despite the breathing apparatus, she crossed the room to stand by the open windows. Her hands were clammy now inside the latex gloves. Even though she had rehearsed this moment many times before in her head, she felt her heart racing. It was, she knew, the most dangerous part of the operation. She watched the crucible intently as the solvent evaporated away until there was barely any left. Then, she strode across the room swiftly and pulled the burner out from underneath it. The heat retained by the crucible would be sufficient to evaporate what remained.

While she waited for it to cool, Alice pulled together all of the equipment, putting each piece in a sealed plastic bag then adding it to a holdall she had positioned on the floor. Safe disposal of the items would be essential.

Returning to the crucible, Alice picked it up and examined the contents; a large smudge of off-white residue. Three milligrams of ricin was, she knew, enough to kill an adult. She had nearly half a teaspoonful here. More than enough. She sprinkled the residue onto a piece of creased paper then carefully slid it down the crease into an empty plastic nasal spray labelled as medication for rhinitis. On the side was pasted the pharmacist's instructions: ***spray twice into each nostril, twice a day.*** It was identical to the spray Blake received on prescription each month; she had spotted that when hacking into his medical records. After adding a little water, she replaced the top, shook it vigorously, then took the tiny bottle over to the window and pushed the nozzle down a few times to prime it. When the atomised liquid sprayed from the tip in a fine mist, she knew that it was ready.

Still wearing the breathing apparatus, she took the holdall out into the garden, then went back inside and fetched a bowl of hot, soapy water. Cleaning each item from the bag thoroughly, she removed all traces of the castor beans. She had considered just washing them in the sink, but that was out of the question. There was too much risk of putting traces of the deadly poison into the water supply.

As she cleaned, she thought again of her mother. What would she be thinking if she could see Alice now; her daughter, an assassin, preparing a poison to kill her grandfather; what on earth would she make of that? She had loved her mother, but they had never been close, not really, not like some of her friends at school with their mothers. Oh, they had got on well, spent time together, enjoyed each other's company, but they had never talked about anything deeper than school, work, holidays, the day-to-day stuff. And hugging; there had been very little of that, particularly once she had hit her teen years. In many ways, her grandparents had been more affectionate towards her than her mother. When her mother had been near the end, Alice had told her that she loved her. She remembered her mother's thin, pale smile. She had said, "I love you too darling." Then she had paused before saying, with a deep sadness in her voice, "We should have said that to each other more, shouldn't we." The regret in her tone had stayed with Alice long after her mother's death.

Many times, during her teens, Alice had asked about her father, but her mother had simply shaken her head and withdrawn from her. When she had asked if she had tried to find her real parents, her mother had answered that Nanny and Grandad were the only parents that mattered to her. Alice wondered, not for the first time, whether her mother had really been unable to connect with her at that more intimate level, or whether she was just trying to keep her at arm's length to protect her from her past. If it were the latter, then she would clearly be distressed that her daughter was engaging in any way with her grandfather. And as for killing him ...she would probably be horrified. If her mother were still alive, she reflected, she would have to carry her plan out without telling her, for the assassination of Blake Montague was non-negotiable.

When the realisation had first hit her, the realisation that she intended to kill Blake, it had shocked her. She couldn't understand where the impulse had come from, only that it was strong and undeniable. This was before she knew that he was her grandfather, though her instincts told her that he had blighted her life in some way, and her mother's, and the lives of many others besides. Night after night she had lain awake, upset at the emotions coursing through her body, impelling her to commit murder. It was as if the compulsion had been planted in her, like a seed, or else it had always been there but it had only just made its presence known. It was only through the knowledge that had come to her through the death of the tree, the discovery of the evil contained in the time capsule, the testimony of Dora and Gabriel and Winston, that she had come to understand the full horror of Blake's life and the damage he had done to his family, her family. Only then had it all made sense. Now it was clear. He was evil. He had to die. And she was the only one who could do it.

Once she was satisfied that every trace had been removed, she placed the items back in the bag. They would be disposed of while people were still asleep in their beds, pushed deep down into some of the many skips hired by local builders for the home improvements going on in the area. The only item that she would retain, apart from the deadly inhaler bottle, was the breathing apparatus. She would need that.

Only the contaminated water remained now. Alice had already planned its disposal. She walked down the garden to where the tree had been torn from the ground by the lightning strike, uncovering Dora's time capsule, connecting the past to the present. What better place for the by-products of the poison that would kill Blake Montague, she smiled, as she poured the still warm, soapy water down the hole that was all that remained from that cathartic, stormy night. It was only when she was back inside the house that she felt that it was safe to finally remove the mask.

Chapter 28

The following day, Alice had been tempted to go and check on Adam. It had been a long, largely empty, day. All of her plans were laid; her exit strategy was complete. There was nothing to do except wait for night to descend. She felt guilty about Adam; despite wanting to spend some time with him, she had resisted the urge. She knew that he was distressed by her plan and would try to talk her out of it.

Now she was sitting in her car, parked in a passing place in a narrow dark lane, a short way from Blake Montague's mansion. Squally rain was beating down upon the windscreen, driven by mad, gusting winds. Earlier, as she had driven towards her destination, there had been growling thunder in the distance and an occasional flash of lightning. It was a good omen, she decided. It would keep people in their houses. She had dressed herself in a black nylon overall which could be disposed of when she had finished her mission, her hair pinned up onto the top of her head, topped by a black baseball hat. A little bit SAS, she had reflected, catching sight of herself in a mirror before leaving the house, but there was unlikely to be anyone to see her so it mattered little.

Opening the laptop on her knees, she started by checking the emails and social messaging sites for Blake Montague and Tabitha Watts. Blake was due to be away at a conference in Brussels that night with Tabitha in attendance; she wanted to check that there had been no last-minute changes before she moved to the next stage of her plan. She nodded as she scrolled through their communications. Everything checked out. There was some Twitter feed about Blake's speech four hours previously. Excellent. She checked her watch. 1.30 am. It was time to make her move.

She proceeded to access the CCTV and alarm system for Blake's mansion and grounds. She had set the hack up the previous day, leaving a back door so that she could get in easily tonight. Before disabling it, she checked all of the cameras, inside and out, just to ensure that there were no signs of life. With Blake and Tabitha away, she was confident that the housekeeper would not be there, but she took the opportunity for a last check. There was no one. Once the system was disabled, she anticipated that the company that supplied it would be alerted. It was doubtful that they would come to fix it before the morning, but not impossible. She took a deep breath, closed the laptop, placed it on the seat beside her and started the car. She would move quickly now. If everything went according to plan, she could be in and out in less than ten minutes, reboot the alarm and CCTV systems and be on her way in a further five minutes. The apparent fault would be fixed before the repair company could even make it to the door.

The front of the mansion was gloomy, foreboding. A lightning flash illuminated it momentarily, then it was dark once more. Alice drove right up the wide driveway to the front door; there was, she reasoned, no reason to hide herself. With the cameras turned off and no one in the house, she might as well get close; no sense in getting soaked. Turning round, she picked up a small rucksack from the back seat, holding it by one strap, opened the car door and slipped out onto the gravel drive. The wind drove the rain into her face, making her overall flap, pulling at the hat. She slammed the car door shut, held the hat on with her hand, and made a dash towards the porch.

Once within the refuge of the porch, she put the rucksack down and paused to catch her breath. Even in that short dash she had become quite wet, but the nylon overall had kept the worst of it from penetrating to her skin. From the rucksack, she pulled out a thin pair of latex gloves and pulled them carefully over her hands. Although she wasn't expecting an investigation into Blake's death, she wasn't going to run the risk of leaving fingerprints within the house. From the breast pocket of the overall, she withdrew a key to the front door. She had ordered this from an online company that specialised in cutting keys from photos. She had wondered whether there would be a problem that all of her photos had come from the CCTV camera on the porch that she had hacked some time earlier, but there had been no communication from the company at all apart from the key and the bill. Apparently, business was business as far as they were concerned. As always, she had used proxy servers and a PO box to cover her tracks.

She had done her best to clean up the images with some fairly sophisticated software, but still, she wasn't one hundred percent confident that it would work.

Breathing deeply, she slipped the key into the lock. It needed a firm push but it penetrated all the way. Brilliant. She turned it gently, but felt resistance. Damn. She tried it more forcefully, turning it clockwise and anticlockwise, but still there was resistance. Her heart was fluttering now, her breath coming in short gasps. She let go of the key and dropped her hands while she re-gathered herself. It would be disastrous if the key snapped off in the lock. It would be like a calling card, and Blake would be in no doubt who had left it. Feeling calmer, she took hold of the key again between finger and thumb, turned it with gentle pressure and jiggled it forwards and backwards at the same time. After a few tense moments, she felt the key slip past the resistance and begin to turn. With a sigh of relief, she rotated the key further and pulled at the door. She was in.

She bent down, took a slim torch from a pocket on the outside of the rucksack then picked it up by one strap, hoisting it over her shoulder as she straightened up. Stepping inside the house, she waited until she had shut the door behind her before she turned on the torch. She had studied the plans of the house and the internal CCTV to give her some clues about how to navigate through the rooms to find the staircase, but still the thin beam of the torch in the huge space of the hallway created an eerie effect which was quite disorientating. Sweeping the light across the room, it illuminated all the trappings of wealth and privilege; dark, gilt-framed portraits, swords, guns, the stuffed head of a stag. It was oppressive, disturbing. It stank of exploitation and oppression.

Catching sight of the doorway she had been searching for, Alice moved forward quietly and purposefully towards the ballroom. As she approached the doorway, a dim light snapped on inside the room. Alice froze, poised on the threshold of the room, stunned by the sudden action. Could it be that lights were operated by timers? For what purpose? She hesitated, unsure what to do. Surely there couldn't be anyone in the house. She had checked so carefully.

"Come in Alice. I've been expecting you."

It was a female voice. The tone was calm, the accent was RP, but there was just a trace of working-class London vowels there too, nothing like the friends and cronies of Blake Montague. It could only be Tabitha Watts. But, how could it be? She was with Blake in Brussels. Alice felt the bile rise in her throat. What if Blake were here too?

"I have a gun pointed at your head Alice. You need to come in and sit in the chair by the table lamp." The tone remained calm but the intent was clear. Running away was not an option; Alice knew that Tabitha was no stranger to guns and to violence. Walking, with trepidation, towards the chair, she tried to catch sight of her, but the area of the room from which her voice came was in deep shadow.

"Put your bag on the table where I can see it before you sit down," the voice said. Still Alice could not see her, but the light from the lamp penetrated into the shadows enough to dimly reflect the metallic barrel of a gun.

Only when Alice was seated with the bag on the table, just out of her reach, did the dim figure of Tabitha Watts emerge from the shadows. Alice could just make out a dark jumpsuit and black pumps in the low light and the glint from her gun; clearly, she had been expecting her, as she had said. She crossed the room with cat-like grace, the gun always pointed at Alice, sat down in the chair opposite hers and lowered the gun onto her lap, still pointed in her direction. There was sufficient light from the lamp to see the outline of her face but not to read her expressions.

"I'm Tabitha Watts," she began. "And you are Alice Liddell, otherwise known as Emma Reynolds."

"I thought you were in Brussels with Blake Montague," Alice responded. Despite the gun, Tabitha's manner did not seem angry or threatening. She dared to ask a question. "How did you know I would be coming here tonight?"

The dim light reflected back from Tabitha's teeth as she smiled. "Karen told me to expect you, just in case Gordon didn't deter you. She's been keeping an eye on you. She recommended that I tell Blake at the last minute that I was too sick to accompany him; she thought, if you were looking for to pay us a visit, the Brussels trip might be the opportunity you were looking for."

"Then you know why I'm here," Alice responded coolly. There was no point in trying to hide anything now. If Karen had been confiding in Tabitha then she clearly trusted her. Alice had made her play. Now it was time for Tabitha to reveal which side she was on.

Tabitha smiled again. "I'm pretty sure I know what your intentions are as far as Blake is concerned." She paused, considering her words carefully. "Karen and I are less clear about what your intentions are towards us." There was an edge to her voice. Was that intended to intimidate Alice or was she genuinely concerned for her own safety?

Alice shook her head, as if to deny Tabitha's misgivings. "I'm not here for you or Karen." She shook her head again to underline this. "Just Blake. I'm going to kill Blake." She waited for Tabitha to respond but she remained silent, the gun still pointed towards her. She wanted more assurances than a simple denial of malice.

"You don't trust me," Alice stated simply. "I hear it in your voice. And I don't blame you; I understand the risks involved. But I have no argument with you. You and Karen are just two of the many people caught up in Blake's web."

Once again there was a long silence. Alice allowed it to hang between them. She needed Tabitha to articulate what was on her mind.

Tabitha finally broke the silence. "Who are you? I know you're not Alice Liddell, despite the fact that you do indeed appear to have popped out of a rabbit hole. I know that you lived as Emma Reynolds before that. Karen told me all about your mother's adoption, your early life, never knowing your dad, your mother's death. The thing is though, what earthly reason does Emma Reynolds have for wanting Blake Montague dead?"

Alice took a deep breath. "I'm Emma Montague. My mother was Evie Montague. Blake Montague was her father, my grandfather. I'm not sure if she ever knew that, but I know it and I have the proof."

The table lamp snapped on next to Tabitha. Alice heard the click of a safety catch as she placed the gun on the table and faced her, nodding slowly. "The proof is right in front of me. You have his eyes, Blake's I mean. When Karen told me I just couldn't believe it, but I see it now, even through those Plain Jane spectacles you try to hide them with."

Alice found herself smiling reluctantly. There was something very engaging about Tabitha; it was not hard to imagine how beautiful she must have been in her youth. No wonder Blake had kept her close to him all of these years.

"Did Karen know that Evie had survived after Audrey's murder," she asked.

Tabitha shook her head. "Evie," she mused, looking off into the darkened room. "Evie." She smiled. "It's a lovely name." She looked back at Alice. "Nobody knew except the doctor, her grandmother, and me." She frowned. "I couldn't trust anybody at that time. I was terrified of what Blake would do if he found out the baby had been born. At the trial, he made sure that no mention was made of Audrey's pregnancy. It was as if the baby had never existed."

"And the doctor told no one?" Alice queried.

Tabitha gave her a bitter smile. "Blake wasn't the only member of the family who knew how to get what he wanted. I presume that Grace paid him off before she took the baby away and arranged an adoption. All I was allowed to know was that the baby would have a new life with a new family. I told Winston about the adoption later because I thought he might be the father. Huh," she snorted, "apparently, I got that one wrong. I told Gabriel too, just because Freddie was accused of being the father." She shrugged. "I never knew whether she had thrived or not. Never even knew her name till now." She smiled gently. "I'm glad it was Evie. Audrey would have liked that."

Turning her gaze back to Alice, Tabitha's tone changed; the cautious edge was back. "It still doesn't explain why you and your lovestruck neighbour are risking your lives. You've never met Blake; he's done nothing to you personally. Dora has reason to hate Blake, so does Karen, so do I. She looked down, shook her head, and muttered to herself. Engaging Alice's stare once more, she narrowed her eyes suspiciously. "You never even knew Audrey and Freddie. You've only just discovered you're one of the family. Have you developed a sudden sense of responsibility for defending the family honour or do you see yourself as some kind of avenging angel? Hundreds of people have reason to hate Blake Montague enough to want him dead. You don't!"

Alice nodded her assent. "Hundreds of people have reason to hate Blake Montague enough to want him dead, and yet he's still alive. Why is that?"

Tabitha snorted in frustration. "You don't understand."

Alice held up her hands. "I do understand. I know why none of you have killed him, and that's why it has to be me. Because I can. I'm the only one who can. It's precisely because I'm not caught up in his web, like the rest of you, that I can do it. I'm Alice. The rest of you are ..." she looked up, searching for the words to express herself ... "well, you're infected by him."

The fury on Tabitha's face told Alice that this had not been well received, but she pressed on. "He is a malevolent creature who controls his environment and everyone in it. But even as you hate him for this, you also feel admiration for his control and, well, you feel indebted to him for what he has done for you. You are what he has made you. That's why you can't kill him ... and that's why I can."

Tabitha felt the blood rush to her face. When Karen had told her what she knew about the deaths of Audrey and Freddie she had been filled with rage. Feeling the rage welling up inside her now, once again, she struggled to suppress it. She looked down at the antique Persian rug that had been on the floor in that exact same position when she had first started to work for Blake all those years ago. She lifted her gaze, staring into the gloom, knowing where each picture, each ornament, was positioned, even though she could only see shadowy outlines. Nothing had changed. Nothing had moved. It was as if Blake could control time itself, even as he controlled his filthy, corrupted empire. Tabitha's rage was as much with herself as with Blake. She had moved within these walls, year upon year, aiding Blake as he altered reality, rewrote the narrative to fit his own perverted ends. Had she really not known that Blake had murdered Audrey and Freddie? Had she really believed his distorted version of the truth? It was as if she had sleep-walked through forty years, believing she was detached from Blake's influence, merely an employee. In reality, she could see it now, she had become tainted by his lies, permanently in thrall to the power of his will. She listened to the sound of the rain, angrily pounding upon the roof and walls of the ancient mansion, trying to force entry. How could she have allowed herself to become yet another victim of Blake Montague?

Alice watched as the fury gradually seeped out of Tabitha's face, to be replaced by perplexity. When Tabitha's eyes looked up to meet hers, she became aware that she was being studied, evaluated.

"I still don't buy it," she said finally. "Take your glasses off."

Puzzled, Alice removed them. Tabitha had been correct; she wore them more to hide her eyes than out of a need to see more clearly. Now she could see that Tabitha was staring intently at her and nodding grimly.

"What?" exclaimed Alice sharply.

"Pure Montague," Tabitha responded. She grimaced. "If anything, your eyes are even colder than his."

"Meaning what?" Alice fired back.

"Meaning I believe you now, you do have the capacity to kill Blake, but I worry what you'll do after you've killed him," she replied.

Alice was a little taken aback. She had not expected this. "I've already told you that I mean no harm to you and Karen," she protested. "You're not to blame for what he made you do. Well, not entirely anyway. You're as much victims in your way as Dora and Audrey and Freddie."

"I'm not worried about myself or Karen." Tabitha was very sombre now. "I'm worried that I see Blake in your eyes. Maybe you aren't aware of it yet, just who you are, just what you are capable of, but I worry that you're killing Blake in order to become Blake. You see, I think it very possible that you carry the seed of his cruelty and ruthlessness within you. After all, this is murder you're planning to commit isn't it?"

There was a long, uncomfortable silence; Alice was too shocked to speak. That Tabitha could think that she might be a monster, like Blake, well, it was too awful to contemplate. Why would she say that? She had come to save the world from Blake, not to become him. Her mind struggled with the image of herself that Tabitha had presented. Never had she wanted to become like Blake. He disgusted her. Yes, she was going to kill him, but it was wrong to think of it as murder. This was justice. This was something that should have happened a long time ago, but it hadn't because only she, Alice, could do it.

Tabitha watched Alice carefully, trying to gauge the impact of her words. She had seen it before on the streets, the ambitious newcomer, plotting the murder of the local drug lord in order to steal his empire. And yet she wanted to believe in Alice, desperately wanted to believe in her and trust her. Things had changed now; Karen had finally told her what she had suspected, but never been able to prove, for so many years. She had told her about the cover up of Freddie's death in prison. She had told her that Martine's alibi for Blake on the night of Audrey's murder had been a lie, and that that probably accounted for her death, swimming off Blake's yacht while he had conveniently gone ashore to buy provisions. And now that she knew, for absolute certainty, that Blake had murdered his own wife and then cold-bloodedly ordered the murder of Freddie in prison, she could hardly bear to be in the same room as him anymore. She so wanted to believe that Alice was sincere and honest.

Chapter 29

Adam lay awake on the bed, wondering where Alice was, what she was doing. The ponderous tick, tick, tick from the clock on the landing pedantically measured out the unbearably slow passage of time. From time to time it was drowned out by another burst of rain beating upon the window, only to take control of the silence once more as the rain subsided. The curtains were not drawn so he could see the gritty gloom outside. Earlier there had been some flashes of lightning and the distant growl of thunder. It had been dark for some time now; he guessed that it was the early hours of the morning. A few hours ago, he had heard her car leaving. He had struggled over to the window, opened it, and called out to her, but either she had not heard him or she had ignored him.

When she came back, would she be a murderer? The very thought of it chilled him. If she was, and he didn't report it, he would be an accessory. And yet, she was such an ordinary woman in so many ways, and he had never loved anyone like he loved her.

He adjusted his position a little to relieve the ache in his ribs, pulling the duvet a little higher where his shoulder had been exposed and was starting to chill. On reflection, he had never actually loved anyone, really. Not before Alice ... or Emma as she was really. And that was the problem, wasn't it? He wasn't sure whether he was in love with the real Alice, or what he imagined her to be. But he did love her. He was sure of that.

It had been a whirlwind fortnight. Two weeks ago, he had been stumbling drunkenly out of a taxi after yet another party where he had propositioned yet another clone of the sort of woman he thought he wanted to be with. He sighed and shut his eyes. It was like waking up after a long, meandering dream. Alice had swept him off his feet, shown him the emptiness of his life, given him a new sense of who he was and where he was headed. She had shown him what a true relationship could be, unleashing feelings and emotions he never knew were in him. An odd thought occurred to him; would his mother and father like her? He smiled to himself. Ironically enough, they probably would; just as long as they didn't know what she was out doing at this very moment. Then again, did his parents actually care that much? Why would you have a child, only to pack him off to boarding school or dump him on a nanny?

As tiredness overcame him, he crossed the fingers of both hands. He just wanted her back, safe. He just wanted the whirlwind of Alice to continue. He slipped into a fitful, troubled sleep.

Chapter 30

It was Tabitha who broke the silence. "So, Alice, these are my options as I see it. Option one, I could try to talk you out of killing Blake, but, realistically, you would probably tell me that you had changed your mind just to get out of here and then come up with another scheme to get him. Judging by what you've risked so far, I don't think I could persuade you to quit now."

Alice nodded, almost imperceptibly, as she registered Tabitha's shrewd insight. "How about option two?"

"Well, I could pick up the gun, shoot you and tell the police you were an intruder who broke in and threatened me." There was a hard edge to her voice now, the accent of her youth just a little more pronounced. Alice froze in her seat. This had, of course, occurred to her as a possibility, but the calmness with which Tabitha suggested it as a possible option was chilling.

"Or you could just let me go ahead and kill him," Alice offered. "It's what I came for."

Tabitha nodded. "That's option three. And it's a risk." She shrugged. "But then they're all risky in one way or another aren't they?"

"Well?" Alice asked. "What's it to be?" She hoped her voice sounded calm but her stomach was churning and she could hear the blood pulsing in her ears.

Tabitha sighed. Alice was right. No one had dared to make a stand against Blake in the forty years that she had worked for him. Now that she had been awoken, now that she knew the truth about Audrey and Freddie, now that she had been forced to recognise her complicity in Blake's crimes, it was time to act. "I suppose that only one of the options has the possibility of a good outcome. I'm going to go with option three. In fact, I'm willing to help you with option three. Now that I know for sure that Blake had Freddie murdered, I can't excuse his behaviour any longer, nor mine for working for him for so many years. But I'm warning you now, young lady, if I see any sign of Emma Montague emerging from Emma Reynolds, I'm going to bring you down any way I can."

Alice took a deep breath and exhaled slowly before she spoke. "Thank you, Tabitha. I won't let you down."

Chapter 31

Karen Turner swirled the whisky in the glass, took a small sip and stared into the gloom. One small table light cast long shadows across her lounge. She knew she should stop drinking; she had drunk more than enough already tonight, but holding the familiar glass in her hand gave her a measure of comfort.

Outside, the traffic had subsided to the occasional car shushing through the puddles in the street below her window; mainly taxis, probably, at this time of night. The rain had nearly stopped now; the wind had dropped. She glanced at her watch. 2.15. She held the glass against her cheek, felt its cool, hard surface.

Alice was at Blake's house, she felt sure of it. Back when she had been DCI, she was known for her hunches, her premonitions. But there was no trick to it really, she reflected. It was simply a matter of understanding all of the people in play, the issues at stake, the emotions, the motivations, the histories. If you knew all of those, people were actually very easy to predict. Alice was at Blake's house. She could feel it. She had come too far to give up now; she was a very determined young lady and she clearly felt, for some reason, that it was her destiny to bring justice to Blake.

She swirled the glass again, held it to her nose to inhale the creamy, buttery aromas, the scent of peat, but she did not drink. There was always the possibility that she might need to undertake some action tonight to protect herself. She took some comfort that Tabitha would be in charge of the situation. They were not friends, could never be comrades; there was too much history between them for that. But she trusted Tabitha. They had shared interests. And Tabitha would ensure, as best she could, that they were both safe.

What did this mysterious young woman, Alice Liddell, Emma Reynolds, have in mind? And what did she, Karen, want it to be? She leaned back in her armchair, pulling the glass down onto her tummy and holding it there with both hands. For him to suffer; that was what she wanted. She nodded slowly. For Blake to suffer, and be humiliated, and for everyone to know who he really was and what he had really done. That was what she wanted. She let out a deep sigh. The stakes were high. If Blake got wind of any of this, they were all in danger. And then again even if Alice did manage to deal with Blake, what did she have in mind for her and Karen? After all, they were complicit in so many of his crimes. But, the fact was, it was time. Alice Liddell had broken the hold Blake had over her, over them all, and there could be no going back now. She lifted the glass to her lips and drained the contents. Tabitha was in control now. She could be trusted to make the right decisions.

Chapter 32

From under the coffee table, Tabitha pulled out a flask and two cups. She laughed at Alice's raised eyebrows.

"I had a hunch this would go well," she said. "I thought coffee would be like a peace offering." She shrugged. "I did have a gun pointed at your head, after all."

Pouring the coffee, she took one cup and crossed the space between them, lifting the rucksack and offering it to Alice before placing the coffee on the table. "Don't worry about the alarm company; I've already told them that I took it off-line manually. We don't want any interruptions, do we?"

Alice nodded gratefully.

As Tabitha sat back in her chair, Alice opened the rucksack and carefully took out several items, placing them on the table.

Tabitha surveyed the array of objects, intrigued. "I hope your plan is a good one. There won't be any second chances with Blake."

Alice smiled grimly, pointing to the medication bottle on the table. "Ricin. One of the deadliest poisons in the world. One good sniff of that and he'll be dead within 72 hours, probably a lot less at his age."

Tabitha screwed her face up. "72 hours? That's a very long time. He could be diagnosed and cured in that time."

Alice shook her head confidently. "For a start off, it's very unlikely that any doctor would make a diagnosis of ricin poisoning. It's incredibly rare and the symptoms look like a whole bunch of other respiratory and cardiac illnesses which are much more common." She held her hand up as she saw Tabitha opening her mouth to object. "And even if a doctor did diagnose ricin poisoning, it wouldn't matter. There's no antidote; there's nothing the doctors could do for him. Once it's inside his body, he's as good as dead."

Tabitha took a deep breath then inhaled slowly, nodding gravely as she considered Alice's plan.

"And how do you plan to ensure that he inhales it? What if he smells it and becomes suspicious?"

Alice shook her head once more. "It's colourless and odourless. The container I've put it in is indistinguishable from the one he gets from the chemist.

It's identical in every way to the medication he takes twice a day."

Tabitha relaxed a little in her chair, then sat up again as a thought occurred to her. "Wait a minute. This stuff is deadly. So … what … you were planning to swap it with the one in his cabinet and wait for him to use it?"

Alice smiled her assent.

"But if I hadn't been part of this plan, I would be left in the house with a bottle full of deadly poison." There was an edge in Tabitha's voice. "It could have killed me as well." She considered for a moment. "It could have killed lots of people if I had thrown it out and the bottle had burst."

Alice's response was equally firm. "The chance of you inhaling from the bottle would have been very remote, but, yes, I admit that it's not impossible. I'm sorry, but you must realise that I couldn't tell you about it without risking the whole operation, not until I knew that I could trust you. And, as for the problem of disposal, well, my plan was to come back, once Blake had been taken to hospital, find it and dispose of it myself."

"And now?" Tabitha queried.

"Well, if you're willing, you can help me."

Tabitha remained impassive, waiting for an explanation.

Alice continued. "You are the best placed person to swap Blake's real inhaler for this one." She pointed to the bottle on the table. "As long you don't push the nozzle down to activate the spray, it's perfectly safe." She picked it up, as if to demonstrate this. "When Blake has had his prescribed sniff in the morning or the evening, he replaces the top, yes?"

Tabitha nodded slightly.

"Okay then. Nothing can get out when that top is present."

Tabitha nodded again.

So, once he starts showing symptoms, you swap this one back for the real one and then bring this one to whatever hiding place we decide upon. It will need to be outside the grounds so that I can access it easily. I can dispose of it safely from there. I still have the breathing apparatus I used to make it."

Tabitha's eyes opened wide. "You made this stuff?"

Alice shrugged and smiled. "It's not so hard, really. The instructions are all there on the dark web. It's just very, very dangerous, that's all. Get one thing wrong and you die a horrible death."

Tabitha shivered visibly. "No shit," she muttered. "Let's hope no other dudes fancy their chances as amateur chemists."

There was a long silence while both women assimilated what had just taken place. Finally, Tabitha looked up and gave Alice a grim smile. "Okay then, I'll do it. Better tell me what symptoms to look out for."

Alice smiled, pleased. "Sure thing. Well, to begin with, it will appear like a respiratory disease. That should come anything between 4 and 8 hours after he inhales it." She considered for a moment. "He might actually give himself a second dose before any noticeable symptoms appear, so don't swop the bottles until you're sure."

Tabitha nodded thoughtfully. "So, what, coughing, difficulty breathing, that kind of thing?"

"Exactly," Alice agreed. "He might be sweating as well, a bit feverish even. He's likely to think it's flu or some other cold virus at this stage."

"Should I hold off calling a doctor?" Tabitha queried.

Alice shook her head firmly. "No. Act exactly as you would do if it was a real chest infection. Suggest he call a doctor if that's what you would normally do. Insist upon it later when it starts to get worse. It's really difficult to diagnose ricin poisoning. The doctor will just presume it's a respiratory illness."

Tabitha shrugged. "Okay then. So, how will it develop?"

"Probably fluid on the lungs," Alice continued. "The doctors will diagnose that with their stethoscopes. Then low blood pressure. They'll pick that up too. They might be thinking pneumonia. Then again, there could be vomiting or diarrhoea. That could have them thinking something else."

"And you say he'll be dead inside 72 hours," Tabitha checked.

"Mmm, Alice agreed. Could be much less though. Could be only 36 hours. It depends upon how much he inhales and how fit he is. His body will simply shut down, probably through multiple organ failure."

"And it's unlikely that they will ever know it's ricin that caused it." Again, Tabitha was checking she had understood.

"Very unlikely," Alice assented. "You have to do very specific tests for ricin. The doctors would need a reason to suspect that he had been poisoned. By that time, all of the evidence would be gone anyway."

Tabitha sat back in her chair and considered what she had heard. This young woman was so cool and controlled. It was both reassuring and terrifying. She truly hoped she was doing the right thing here.

Chapter 33 The next day.

Adam woke to feel Alice stroking his hair. He opened his eyes and found her lying next to him, propped up on one arm so that she could look down into his face as he woke. She smiled affectionately and moved her hand onto his cheek, rubbing his lips gently with her thumb.

"I was worried about you …" he began, but she put her fingers to his lips to interrupt him then leaned over and kissed him.

"There's nothing to worry about any more, Adam." Her voice was reassuring, almost motherly. It was like she was soothing a little boy who had woken up from a bad dream. "It's all taken care of."

Adam was not reassured. "What have you done Alice? Tell me what you've done."

She smiled indulgently. "It's important that you find out what has happened at the same time as everyone else finds out. You'll see why later. In the meantime, I think you might be ready to move around a little."

She crossed to the window and whisked open the curtain. Sunshine streamed in, lighting up the side of her face then flooding the room.

"It's lovely out there. Let's see if we can't get you out into the garden for a while."

As she turned to face him, Adam was stunned at how beautiful she looked. She seemed to have a new radiance in her face.

"Come on lazy bones. It will do you good."

Adam was happy to be assisted with dressing and washing. This attentiveness was something new. He liked it. He allowed her to lead him down the stairs and out of the back door.

It was cold in the shadow of the house, but, as they emerged into the sunlit garden, he felt the warmth of the sun's rays upon his back. She had been right. It was doing him good. It felt as though his broken body was being soothed, healed, restored to its former vigour.

"Look Adam. Snowdrops."

Alice was pointing to the hole which had been left after the tree had been ripped from the ground. And, sure enough, there were snowdrops, little clumps of them in a ring around the hole, their heads pointing shyly towards the ground. She took his hand and led him across to examine them more closely.

In between the clumps there were green shoots, newly emerged from the ground.

"And crocuses," Alice added, excitedly. "Those will look beautiful when they flower."

She looked across at Adam. He nodded thoughtfully then smiled. "Dora," he whispered. Then louder, "It must have been Dora who planted them."

Alice smiled wistfully. "Poor Dora. An attempt to cover up the evil she had buried with something pure and beautiful."

— —

When Tabitha had heard Blake's car pulling up outside, she had scuttled to her room and locked the door, seating herself in an armchair that looked out across the grounds of the house. Struggling to suppress her anger and hatred, she could not bear to be in the same room, did not trust herself to hide her loathing of his hypocrisy and lies. When he knocked on her door, she told him she had a sickness virus, that she was staying in her room to protect him from it. The irony of the excuse did not escape her.

From the sanctuary of her room, she listened as he continued, like a giant spider, to weave and manipulate the threads of his empire, telephoning people, summoning some of them to a meeting, threatening or flattering them, his voice alternately dangerous or unctuous. When he stopped for a shower, she prayed that he would take his medication, inhale the deadly poison that Alice had prepared for him.

Waking with a start, Tabitha realised that she had dropped off to sleep. Disorientated, she rose from the chair. It was still light outside; there was no sound from the rest of the house. She checked her watch, three pm. She had heard Blake arranging a meeting for three thirty. He must have gone out.

Emerging cautiously from her room, she listened again. Nothing. No sign of life. Just the staccato tick of the grandfather clock in the hallway. She was alone once more. Wandering the corridors of the ancient house where she had spent the best years of her life, she saw it all in an entirely new light. Her senses were alive to it; the smell of decay and corruption, the centuries of exploitation and corruption that had forged the house and its contents, the malevolence that Blake brought to her life. She hoped it would all be over soon.

Chapter 34 8 hours later

As Adam sat down, he surveyed the table; pale green table cloth, a candle at each end of the table, an elegant glass vase of pink and red roses in the middle, a bottle of white wine in a shiny silver ice bucket. He raised his eyebrows comically then grinned up at Alice.

"What?" she protested.

He looked down at the table then back up at her again; a mime of surprise and pleasure.

"This!"

"Unfair! I can do romantic!" She playfully assumed an air of injustice.

"I like it," Adam responded, amused by her clowning. "And," he injected a more sincere tone, "I could get used to it."

She smiled, placing two bowls of spaghetti on the table. "Try to focus on the ambiance rather than the food," she instructed him with mock severity. "I think that presentation is probably my forte. My cooking skills still lag behind a little."

Adam twisted the fork expertly into the spaghetti and raised it to his lips. He chewed thoughtfully, swallowed then regarded her gravely. "Splendid, my dear. A triumph!"

Alice narrowed her eyes. "Okay. You've got me. That sounds very familiar but I can't place it."

Adam smirked. "A Christmas Carol. Bob Cratchit to his wife on tasting her pudding."

Alice giggled. "Seriously? We've turned into the Cratchit family now? Well, in that case, God bless us all."

As they ate, Adam looked up at Alice. She seemed so carefree now, so mischievous. Maybe they were safe now. Maybe she really had dealt with Blake Montague.

"We **could** be, you know," he ventured, tentatively, "a family, I mean. If you wanted. Because, well, I would like to, if you did, that is…."

He studied her face, searching for encouragement to continue.

Alice smiled warmly, reached across the table and squeezed his hand.

"So, you can do romantic as well. Good for you." She gave him a pantomime wink. "Let's take it one step at a time shall we, Adam. It's not so long ago that you were a serial dater with polyamorous tendencies. It's a big step to exclusivity and monogamy. Let's just say we're in a relationship, shall we. Will that be okay for now?"

Adam nodded happily.

— —

When Blake started coughing, Tabitha took that as her signal to emerge from her room, apparently restored to good health. She found him in his office, sprawling back in his swivel chair, a large glass of brandy in his hand.

"This bug had better not be from you," he uttered nastily, then erupted into another bout of coughing.

Tabitha shook her head. "Mine was sickness and diarrhoea. Food poisoning, I think. Yours is clearly a respiratory virus. Would you like me to call the doctor?"

Blake shut his eyes and sighed loudly. "Good God woman, it's just a cold." He opened his eyes and fixed her with an unpleasant stare. "You may have the luxury of being able to take to your bed at the slightest sniffle, but I have not."

He swallowed the whole glass of brandy in one gulp then held it out.

"Pour me another glass of brandy then get me Jonty on the line. The honourable member for Uxbridge has got some explaining to do."

Tabitha went about her normal business in the house, executing Blake's plans, giving instructions to the housekeeper, but always listening out for Blake's progress.

As evening fell, she listened at the door of his office. Blake was wheezing now, struggling to fill his lungs. She couldn't resist going in to witness his demise. He had removed his tie and opened the top buttons of his shirt, his face grey and sweaty.

"Sir Blake, you don't look well. Please let me call the doctor," Tabitha began.

"Get the fuck out of my office, you witch," he wheezed.

Tabitha looked at him and shook her head. He looked a shadow of the man who had tyrannised her and the rest of his empire for decades. He looked beaten.

Chapter 35 10 hours later

Alice was woken by the angry buzz of her phone. She tried to reach across to pick it up without waking Adam, but she felt him stir beside her.

"What … what time is it?" he croaked sleepily.

"It's early. Go back to sleep," she whispered.

The text was from Tabitha. It was a bogus message about a parcel, designed to look like a scam message and sent on an unidentified phone that Alice had given her. This was the sign they had agreed on. She had hidden Blake's medication inhaler, with the remains of the ricin still inside it, in the agreed place. It was time for her to go and pick it up.

She slipped out of bed. Adam had fallen back into a doze, snoring gently, but he stirred again as she tried to creep out of the door, holding her clothes in her hand.

"Alice? Where are you going?"

"Shhh." She crossed back to the bed and kissed him gently. "I just need to pop out for a couple of hours."

Adam's eyes shot open. "What? Where? What's happening?"

"Shhh." She kissed him again. "It's okay, really it is. It's all part of the plan. It's just a matter of tidying up a few loose ends. I'll be back in a couple of hours, three at most."

She put the clothes on unhurriedly, trying to make everything seem normal and routine for Adam's sake. Then, crossing to the door once more, she stopped briefly and turned. "Blake will be gone very soon now. You have nothing to worry about. I'm just covering my tracks. Try to go back to sleep."

Stopping at the cupboard by the front door, she took out a rucksack. It contained the breathing apparatus and all of the equipment needed for the safe disposal of the ricin. Her mind was clear and calm. She was in command of everything now.

— —

The fact that Blake allowed Tabitha to feel his forehead was a sign of how sick he had become. "Oh my God Blake. You're burning up."

She stepped back and regarded him with mock concern. He was having difficulty focusing on her. His body had gone floppy and lethargic. It was time to take control.

"Blake, I'm calling an ambulance. You should be in a hospital."

As she waited for the ambulance to arrive, she fussed around him, enjoying the role of nurse. Blake was struggling to breath now and complained of dizziness.

When the paramedics arrived, she insisted on holding his hand the whole time, walking with the stretcher to the ambulance, sitting with him as they drove to the hospital. The paramedics saw a faithful assistant and carer, sick with worry about her employer. In truth, Tabitha did not want to miss a moment of the internal disintegration of the monster who had manipulated and intimidated her for so very long. It was the final act of the show and she wanted to enjoy every minute.

Chapter 36 20 hours later

It had been an odd day, Adam reflected. First Alice creeping out to do … well, whatever it was she had done. When he had asked her again, she would not tell him, told him to wait and see. They had spent a lovely day together, walking down by the river, lunch in a pub, driving into town to watch an old movie at the cinema, dinner in a romantic little Italian Trattoria. And now they were having sex. He lay back, watching her smiling face rising away from his then sinking back down towards it as she lifted herself almost clear of his erection, twitched her hips artfully to caress the end of his erection with her labia, then plunged down until he was deep inside her once more. From time to time, she playfully placed her hand over his mouth, forcing him to breathe through his nose, removing it only to smother him with kisses, then replacing her hand again. When he felt himself rushing towards his climax, she sensed it too, gluing her lips to his, sharing her breath with his as he panted his way towards an almighty orgasm that shook him to his very core.

As he panted his way back to recovery, she stroked his hair, his face, his torso, tender and gentle in her attentions. He fell asleep in her arms, exhausted from the day's activities.

— —

Several times during the last few hours, Tabitha had closed her eyes, weary from the demands of the bedside vigil. The nurses had offered her a room to sleep in, but she had refused. Once she had dozed for a few moments, head lying on the bed next to Blake's tortured body, but she had woken up with a start, angry with herself for not staying awake. She did not want to miss the passing of Blake Montague from this life.

The perpetual bleep of the heart monitor testified to the continued existence of the man she had come to loathe. The drip in his arm sustained him, trying to hold on to him, keep him from drifting away. His breathing was laboured, ragged. His whole frame lifted slightly from the bed each time he tried to draw a breath. Meanwhile, three doctors stood in the corner of the room, muttering anxiously.

"I don't get it? He's not responding to any treatments."

"His organs are close to shutting down."

"Well, I think we've done everything we could."

They looked across at the devoted assistant who had stayed by his side since he'd been brought in. She gave them a brave smile then focused back on the dying man. Blake had lapsed into a coma by now.

Tabitha felt that he could not be aware of her by his side, holding his hand, and yet she did not relax her grip for a moment. She wanted to feel it. She wanted to feel the life drain out of him. And finally, it did. She felt the tension oozing out of his body. His entire skeleton seemed to collapse as his breathing stopped, like a giant airship deflating. She squeezed his hand hard, just to make sure he was really dead.

For a long time. she just watched him, hardly daring to breathe herself, fearing that his life might fan itself back into flame. Only slowly, slowly did she become aware of the massive weight lifting off her, leaving her giddy with freedom. What would she do now with the rest of her life? She was no youngster, but she might still have many years before her. And then it hit her, a dread sense of foreboding. When a gang leader on the streets was killed, there were always contenders to fill the vacuum. She hoped it wouldn't be Emma Montague.

Chapter 37 4 hours later

Adam and Alice were sleeping peacefully when the buzz of her phone woke them. It was a message from the unidentified phone once more. It simply said, ***callooh, callay***.

Looking over Alice's shoulder, heavy with sleep, Adam gawped at the message. "That's from The Jabberwock isn't it?"

"Mmm hmm," Alice agreed. "It comes from this bit:

And hast thou slain the Jabberwock?

Come to my arms, my beamish boy!

O frabjous day! Callooh! Callay!

He chortled in his joy."

"So, does it mean...?" Adam left the sentence unfinished.

"It sure does," Alice declared, with a flourish. "Blake is dead. Let's put on the TV and see if it's hit the news yet."

The news was full of it. Blake Montague, the famous Tory MP had died of a respiratory disease. There were accolades from former colleagues and friends, tributes to his skill as a statesman, expressions of gratitude for the service he had provided to the country.

Adam hugged Alice with relief. "That was you, wasn't it. You did it." He paused in thought for a few moments. "But they said it was a respiratory disease. So **how** did you do it?"

Alice smiled smugly. "That, my handsome young man, is for you to decide."

"What?" Adam propped himself up and one elbow and gave her a quizzical look. "How is it for me to decide?"

Alice snorted with amusement. "Well, we can't have Blake Montague going into the history books as a great hero, can we? You have a film to make, Adam. It's for you to re-write the narrative. We'll need to protect some people, me and you, obviously, and I've made promises to Tabitha about her and Karen, and then there's Dora of course, but I think there's still plenty of scope for you to turn the reputation of Blake Montague from hero to villain."

Adam shook his head as he tried to comprehend this. "Re-write the narrative?"

Alice kissed him fiercely. "Exactly. We owe it to all the people he has hurt, to Audrey and Freddie, to Martine even, despite what she did to protect Blake."

Adam lay back and stared at the ceiling. It was a lot to take in. The girlfriend he adored had just killed someone, actually killed him. Now she was encouraging him to make a film that would upset a lot of powerful people; it would drag the reputation of a famous Tory MP through the mud and his confederates, by association, would be smeared with the same scandal.

He propped himself back up on his elbow and peered into Alice's face.

"So, Alice, who will inherit Blake's estate? I mean, he must have been very wealthy. There's bound to be a lot of money as well as the house and everything that goes with it."

Alice flashed him a winning smile.

"Well, I did tell you that I was setting up my own genealogy business, didn't I? So, I took the liberty of completing the family tree that Dora started. And guess what? Since Blake killed off most of his close family, there are only two close members of kin surviving. One of those is, of course, Dora Brooke. The other is a young lady who the rest of the world doesn't know about yet, but they're just about to discover her. She's called Emma Montague."

More Publications by Russell Gregory

The People In a Town Like Yours (Number 1 in the **Town Like Yours** Series)

Do you ever wonder about the people you see every day on the bus, in the supermarket, down the pub? They live in the house down the road or in the next street or on the other side of town. Their lives run alongside yours and yet you know little or nothing about them. What dramas are being enacted behind closed doors? What are they thinking or doing as you pass them in the street? Here is a selection of those people and their dramas, a collection of short stories, about shopkeepers, librarians, bouncers, beggars, con artists, lovers, unfaithful partners ... the people in a town like yours.

More People In a Town Like Yours

(Number 2 in the **Town Like Yours** Series)

Do you ever wonder about the people you see every day on the bus, in the supermarket, down the pub? They live in the house down the road or in the next street or on the other side of town. Their lives run alongside yours and yet you know little or nothing about them. What dramas are being enacted behind closed doors? What are they thinking or doing as you pass them in the street? Here is a selection of those people and their dramas, a collection of short stories, about shopkeepers, crooked bank managers, wannabee rock stars, loan sharks, yummy mummies ... the people in a town like yours.

Printed in Great Britain
by Amazon

61992495R00167